The Book of the Needle

A time to rend and a time to sew.

Eccl. 3:7

MATTHEW FRANCIS

Cinnamon Press

Published by Cinnamon Press,
Meirion House,
Tanygrisiau,
Blaenau Ffestiniog,
Gwynedd,
LL41 3SU
www.cinnamonpress.com

 ISBN 978-1-907090-25-6
British Library Cataloguing in Publication Data. A CIP record for this book can be obtained from the British Library.

Designed and typeset in Bookman Old Style and Garamond by Cinnamon Press. Cover design by Jan Fortune, from original artwork 'Tailor Book of Trades' from *Das Standabuch* by Jost Amman.

Cinnamon Press is represented by Inpress and by the Welsh Books Council in Wales.
Printed in Poland.

The publisher acknowledges the support of the Welsh Books Council.

Acknowledgements

This novel originated many years ago in the Learning Resources Centre of the University of Glamorgan, when, bored with the work I was doing, I wandered over to the shelves and took down a book. It was Christopher Hill's *Change and Continuity in Seventeenth-Century England*, and I opened it at the chapter entitled 'Arise Evans: Welshman in London'. Hill's essay is a small masterpiece of historical biography, and highly recommended to readers of this book.

I would like to thank Yr Academi Gymreig for the award of a Writer's Bursary which enabled me to take time off lecturing to write, the Department of English and Creative Writing at Aberystwyth University for allowing me two periods of study leave, one of them extended, and the Founder, Director and Trustees of the Hawthornden Foundation for a Hawthornden Fellowship which provided a month of ideal writing conditions at a time when they were much needed. Thanks also to the Director and the other Hawthornden Fellows for being such good company. I am grateful to Jayne Archer and Jane Huggett for helpful responses to queries, staff and students at Aberystwyth University for many fruitful conversations, the staff at the National Library of Wales for their unfailing courtesy and efficiency, and Creina Francis for living with all of it and listening to some hopelessly inadequate drafts.

Of the many primary and secondary sources I have consulted I would like to single out Diane Purkiss's rich and humane *The English Civil War: A People's History*, which proved a perfect introduction to the period; the superbly researched series of pamphlets on aspects of seventeenth-century life published by the Stuart Press and written by authors including Jane Huggett, Robert Morris and Stuart Peachey; and Liza Picard's delightful *Restoration London: Everyday Life in the 1660s*, together with its inspiration, *The Diary of Samuel Pepys*. None of my sources is to blame for any of the liberties I have taken, consciously or unconsciously, with history. Readers are strongly advised not to try any of Maud's remedies, especially the bluebottles.

My greatest debt, of course, is to the writings of Arise Evans himself, particularly the pamphlet *An Eccho to the Book Called A Voyce from Heaven* (1653), which I accessed, along with many other texts by Evans and others, through Early English Books Online. *Diolch yn fawr.*

Er Cof Am

Arise Evans

(1607 – 1660?)

The Book of the Needle

Or

A Compendium for the Use of Prentices and Journeymen, Aptly Design'd to Instruct them in the More Perfect Accomplishment of Sewing, Cutting, Fitting, Pressing and Botching *&c. &c.* with some Commemorations of the Late Time of Confusion Call'd the Great Rebellion and Commonwealth of *England*, and of his Part in Bringing All to a Joyous Resolution,

by *Arise Evans*, Tailor and Prophet.

Given by me at my house in *Long-alley, Black-friars,* this Year of Grace 1661, and is to be sold by Mr. *Lowndes* at the *White Lion* in *S. Paul's Church-yard.*

Contents

Chapter

Chapter I
The Needle Vindicated from Holy Writ

If it be true that a man must have a trade, it is also true that he must have clothes, and so must his wife and children, else they would be everywhere naked to their great shame and discomfort. The trade of tailoring, then, answers to a general need, and it is one of great antiquity and respectability. The first tailor was Adam, for he sewed fig-leaves together to make aprons, as did also his wife Eve, who was thus the first seamstress. In this, they disobeyed the will of God, and therefore it may seem that tailoring was the Original Sin of which the divines speak, or at least the Second Sin, following that of pilfering fruit. And it may be indeed, but the Lord sanctioned it hereafter, for when he cursed the woman to bring forth children in pain and to harken to her husband, and the man to eat bread in the sweat of his brow, the Lord himself made coats of skins sewn together and clothed them. Thus was the Lord God the second tailor, and thus was tailoring the only thing in the world to be devised by man first and God afterwards. And ever since that time tailors have been curious men given to dreams above their station.

The Israelites in the time of Moses were skilled in many trades. One Belazeel and his fellow Aholiab, we are told, had the wisdom of heart to do the work of the engraver and of the embroiderer, in blue, and in purple, in scarlet and in fine linen, and of the weaver, and of those that devise cunning work. They were also tentmakers, as the Apostle Paul was at a later time. This trade is the cousin of tailoring, the tentmaker making, as it were, garments affixed to the ground instead of to the person, which a man can step into and out of without touching them; to be more exact, it seems to me that a tent is a sort of pocket that has got out of hand and lost all contact with the body. The tent they made was called the Tabernacle, and it had ten curtains of fine twined linen and blue and purple and scarlet, coupled with each other in two sets of five, and each curtain had fifty loops; there were also eleven curtains of goats' hair to cover the top of it, over which was another covering of rams' skins dyed red, and over that yet another, of badgers' skins. So we see how skilled were these Israelites in the use of many stuffs or materials that it would defy a tentmaker or tailor of these days to work, for there is nothing tougher than a goatskin, and as for badgers' skins I know not where to find them in sufficient number to cover such a tent when each of the curtains that formed the innermost lining was twenty-eight cubits long by four cubits wide, and there were, as I have said, ten of them. My yardstick is insufficient for such a calculation, and no workshop I have wrought in has had space enough to lay such curtains out, but I doubt not it would require a mighty slaughter of badgers.

Afterwards they made holy clothing for Aaron and Aaron's sons. They made the ephod of the same stuff they had used for the curtains lining the Tabernacle, but this time with the addition of gold, which was beaten and cut into wires and worked in with the blue, the scarlet, the purple and the fine twined linen, that is, they sewed it up with gold thread, which is another costly item and hard to work with. But what an ephod is no one knows to this day, for the pattern has been lost, but it must have been some kind of tunic or doublet, since it had shoulder-pieces and a girdle, which shows us that it covered altogether the upper body. This ephod had a cover or outer layer which the Scripture calls the robe of the ephod, all of blue with a hole in the top, and on the hem of it were embroidered pomegranates of blue, purple and scarlet, with bells of gold between them. They also made a coat of fine linen for Aaron, and a girdle of needlework, and a mitre of fine linen, this last being properly the labour of the milliner. For Aaron's sons, they made coats, girdles and bonnets, for glory and for beauty, and also breeches which reached from the loins to the thighs. What kind of stockings they wore with them, woollen or linen, the book does not say, but it is evident these were breeches such as any tailor of our days might make, though whether they were galligaskins, scabilonions, sliding hose, scaling hose, gregs or slops I know not.

Our Lord Jesus himself was wise in the ways of tailoring. When he said that it was easier for a camel to pass through the eye of a needle than for a rich man to enter the Kingdom of Heaven, it seems to me that he must have meant some thread or twine made of the hair of camels, which was doubtless too coarse for the needle; I suppose they made rope from it for tying packs to the camels and did not use it for sewing. For our Saviour showed that he understood the craft and would never imagine a camel in a workshop when he declared that no man sews a piece of new cloth on an old garment, or else the new piece that filled it up takes away from the old, and the rent is made worse. Here we see him, as it were, in the tailor's shop, sorting through the basket of rags and snippets that all such places have, and choosing one that will match the cloth to be mended for colour and weave and wear. Thus he shows his humility, for he was not above botching, which is as much part of the trade as making is, and a thing every tailor must learn.

From these examples we see that the calling of a tailor is an honourable one, vouched for by Scripture, and that God himself followed it, though he did not lead it. If, sir or mistress, your son yearns to be apprenticed to a tailor, or if he does not but you wish it for him, none of you need be ashamed. But you may have heard it said that tailors are small of stature and puny of limb, that they lift no heavy weights and swing no hammers or axes, and on account of this that they are no true men, but cowards in a battle or a brawl, and other things are said of their privy powers that I shall not repeat, but men call them scurrilous names, such as pricklouse. What, is a bolt of cloth not a heavy weight? Have you tried to lift one? And though a needle is not a hammer, nor a pair of shears an axe, yet there is strength of a subtle and intimate kind needed to wield these, too, when the cloth is heavy or tough, as leather or canvas are. And remember too that a tailor, at any rate when he is an apprentice or a journeyman, spends most of his life in one position, sitting crosslegged on the wooden platform we call a shopboard with the cloth draped over his lap, sewing. And though the muscles of his thighs and calves ache yet he may not uncross them, nor move to relieve the pressure of the board against his buttocks, and he continues, pressing and pulling with thimble and needle till his fingers are weary. When it grows dark, he does not come home like the ploughman or the farmer, but most often works on by candlelight while there is work to be done, for of the making and mending of clothes there is no end. Thus many tailors wear out their eyes before they are old. Therefore I say to you that a tailor is a true man as other men are, and that his labour is no less than theirs.

Nevertheless, to be of small stature is no handicap to him, and rather an advantage if he is to spend his days all folded up and perched upon a shelf. The legs will bend easier if they are more like wires and less like tree-trunks, and a slight frame will spring easier from the floor to the shopboard and back again. So if your son is like to be a small man you may ask him to consider this trade. I am of no great size myself, and so it was thought good that I should become a tailor though my brothers, who were sturdier, followed my father's profession of sheepfarming in the mountains of Wales, and one of the brothers is there still, minding his flocks in the mist, though the other is dead. I was but nine years old when this course was chosen for me, for I do not remember that I had any say in it, though wise beyond my years as all confessed. And though small, I understand not how they could be sure I would continue so and not suddenly grow to a full height and breadth at twelve or fourteen as some do. But perhaps it was not my stature that persuaded them so much as my nature, for I was even then a person given to deep thought and melancholy and dreaming, and, as I have said, tailoring is a brooding sort of labour.

My name is Arise Evans, and I have spent my life in this way, cutting and sewing, making and botching, and though never a master tailor, for I had neither the means nor the influence with the Guild, yet I have sat on shopboards enough and sewed seams, gussets and buttonholes enough to instruct any apprentice. Also, unlike any master tailor you will find in this kingdom, I know how to write, not merely inventories and accounts, but whole books with prologues and colophons and all the other tassels and froggings you could require. (I take no credit for this, though I was always quick at learning as a boy – it was the Lord God himself who instructed me in book-writing, whom I obey in all things.) I was pretty famous a few years back during the late troubles when the world was turned upside-down and none knew how to stand it rightway-up again. Yet I had never enough to live by from it, so little did I seek my own profit, and now that the kingdom is restored and all my words have proven true, I have nothing to show for it. None likes to think now of the times we have lived through and the perils we have faced, and so even those who guided us out of them to the bells and the bonfires, the incense and the ointment of our present glorious age are forgotten. Yes, sir and mistress, I am the very same Arise Evans. How many of that name do you know of?

Chapter II
The Book of the Needle Conceived

This is the reason I have decided to write what I never wrote yet, a book that shall contain all my understanding of this, my profession. It was my wife set me on to it, when she comes in from visiting a sick neighbour and sees me writing as she has done so often before. What are you writing, husband? says she.

A letter, wife, to His Majesty the King.

Only a letter? she says, coming up and standing close above me to read what I am writing. I had thought it was another book.

Indeed, it will be a book when I have finished it, for I shall have it printed, as I did formerly my letter to General Monk, and my letters to the Lord General Cromwell.

Oh, says she, a letter of that kind. There were not many that bought the other letters, as I recall. Why should anyone buy a letter that is addressed to someone else? I would not.

That is because you are a woman and not concerned with controversies.

What is in the letter? I cannot read it in this gloom. I wonder you can see to write at all.

It is a letter of thanks to His Majesty for his healing of my nose.

Is it healed? says she. Come out into the daylight where I can see it. Very well, then, move a little closer so the light falls on you when I open the door. I believe it is a great deal better.

And she pokes at it with her finger. Her sight is become weak these last few years, which causes her to move her head back and forth, half-closing her eyes as she peers at me.

It is healed, I tell her. His Majesty laid his sacred hand on me, and the poisons gushed forth at his command, in the same way as he cures the King's Evil. I do not say this was the King's Evil, for the look of it is different, but it must obey him just as that does.

There is a bit more swelling here, she says, above the right nostril. It is very red, and somewhat bloody and pustular. I wish you would let me apply some *unguentum album* to it. (For my wife is become a sort of woman apothecary or physician from years of ministering to her children, and anyone else who will let her.) A needle, she says. A needle and we will light a candle, for it must be hot. And some *unguentum album*. I would use plantain water and loose sugar, but we have no sugar.

No wife, that is blasphemy. Only God can heal, and the agent of God, who is King Charles Steward. She frowns and is about to speak further, when I say to her, Remember your promise, wife.

Wrongly called Stuart by the vulgar who know not the meaning of his name.

My promise, says she, then, with a pursing of the lips and a little huffing sound, always my promise.

It seems I must always remind you of it.

It seems you must. Well...

And she shrugs and is silent, standing in the doorway with a fidgety rain falling behind her, and a smell of coal-smoke, ordure and dust coming into what I call my study, though it is also our bedroom and parlour.

Shut the door, I say. It is cold.

I return to my desk and she shuts the door as I instructed her and comes over to me again, taking off her hat, which drips on the straw matting of the floor, and adjusting her kerchief.

This letter will not sell, says she. It will make us no money.

I do not write it for that.

Have you heard from Mr Satterthwaite?

I do not think we will hear again from him now the King is restored.

And the last of his money is almost spent. Husband, you must go look for another position.

The King will remember me. He promised to do so when he healed my nose. Besides, my tailoring days are done. I could not sit now on the shopboard above an hour. My knees will not allow it. If I were a master, and could stand at the cutting board...

You know as much as any master. Why, you could write a book on tailoring. People would wish to read that. They would pay well for it, I have no doubt.

Mrs Evans, I tell her, I do not write of earthly things but of spiritual things. All I have written has been to glorify the King, to foretell the upheavals and restoration of the kingdom, and to open men's eyes to the heavenly truth. In the earthly realm I am a tailor, but in the spiritual realm I am a prophet, and must speak God's word.

Well, says she, and does not God speak through needles and stitching, and shopboards and shears and thimbles and doublets and gowns? Did not our Lord wear clothing like other men, and did not he use men's trades to enlighten them in parables? Did he not speak of labourers in vineyards and fishermen and sowers of seed? Mark, husband, I do not contradict you, but you may prophesy by way of tailoring as much as by any other matter, and make some money into the bargain.

Prophesy, say I, what shall I prophesy now? The future has already happened.

Chapter III
The Appurtenances Held Up to the Reader's Gaze

This morning I am alone in the study, for my wife is visiting our daughter Willis in Fetter Lane; I sit at my desk with pen, ink and sandbox before me, yet, though I dip the pen a hundred times, I let the ink dry again on the nib some ninety-eight times, and the ninety-ninth time a blob falls on my paper like a great dark tear. I have, it is true, written a good first chapter, which thoroughly vindicates and justifies the profession from the Word of God, for there never was a tailor that knew his Scripture as I know mine. But my second goes astray with talk of my wife, who ought never to be in a book of tailoring at all, for she knows naught of it. I shall mend all presently. But for the time being, I must concentrate on the tools, armoury or equipment of my craft, which I have fetched from their various hiding-places, rooted out rather, for they have not been used these five years, no, nearer ten.

This being *The Book of the Needle*, I must say something of needles, and of the other appurtenances of tailoring, for your son, sir or mistress, must be equipped with these before he seeks a post, or no master will take him on. A needle is but a fine piece of wire, sharpened at one end and with an eye at the other to take your thread, the whole carefully straightened, tempered and polished. Though there may be some in the shop, yet more are always wanted, for a needle does not last long, and therefore your son will need a wallet of needles of various lengths and finenesses. These needles, being of steel, will rust if not kept dry; the smaller ones may break and the others bend, and all will lose their point with much use. You may sharpen a needle on a whetstone, but it is tedious work, and the metal is soon worn away. They may be bought from most chapmen, or from a haberdasher's stall in a fair or market. Look at them carefully before you buy, to see that none are rusted or out of true or have flaws or burrs in the eye that will break your thread.

My own wallet is before me as I write this, and I take the needles out one by one and drop them on the desk. This one is so fine from much use I can hardly see it now; this one is so much rusted it would break if I tried to use it; this has a broken eye and this one I broke by sewing too vigorously or by picking my teeth with it, though why I kept it after such a mishap is more than I can now say. Here are the great darning needles with eyes wide enough to take a strand of wool. They are so like weapons, when I was first an apprentice I could not refrain from waving them about like tiny swords, dreaming of myself as Tom Thumb, who used such a needle in defence. Another thing I cannot refrain from with a needle is trying the point of it, and indeed I have pricked myself now as I always did. If it is not sharp, Arise, you will find out in the sewing, so said my master, Hugh Jones, it is no good bleeding on the customer's linen.

Your son will need abundance of pins besides, for tacking one piece of cloth to another, and these will be familiar to you, being always about the house, for gentlewomen use them for attaching ribbons and suchlike fripperies to their persons. My mother, who cared little in other respects where I went and what I did in my childhood, would never allow me outside without one, for, said she, you must have a pin for when you pass the witch's house. For pushing the needle, your son will need a thimble, which must be of a size to cover the tip of the second finger, of steel or brass, or leather. My thimble is brass and too large for my finger, for I had it from Mr Jones when I left his house for London. It is colder in my hand even than the air around me, and has a slight oiliness. It smells of copper coins, and it tastes of them, too, a sourness and a kind of ringing in the mouth. Mark you, I lick it only for old times' sake, since that is what I would do in my prentice days. Do other boys do this, and do other trades have such an abundance of small playthings for them?

Thread also may be bought from any chapman or haberdasher, of silk, linen or wool, and in all sorts of colours, of which white, black, red, green, brown and blue are the main ones. Buy what you can; there will be more in the workshop, and no master will grudge its use, though the silk thread and some of the colours, in particular blue and black, are more expensive. As for cloth, that is purchased by the client and brought into the shop with his order, and whatever is left he takes away again. The snippets are stored in a box as I said before and sorted through whenever a garment is to be mended. Since these snippets belong to the customer, the purloining of them is a petty crime, though one which is only to be expected in a man whose profession is descended from the sin of Adam and Eve. The tailor therefore conceals the offence behind his own canting language. The snippets he calls cabbage, and the box where they are kept he calls hell: if the customer asks what has become of the other pieces of his cloth, it is the tailor's custom to reply, They are in hell, sir, for all I know. Other things you will find too lying about in this box or another, such as buttons and tassels and loops and stiffenings and other embellishments that have been cut from this garment or that, and a good master will find uses for them sooner or later.

Before the master cuts, he must measure, which he does with his yardstick or rule, marking the cuts to be made with tailor's chalk. For measuring the cloth when it is draped over the customer's body instead of over the cutting board he uses a strip of parchment or waste cloth on which he has marked the measurements with ink or chalk, or with stitches or scissor-cuts. This does not concern you yet, for it is his work, but I have a yardstick of my own, again from Hugh Jones, who fondly imagined that as I was going to London I would be a master myself presently. However, it is always as well to have some chalk in your pocket or bag for marking any alterations, and also for giving to the master when he strides up and down the room cursing because he cannot find his own. Thus an apprentice gains credit, and saves his ears from profanity. There are also irons, which are heated over the fire and pressed over the damp cloth to set a seam. The master will most likely have several and expect you to use them. Other tools you may make for yourself, such as a small cushion of cloth stuffed with snippets to hold the material in a given shape, as the master directs.

For cutting there are two implements, scissors and shears. The scissors are two blades joined in the middle with a pin which forms their pivot, while the shears are larger, composed of a single piece of steel bent in the middle to form the two arms and blades, with a curved piece of metal between them which acts as a spring to keep the tension. Your son will need scissors for the trimming of edges and cutting off of thrums and other finishing work. However, it being a rule of the trade that *the master cuts, the others sew,* he will need no shears of his own, for most of his labour will be in sewing up the pieces which the master has cut out for him. Here are my shears, obtained from my master as the other things were. I wish I had some cloth to cut with them. There, I have taken a small snip at the hem of my doublet, and it is very good, they are sharper than I thought, although I cannot remember when I last whetted them. And only a little rust on the blade which I should clean off – not that I ever expect to use them, but in honour of Mr Jones, who gave me these, too. No master after him ever trusted me enough to stand at the cutting board and cut, so the shears got no more use than the yard did. It is like looking at the possessions of a different man, as if a stranger had lived close up against me all these years, going out to the workshop when I did, but standing in a different place, and all his thoughts were of cutting and measuring while mine were of God and the King and war and angels.

I do not find much in Scripture of shears, but all that is related there is of the shearing of sheep. It is true that a shepherd uses these tools as well as a tailor, though a tailor's are somewhat finer. My father carried a pair of shears, and a whetstone for sharpening them everywhere he went, for there were always tangles and brambles to be clipped off, or a ewe might catch her wool in a thornbush. After all, what is a sheep but cloth in the raw? This was another reason my family had for choosing my profession, to have an agent in the other end of the business. For much of the wool we sheared from our flocks was carded, spun and woven by my mother and the women of the farm, for making into a material they call Welsh cottons, which we sent to the fulling mill to be shrunk and hammered, and thence to Oswestry to market (the remainder being sold to other weavers and clothiers round about), and so we were up to the elbows in cloth. Our own clothing, however, we bought from the travelling tailor who came to see us every year in the autumn, and measured all of us, to take orders for a suit of clothes for each. I remember all this well, small as I was, and how my suit of clothes was always cut down from my brother Griffith's, just as his suit was cut down from my brother Owen's.

Chapter IV
Welsh Cottons, Though Humble, Not to Be Despised

The cloth called Welsh cottons is a loosely woven wool with a fluffy nap. Because it is cheap and more for utility than decoration, it is commonly undyed, its natural colour being a greyish or brownish white, though some dye it, not so much for ornament as to keep away rats, which love wool but not the smell of the dye. As it is soft and light it is exceedingly warm next the skin and so is much used for lining garments such as coats, cloaks, bodices, petticoats, and for men's and women's stockings. It is a humble cloth, made from the fleeces of Welsh sheep which, living on poor mountain pasture in the wildest of weather, have coarse and greasy wool, though the meat is the best eating of all. Still, it is in wool, not in meat, that the wealth of the sheep-farmer resides, for you may only kill the animal once, be it sheep or lamb, while you can shear it half a dozen times or more before it loses its value. And though the wool be poor, yet if you have enough sheep and weave the cloth yourself, you may have a good living of it.

Where I lived in my childhood sheep outnumbered people. On each of the hills round about were my father's flocks, in one walled field or another, drifting from one corner to its opposite, with or against the slope, as if impelled by some power. I heard them day and night, for sheep continue to call after dark, either in their sleep or because one of them has woken and cries out, having had whatever kind of nightmare such an animal may have, and when one wakes and cries they must all wake and cry, for such is their nature, to do always the same as their fellows. And just as they filled my ears at all times, so they filled my nostrils, though it was not so much the animal itself as what it was anointed with, a grease of pitch, tallow and wheatgerm that my father and brothers boiled in a great iron cauldron over a fire in the courtyard. It was black and looked like burnt lard, and after they had done it not only the hog lambs but father, brothers and myself and everything else smelt of grease, an essence of pinewood and bonfire and cured meat and rotten meat and candles and hay and vomit and sheep dung. It never seemed to me then that I would have any other life than washing and shearing and lambing and slaughtering.

I am a Briton by nation, what you would call a Welshman; my county is Merionethshire, and it is a bony land, having many mighty hills, and one in particular a few miles off from our house that was called Cader Idris, which is the highest hill in the kingdom, and no doubt also in the world. I will lift up mine eyes to the hills, so David sang, from whence cometh my strength, and indeed wherever I went in my childhood I lifted up my eyes. I know not if it made me strong, but it transported me after a fashion because hills bring distant places close up, so that in a moment you feel yourself elsewhere just by looking. You even feel, if you gaze long enough at them, that you are no longer standing on the earth but flying or falling, since everything you behold is at the wrong angle, sheep, stone walls, rocks, thornbushes. Our house was on a slope, so that when you went in through the front door and stood in the dark passage, the warm gloom of the hall, with a fire smouldering in it and the smell of smoke and, oftentimes, of boiling soup, was to the right and down, while the parlour was to the left and up. There was a fireplace in the parlour too but it was seldom lit, so the place always smelled of damp. The smells of the house lay one on top of another, and over all was the smell of sheep grease.

Through the passage and out the other side was the farmyard. It was full of mud, with which I made myself intimately acquainted, and so learned that much of it was dung. The cock crew at daybreak but he ended not there, for crowing rather than connubiality or cantankerousness was the greater part of his business, and so he continued at it twelve times an hour for the duration of the day and twice an hour at night. The pigs fattening in the boarhouse ate mightily of their dry peas, whey and warm washings, making a noise like a heavy man snoring, which noise they made just as heartily if it chanced at any time that they were not eating. Here also were the dogs Geraint and Pero tied up when they were not herding sheep, barking whenever anyone came into the yard, and howling in between. And here was the barn where the fleeces were kept, and on a fine day you would find my mother and Bethan sitting outside it, carding the wool.

For wool is woven by God in a manner so multifarious and confusing that it cannot be worn by any but a sheep until it has been taken apart and put together again by the art of man, or rather in most cases by the art of women. The fleece, which seems so solid, is made up of thousands of hairs as fine and white as the gossamer of a dandelion. Before they can be spun on the wheel into thread, and woven on the loom into workable cloth (both which activities were performed by my mother and Bethan in the hall), these fibres must be straightened by teasing them with a teasel (which is a dry and spiky flower), or by combing them with a comb, or as my mother and Bethan did outside the barn door in the muddy sunlight, by carding them with a pair of cards, which are paddles or bats covered in sharp points. Each woman would hold one card in her lap, her left hand resting on the dropcloth, and, wielding the other in her right, would pull and tear at a clump of fleece until the fibres were transferred from one card to the other. Then she would change hands and pull and tear again, repeating this as many times as needful till all was straight, when she would lay it in the basket beside her for spinning later, and take a new clump. It was a loud and cruel kind of work, and each woman seemed to me, as I sat at their feet in the faint smell of sweat, to be fighting with herself, so clatteringly did they go about it, burrs and bugs scattering on the dropcloth at each skirmish. What was strange was that for all the noise they made, they could talk at the same time, or rather my mother could talk and Bethan could grunt, which was the kind of converse she made for the most part.

I never knew and none ever thought to tell me who Bethan was to us, whether a servant or cousin or some other kinswoman. She was old enough to be my grandmother, or sometimes, as I thought, my mother's grandmother, and my mother at times talked to her deferentially and asked her opinion as if she were an aunt at least, but at others she instructed her, and it was true that Bethan did more and humbler work about the house and farmyard than my mother did, though less than the girl. All the while they carded, my mother talked, not caring whether or not she could be heard above the battering and rending, and Bethan made sounds which to my ears sounded like discouragement and disapproval. My mother ignored them, but continued her talk of what concerned her that morning, which was generally something she had heard from the neighbours. Thus she might say that a servant on such a farm had been walking through the fields before sunrise when he passed a group of people in white aprons, and thought them to be a marriage company, but when he called to them they made no reply. Then when the sun was rising, he saw that they cast no shadows, and the hair moved on his head. He drew his knife then, and they vanished, because the *Tylwyth Teg* were, do you know, Bethan, afraid of iron? There is nothing else they fear, but only iron.

All the while she was battering and battering with the two cards, and Bethan grunting and frowning on the other side of the barn door. Then my mother would stop and pick the wool out of the teeth of her card and I would ask her what were the *Tylwyth Teg*, for at that age I asked questions at all times. The words meant Fair People, but my mother never mentioned them without a fearful excitement as though their fairness frighted her.

There are no *Tylwyth Teg,* Bethan would say.

If it was not the Fair People she talked of it was ghosts, or else witches. There was an old woman in an ash-coloured gown, her apron thrown back over her shoulder who would walk before you on mountain paths in the mist carrying a milk-pail and crying Wow up! the apparition of which was a certain sign that the beholder had lost his way. And other things might go before or beside you, having the appearance of a round bowl, a goose, a lovely young woman, a stern man who walked always on the left side, never turning his face, or a great mastiff that burst into flame and became a fire the size of a field and crackled like burning gorse. And, my mother would say when I had tired of hearing of all these and rose to leave the farmyard, if you are going past the witch's house, forget not to take a pin with you, for a witch cannot harm you if you draw her blood. Then she would take another hank of wool and commence battering at it again.

Chapter V
A Diseased Nose No Disgrace to a Prophet

This morning when I rose from our bed against the wall of the study and went to write, I found my wife there before me, reading my writings. Wife, said I, what is the meaning of this? Did you not swear not to do such things?

No, Mr Evans, says she. That was not what I promised at all. I like not this chapter.

She is seated at my desk in kerchief and waistcoat and apron, holding the last sheet of my chapter away from her face and peering. Sheep, says she, farmyards, carding, the *Tylwyth Teg*. Who will buy this? Let me look at you, she adds as I come closer. I think it is worse today. You must let me try the *unguentum*.

My friends say they do not know me, I am so changed since His Majesty's touch.

What friends?

Mr Lowndes, for one.

Hm, she says, a poor friend he is. But do you see, husband, you waste too much time at the beginning with all this talk of Adam and Eve and the Tabernacle. This is a book of tailoring. Such things run not in this new age. Keep you to stitches and hems and gussets, or people will call you a Puritan.

Puritan! I have been called many things, but never that. And by my own wife, who, by the by, was more than a little of a Puritan in her day. Do you not recall how you panted to hear Mr Cradock preach in Wrexham, and how the first question you asked me when you heard I lived in London was of Dr Gouge and whether I was of his congregation at Blackfriars Church?

That was before the late troubles. Preachers were all the rage then, and I was young and could not hear enough of them. All the maids were the same, they thought only of sermons and hell and lean, deep-voiced men in gowns and clerical bands. But in these times they think of different things, of the theatre, or of the shows of gallantry in St James's Park. No one is Puritan nowadays.

She puts down the paper and rises from the desk, and I know by the way she squares her shoulders and pulls the apron tighter about her waist that she means to fetch her ointment and be a physician again. It is her revenge because I twitted her about her fanatic past. But I will stay her.

And your own son, Mrs Evans? Is not he one of those Puritans you believe have died out in this age?

Owen is not a man yet. He is young as I was, and he will change as I did. Besides, he is not so fanatical when he talks with me as he is with you. He does it to annoy you, as a young man will with his father.

I never did so with my father.

She has gone to her chest in the corner, and is bent over searching, with her rump in its threadbare red petticoat facing me. When did she become so broad, with the first child, or a later one? She mutters to herself: Wintergreen, treacle-mustard, *carduus benedictus*, now where is it? Bastard rhubarb, star thistle, alehoof. What would you call this affliction of the nose, husband? A *noli-me-tangere*? Alehoof is good for a *noli-me-tangere*, if I cannot find my *unguentum.*

It is cured, say I, and I tell you I never spoke to my father as Owen does to me. He wants to go to America. I would as soon he went to Hades.

Your father, she says, your father. How long has he been dead? Ah, here it is. Hold still, husband, let me apply it.

It is wrong, I tell her, it is outrageous. But she has already smeared the stuff on my nose very liberally, so some of it has gone up the nostril. The first instant I feel a burning on the flank of the nose, but it is quickly replaced with a delicious coolness, only the stuff in my nostril discomforts me, and the odour is smothering, a heavy sweetness mingled with something of bitterness. Like greasing a hog, I murmur.

What did you say? my wife asks, searching inside her apron for a bit of cloth to wipe her hands.

A hog lamb. I wrote of it in the chapter you read just now.

Oh.

What is in that stuff?

Wax, oil of roses, hope, fat and ceruse. Do you feel better?

Ceruse is white lead. I know not if it be poisonous.

I was already better. I cannot be better than I was.

Perhaps I should prick it with a needle.

I am about to protest at this, but the mention of a needle has set her thoughts going in their former direction. Sheep do not belong in a book of tailoring, says she.

The sheep must be in the book because they are a source of cloth.

And do you intend to write a chapter of hemp and a chapter of flax, too? And, what do you call them, silkworms?

I write not of them because I know nothing of them. I can only write what I know. And it seems to me, wife, that you are contradicting me.

For this was my wife's promise at our betrothal, that she would never contradict me, which handicaps her greatly in any argument.

Husband, she says, I wish only to save our old age from poverty. Our daughter Willis will have children of her own to care for presently. Our son Owen is as yet only a prentice. They cannot help us much. Write us a book that will help Owen, that will help other parents to choose a trade for their children. Your trade is tailoring. Let us have no more sheep or Scripture.

Yes, it is my trade, but to tell the truth I never loved it. I did not choose it for myself, nor would my father have chosen it for me if he had lived. I was to be a shepherd and live on the farm. As for writing, that is my trade, too, and you must trust me to know it, for I have writ some fourteen or fifteen books and you never wrote any. If I write of Scripture it is because nothing of any sense or value can be understood except with and by means of Scripture, as all men of learning agree, be they Puritan or Episcopalian. And if I write of sheep it is because all I can write of tailoring is my own life, and to understand my life one must understand, must understand sheep.

My face is grown hot, all of it but the nose. This is strange; it was but lately the other way round.

Chapter VI
The Author Catechised

When first I brought forth a book, there were many who said, What does this Welshman know of battles or politics? And how shall a tailor give instruction to a King or a Parliament or a Protector? And a kind of hypocritical persons they call Presbyterians went yet further, saying, He is not godly like us, for this land of Wales where he comes from is one of the dark places of the earth: they scarcely know God in thosc parts, or if they do he is certainly a Papist god. Well, I suppose I may write a book on tailoring, being a tailor, and besides these same Presbyterians are confounded now. Nevertheless, there will be some who question my right even to the authorship of this, the humblest of all my books. Well, they will say, you may know tailoring, but are you wise, are you learned, are you Christian? Will your book make my son a good tailor but a wicked man?

Even my son, Owen, whose name is Welsh, though he understands nothing of the language of his fathers, asked me once when he was younger, Father, were you baptised in those old times in Wales? Were you confirmed? Did you go to sermon, as Christians do? Did you sing psalms? Did you know your catechism?

Yes, said I, and what is more it was my father asked it of me, not me of my father.

For the catechism, then as now, was the asking and answering of questions for the establishing of one's faith, and until you had the answers off pat you had no faith and could scarce be said to exist, for what is anyone without faith? You might as well not know your own name (which indeed is the first question you must answer). It was an amazement to my son Owen that in this land of Wales, which he has never visited and which his godly friends call dark *&c*, there were churches and ministers, as there are in England, and in our house were both the Bible and the Book of Common Prayer. And indeed my father catechised me, as I lay in my bed under the eaves in the sheep-smelling gloom.

Being the smallest, I was put to bed in the summer months while it was still light, in the space under the thatch. My father, when he came in from the fields, always climbed the ladder to the upper storey and picked his way across the floor, dodging the beams with their hanging tools, to say goodnight to me; although I must have been asleep hours before, I always knew he was coming and woke to see the sputtering flame of his candle like a greasy star. Then he would sit beside the bed and ask the questions, while I fingered the crinkles in his forehead, which puzzled me greatly for my own face was without lines. His face was large for his body, flat and shaped like a shield, and this forehead of his was, as it were, the crest or banner across the top.

And if most nights I got no further than my name, what of it? I was young and half-asleep, and besides the name was not the simple N or M of the Prayer Book:

Question. What is your name?
Answer. N. or M.

In Wales, a name is a catechism in itself, and I doubt that my son Owen can recite his name as I mumbled mine:

Q. What is your name?
A. Arise the son of Evan the son of Arise the son of Owen the son of Arise the son of Evan the son of David the son of Arise the son of Griffith the son of the Red Lion the son of the Ren.

To be fair to Owen, he has one more name to learn than I did, being Owen the son of Arise the son of Evan the son of Arise the son of Owen the son of Arise the son of Evan the son of David the son of

Arise the son of Griffith the son of the Red Lion the son of the Ren, for a Welsh name gets longer with each generation. When it was my turn to catechise Owen, and bearing in mind the nation and city and times we live in, I taught him that his name was Owen Evans, and so he believes. Does he even know that he is descended from a Red Lion, and from a Ren? I cannot remember if I told him. These things are easier to say in Welsh, in which language my answer was spoken: *Rhys ap Ifan ap Rhys ap Owain ap Rhys ap Ifan ap Dafydd ap Rhys ap Gruffydd ap Y Llew Goch ap Y Ren.* (For the Welsh of my first name was Rhys, nor did I know the right English of it for many years.)

Q. Who gave you this name?

A. My godfathers and godmothers in my baptism, wherein I was made a member of Christ, the child of God, and an inheritor of the Kingdom of Heaven.

I know this is the answer laid down in the Prayer Book. I can answer it as well as any, and in two languages, but it does not satisfy me. For the part of my name given me by my godfathers and godmothers was only the first word, which is the easiest to remember, and as for the rest, it came from ancestors unknown to me and long dead and was given them by their own godfathers and godmothers. And rightly to understand the name would be to know all these ancestors, both who they were and what the names meant. One of them it seems was a Lion, and that of no ordinary hue, while another was a Ren, whatever that may mean, for I never knew the word in English or Welsh except as a conundrum of my ancestry.

They were men, my darling, like myself, my father told me. The Red Lion had his name because he was bloody and fierce.

The men in those days were greater and more warlike than ourselves, for just as the names get longer with each generation, so the men become lesser. The Red Lion, with only two names, the Ren with only one: these warriors lived close to the beginning of time, when life was simpler than in this corrupt age. They concerned themselves not with shepherding or tailoring or making of books, but only with wielding of swords and hewing of necks. From such am I descended, who had few or no ancestors of their own to recite.

I shall write no more of this catechism, for the reader knows it as well as I, and I hear my wife's voice in my mind reminding me of kersey and fustian. Nevertheless, although I fell asleep most nights before I could get to the end of it, and thus the catechism became mixed up with my dreams so that sometimes I knew not which parts were from the Prayer Book and which from Morpheus, yet I had learned much of it before I was seven years old, the ten commandments in any case, and took to heart the fifth of them:

Q. You said that your godfathers and godmothers did promise for you that you should keep God's commandments. Tell me how many there be?

A. Ten.

Q. Which be they?

A. The same which God spake in the twentieth chapter of Exodus, saying...

I...

II...

III...

IV...

V. Honour thy father and thy mother, that thy days may be long in the land, which the Lord thy God giveth thee...

At this point, how should I not wake up? For it was the voice of my father repeating the words I should have been saying to him if only I had been awake, telling me to honour him, and my mother also, and that only thus should my days be long in the land. I whose days in the land were already long, communing with living sheep and rooting in the grass for the jawbones and shinbones of dead ones, smearing myself with sheep-grease, poking at weeds in the river with a stick, listening to my mother talking with Bethan of the Fair People in the smell of sweat and the sound of clatterings, how could I not wish them to be longer?

Chapter VII
An Alphabet of Woven Stuffs, or The Crisscross Row Unravelled

Alphabetical is the best order, it seems to me. It were a waste of my schooling, which I had at the hands of Mr Beddow, the curate of our parish, in the parlour he had turned into a schoolroom (on land owned by my father) to have mastered the alphabet and not to use it for the better disposition of my material; this being all those cloths other than Welsh cottons, which I mentioned before out of their proper alphabetical place for no better reason than that I was brought up in, under, amongst and between them. But these other stuffs I am less enwrapped in, and can order more systematically. This alphabet of cloths will pass through your fingers, or your son's fingers, in many qualities, spinnings and weavings, and hailing from all parts of the kingdom.

Baize shall be my beginning, a smooth and fine woollen I do not recall ever having made a doublet or gown of. I regret, however, that I have not an A to begin with as Angel to this alphabet, for Angels are the first among created beings and therefore the only right emblem and embodiment of the letter A, as I learned from my hornbook in Mr Beddow's schoolroom, where my brothers and myself and some of the other children of the parish sat at a table as if we were going to eat. The hornbook was not unlike the cards with which my mother and Bethan battered and rent the wool, being a small wooden board with handles, except that instead of spikes it was covered with a layer of clear yellow-brown cows' horn to protect the letters underneath. Under the horn was the crisscross row, which began and ended with a cross and in between were set forth the letters, each with a word and picture corresponding. The Angel A was a man with wings and a body neither clothed nor naked, but blank as though the substance had been left for filling in at some later time. Perhaps he was wearing a garment so fine that my childish eyes could not perceive it, but whether this was a true representation is doubtful, for the Bible tells us how such a one is clothed, as I shall reveal under the appropriate letter. As for B, the point I have arrived at in my alphabet, it was a Bishop wearing a pointed hat and carrying a shepherd's crook in his hand. His gown was not so fine as the Angel's, for it was clearly visible, nor so coarse as broadcloth, which is the second of my Bs and makes gowns and coats and breeches for persons of much lesser dignity than a bishop.

Cottons having been promoted out of their proper station, and leaving aside canvas, which is hard to cut, I must mention calico for aprons, cambric for ruffs, and cock's web lawn for the most delicate of fripperies, and all these are linens of various kinds, which is to say their allegiance is to a vegetable not an animal mother, viz, the blue-flowered plant called flax.

Flannel shall be the next, since I never handled damask and can find no Es worth mentioning. It has an open texture and, being warm, is used in linings and in petticoats. Frieze is a heavy cloth with a raised nap; the word is almost the same as frizz, and the nap being sometimes raised with a furze there is a great congregation of Fs and Zs in the vicinity of this cloth. Fustian is made of a mixture of wool and linen and, like much of the finest cloth, is woven abroad, in the Low Countries. In the hornbook, F was for Father, which is the English for *Dad,* but the man in the picture was not my own father, having a face more oval than shieldshaped and without the banner of crinkles at the top. Indeed he was the same man as the Bishop, only without

God does not allow these knots and kernels of sense to occur by chance.

the hat and the staff, and he walked raising a finger in the air as if explaining something to some other man who could not be seen.

Grogram is a bastard cloth, part wool and part silk, but I ought not to speak so disrespectfully of it for it stands in the alphabet next to God himself, whom I never saw pictured until I went to school. He too looked like the Bishop, all these dignitaries, having a family resemblance, the differences being that he wore a crown instead of a hat and that he was seated on a throne instead of walking at large with a staff in his hand. I studied him well that I might know him when I came to stand before him at the Last Judgement. At the base of his throne there were no clouds or birds as evidence of its heavenly situation, but it stood in a blankness that could have been anywhere.

Here I must mention hemp, which being good enough to hang a man is good enough to hang on him. Holland is an excellent linen from the Low Countries, and the likeliest stuff of any for the gowns of Angels, for Scripture tells us that those that preside over the Last Days will be clad in pure and white linen, which we may suppose to be a fine holland, as it is not to be expected that God would clothe them in housewife cloth, a coarser linen which scarce deserves to share the same letter. Whether the gown was of holland that the Angel wore in my hornbook I know not; its invisibility suggests rather the fineness of cock's web lawn, but I doubt this would be hard-wearing enough for flying in, or for standing next the sun.

K is an uncouth letter, all arms and legs. When I ran my fingers over the letters in the hornbook, I stopped always at the wispy crack over this K, worrying at it with my nails, but it never grew bigger, and the letters stayed safe in their compartments.

I held the hornhook in my left hand and pointed to each letter in turn with Mr Beddow's festraw, saying the letter and the word. Then, when Mr Beddow had moved on to the next child and was making him do likewise, I continued to study the letters and tried to make them signify in my mind as they ought. K in the hornbook was for a Knight, whose attire is not to be discussed here, being of a material wholly resistant to the tailor's craft, and I know not how any ever worked it to such a semblance of a doublet and breeches as this fellow wore, and as the clothing was too hard, by so much was the letter itself too soft, for I could not hear it at all, which is a trick the English sometimes play with their consonants for the deceiving of us Welsh. It was useless to ask my brothers about such things, for their reading and their English were worse than mine was, although they had passed beyond the hornbook. They had a primer each and were learning the grammar and the accidence, and they sat at one end of the bench a little apart from the younger children, muttering to each other when Mr Beddow was not looking. Griffith's eyes went slowly round the room, watching each face in turn, then up to the ceiling, scrutinizing the cobwebs on the beams. Owen did not look up from his book, except to glance down the table at me every now and then and smile. When Mr Beddow stood over them and heard them read from the primer, he told them they did ill, and was sad, but he was sad also when he stood over me and told me I did well. In the woven alphabet there is no such confusion as I felt in the schoolroom, for the first letter of kersey stands out where all can see it, and so does the cloth itself, being coarse with narrow ribs and favoured by countrymen.

A stick of instruction carried by schoolmasters.

Look what a collocation of stuffs I find under L! I have mentioned linen already, and lawn is only a common variety of it. But there is lace, whose weave is so open that there is as much of air in the material as there is of the cloth itself, and there is leather, which is not woven at all, being but the skin of a beast. Then there are linsey-woolsey and lockram, the first a worsted and the second a hempen cloth, so that there is a whole rainbow or gamut in this one letter alone. And I am not halfway through the alphabet yet, so I must hurry myself, though in my fancy I still hear Mr Beddow telling me I do well. Aye, Rhys, he would say, very well, very well indeed, and seemed about to dissolve into tears. He had a black beard and a long bony face like a sheep's.

Rooting further among the cabbage, I find no Ms, Ns, Os, Ps or Qs. It is as if a moth has been at this part of our inventory. I paused indeed for a moment to consider polecat, but it is too small a beast to accommodate many of my words, and has not even the scriptural vindication of badger, which I mentioned in my first chapter. So I proceed rapidly to russet, which is a cloth the colour of decay, as if a bolt of broadcloth had withered on the tree and was ready to fall.

Strange as it is to imagine it, had I been born in India or China instead of Merionethshire I would have grown up among worms rather than sheep, for silk, the most subtle and mysterious of fabrics, is woven from the oozings of such creatures. A worm being so much smaller and exuding proportionally little yarn, I suppose the fields must be thick with them. I have heard that the fibres are not shorn from the outside of the worm, as is the case with a sheep, but that it has a sort of spinning wheel inside its body, as a spider does, and therefore it is only necessary to wind this on to a spool to have a strong thread. This stuff is used in the gowns of persons of quality, and in Scripture we are told that the virtuous woman, whose price is above rubies, though she makes fine linen and sells it, yet the clothing she makes for her own use is of silk and purple. When this silk is so closely woven as to give a cloth that shines on one side we call it satin, a very splendid cloth for court ladies and those whose business it is to dazzle, yet we should note that the angels, as I said before, wear linen and not satin, for the dazzlement that they radiate comes from God and not from a worm.

Velvet also should be mentioned with silk, being the heaviest of silken cloths, with a dense pile. This too is especially used for the business of dazzlement, but would never do for angelic clothing, being far too weighty for flight. They who wear it bind themselves to the earth.

Worsted is a good and strong cloth, woven of a fine, tightly spun thread and used in the gowns of considerable women. And now I am almost, and sooner than I had thought, at an end. Just as my alphabet has no A, so I see that it has no X, Y or Z, all which I remember well from the hornbook. X was for Xerxes, a man I knew nothing of, nor would Mr Beddow explain him when I asked, but he appeared the same man as God, throne and crown and all, only his gown was dyed a dark colour instead of white, shown by a cross-hatching on the picture. This made me wonder if he might not be the devil, but I did not ask this, and kept the question for my father, only I forgot to ask it. And to this day, I know how to pronounce Xerxes, but nothing of his life or character. Y was for Yew, and was the only picture in the hornbook I could compare directly with the thing it described (my father being quite unlikc a hornbook Father), for a yew tree grew just outside Mr Beddow's house and was bowed and gnarled and leafy as its likeness was, and bore berries as that did, though the berries were red rather than colourless. Next to the Yew was Zeal, who was a woman, as evidenced in the smoothness and roundness of her face and the graceful lines of her gown and apron; she walked with a long stride and held out her right hand, exhibiting Zeal as far as could be conceivable when she had no one in front of her to be zealous towards except the yew tree. I looked at her longer and harder than at all the other letters put together, for I have ever found a fascination in Zeal, but at length I would tire even of her, and turn the hornbook over. Here were no more pictures, and no crack in the cow's horn, only the following words: + *Our Father which art in Heaven, hallowed be thy Name, thy Kingdom come, thy Will be done, on Earth as it is in Heaven. Give us this Day our daily Bread and forgive us our Trespasses as we forgive them that trespass against us, and lead us not into Temptation but deliver us from Evil. Amen.*+ These were the words said in church by all the congregation on the Lord's Day, so that I knew their meaning even before I was put to school, and that bread was *bara*, and Father was *Dad*, except that this Father was *Diw*, which is God. Mr Beddow's face when he led us in this prayer in church was as gloomy as it was in school, and it was no less so when he dined at our house afterwards as he did most often on the Lord's Day and many other days besides, and called down God's blessings on my family. And when all had eaten and Mr Beddow had said grace again and risen to leave, he thanked my father and mother for their kindness as if they had broken his heart.

Chapter VIII
Zeal Unfolded by the Youngest of Her Offspring

Zeal reminded me of my mother, though, truth to tell, I cannot be sure now in what this resemblance consisted; Zeal was certainly the younger of the two, though at that age all grown persons were old to me. She looked like the maids in the church that Owen and Griffith gazed at during sermon, but she was statelier, and wore her hair free as I never saw any woman or maid do, and it is not seemly except in a hornbook. She was dressed as only a married woman may be, in a gown instead of a waistcoat and petticoat. The only feature that she shared with my mother was the straightness of her nose. As for my mother's spiritual qualities, whether she exemplified Zeal or no, it was hard to tell, for I was not altogether sure what the word meant; it appeared at the end of the alphabet when I was tired and my mind was full of all the other letters. It was not quite the same thing as hard work, I thought, nor was it earnestness, having a more loose-haired and flowing-gowned quality than either.

There was a man at Llanfihangel y Pennant, my mother said, carding zealously so that the pile of wool beside her grew into a great cloud, who went early to the barn to feed the oxen, and then fell asleep on the hay, which you know, Bethan, is what no one should do. And about midnight they wakened him, the Fair People, dancing all round him in their striped clothes.

Just now you told me they wore white aprons, Bethan said, like a marriage company.

The rest of their clothes were striped, my mother said. This fellow pretended to be asleep, but the most beautiful of the women came and put a striped cushion under his head. There were four tassels on it, do you know, Bethan? He described it with the utmost nicety. But just then the cock crew and all the dancers seemed discommoded by it. So then the woman snatched back her cushion and they went away.

Who was this fellow, Bethan said, who described the cushion so nicely?

Oh, I know not, my mother said. It was in my grandfather's time, I think, and the man is dead.

Then why, Bethan said, do you tell me of it now?

Some might think it was Bethan who was the more zealous in this conversation, but I cannot think of her grey and drooping face as having anything of true zeal in it, even though she carded as fiercely as my mother and was the better weaver of the two. I wondered what colours the stripes might have been, since I had never seen any striped clothing before, but it was no good asking my mother in the presence of Bethan, for she would say the words were not for my ears, or else she would deny having said anything at all.

When Bethan was not about, then did my mother's zeal have full sway, for she would talk to anyone who was with her, and if she thought there was no one with her she would talk to herself. Well, Elin *fach*, she would say to herself when she thought no one could hear her, what must we do today? We must get on.

When she could find nothing to converse with herself about, she would sing zealously, so that the house was always full of her voice one way or another. But when talking to me in Bethan's absence, she cared not a bit if she frighted me, but would discourse of the *Tylwyth Teg* or of ghosts or any other such matters.

Look, said she, there is a bird in the parlour. Get it out, get it out, Rhys!

And when I did nothing, for it was not to be expected I could catch a bird when I was but six years old, she said, Call your father, then (forgetting my father was out in the fields). Is it a sparrow, Rhys? she asked. It seems greater. Oh, I hope it is a sparrow. It is brown, is it not?

I thought the bird was brown, but it was difficult to be sure, because the light in the room was dim and itself of a brownish hue, and besides, the bird would not stay still but flew from one corner to the other panicked by my mother's swishing at it with a broom, and by myself pursuing it with a stool, which I thought to stand on the better to catch it, only I would not have been tall enough even had it waited for me. All the while it made its complaint, so reedy that it seemed not to come from any living thing, yet it had feeling in it, which amazed me that a creature so small and fluttering should express itself so sensibly. And so it continued until Bethan came and the bird straightway flew out the door. It was a sparrow, said she. It was long-bodied for a sparrow, said my mother, and Bethan sighed.

Whether my mother truly believed this sparrow to be the corpse bird, I know not. I had heard its voice calling something like *Whee or Wheedle*, while the true corpse bird is known to say *Deuwch, deuwch*. It is more usually heard at night, beating its wings against a window pane, though there are some that say it has no wings to beat, or feathers either. In any case, neither my mother nor myself died shortly afterwards, nor even Bethan, old as she was, so if it was the corpse bird it had not come for us, but had blundered into the parlour on its way to summon another person. Nor do I think my mother was frighted, but only zealous, which in my understanding of the word, displays many of the same tokens, such as an agitation of the body and hands and a reddening of the cheeks, and the uttering of small cries, and I believe from observation that it is not so unpleasurable as fright, or perhaps this species of zeal may be characterized as fright and pleasure combined. Whatever it is, I believe my mother possessed it.

Aderyn corff in Welsh.

Come, come in English.

Chapter IX
A Prophet Prophesied

I came in, clutching my mother's hand, my nightgown half tripping me, my bare feet pricked by the straw matting, my ankles chilled by the draughts that eddied across the floor. There was a stranger sitting in the best seat, nearest the fire, with Owen and Griffith at his feet, a man dressed in gown and bands like a minister. Though younger than my father, he was heavy and sagging of body, and his mouth was open, the beardless jaw somewhat crooked, which made me want to push it back into place. I hardly knew what was happening when first Owen and then Griffith were asked to stand before him with the primer in their hands and read, the man nodding and half-smiling, helping them along with the sentences when they stumbled.

Have some more beer, sir, said my father.

No, no, said the man, I must hear this first. O bountiful Jesu (these being the words Griffith was just then stumbling over) – Say on, boy.

The fire stabbed between my eyelashes and I held tighter to my mother's hand to keep from falling over, yet I prepared myself inwardly to answer anything I might be asked. Had I not answered a hundred catechisms, waking from dreams to answer my father's questions? But now he took the primer from Griffith's hands and placed it in my own, and the man by the fire said, Read, boy, if it please you, and the words lay before me in a clear yellow light as though I saw them through a thin layer of cow's horn, and then they began to dance, so that first my eyes and then my tongue could do nothing but follow them.

O sweet Jesu, O bountiful Jesu, O Jesu son of the Virgin Mary, have mercy upon me.

The man rose from his seat and threw his arms round me. I felt his empty beer cup pressing against my shoulderblade. Do you hear that? said he. Sweet

Jesu, bountiful Jesu, and in English, too. I never heard a boy read English so well.

Is not my son cunning, Mr Llewelyn?

So he is, yes, so he is. His brothers are fine boys, too, only they do not read so well as this one. This boy will do great things. (He released his embrace a little and laid his hand on the top of my head, grasped it, rather, with a hot, heavy grip.) Bless you, my boy. There is a grace upon you, and your Father has a special purpose for you. I see you speaking with kings and with lords.

Kings, Griffith asked from the hearth, kings? Which kings? The King of England? The King of France? The King of –

I see you famous, a glorious man.

He will be a farmer, Griffith said.

No, no, he will not be that. Never a farmer. A man of God.

A man of God, my father asked, my son will be a minister like yourself?

A man of God, Mr Llewelyn repeated. This is what I foretell for him. There is bad weather coming. I must go. But first I bless this small one (his hand all this time pressing down so hard that I could not stand up straight). O Lord, bless this child, thy son. May he see and hear and speak. Give him wisdom when he asks for it. Chastise him when he needs to be chastised.

Be seated again, sir, my father said, Pray do me the honour to take some more beer.

No, sir, I thank you. I must go now.

But it is late. You must sleep here. This is rough country to travel round at night, and you are not likely to find a bed this side of the Bear Mouth.

There will be a storm, Mr Llewelyn said, and gave a small laugh that seemed part sneeze. Then he wandered out of the room, and my parents hurried after him. I hesitated for a moment, and then followed them all into the chilly passage. The hall door was open on the other side, and I could see Bethan spinning by the dying fire. Mr Llewelyn went to the door that led to the farmyard and opened it, letting in a strong wind and a spattering of hailstones. Look, he said, it is not here yet. Get me my horse, will you? I will ride before it. There is enough of a moon to get me to, where did you say?

The Bear Mouth, but –

The Bear Mouth will do. I will ride to the Bear Mouth. Bring me my horse, if you will, sir, or never mind, I shall fetch him myself, said he, and went out into the dark farmyard, my father running after him calling. But I never saw the man depart, for at that moment my mother took me by the hand and led me back to bed.

We learn from Scripture that some may entertain angels unawares. Griffith said afterwards that Mr Llewelyn was distempered in mind, but all he said came to pass, though some have cavilled at and doubted it. I know not whether he was man or angel, but he was not distempered in mind, that is certain.

Chapter X
Woolach

I wish when I was chasing that bird about the parlour with my mother I had honoured her as the Fifth Commandment admonishes, by paying heed to her words and looking well on its flutterings to see if it were sparrow or no instead of bustling about with stool in hand, placing it, standing on it, leaping off before I could fall, and hurrying on to the next place. All agree that the corpse bird is of no known species, and so I should have been marking carefully the length of its body, the shape of its head and beak, the pattern of its flight, that I might know for certain what it was. I believe it was a sparrow as Bethan said, and there is no doubt that it had wings, and feathers too, for it dropped a couple in its encounters with my mother's broom, but if indeed it was the corpse bird then I missed its meaning.

Though I had been the object of a prophecy, that prophecy was merely that I should be a man of God and talk with kings *&c*, not that I should myself prophesy. I knew not my prophetic nature, and so allowed myself to be ambushed by the future as other men are. And yet, for all we cannot know the future, we believe that we do see it most of the time when what we see is only a reflection of the present, as: The sky is clear this evening, it will be a fine day tomorrow. And then when it rains we shrug our shoulders and put on our kersey or our broadcloth. When I was six, my understanding of the future was just such a haphazard, shrugging business as this. And so it was not till my father lay dying on the floor of the hall after supper that I understood how little I had known of this same future, though I had been told that all men die. And chiefly I reproached myself as he lay panting and shaking, his eyes closed and his broad face crimson, that I had not foreseen this.

Suppose the bird in the hall that day was the corpse bird, come to foretell my father's death, why did it come to a place where he was not? Could such a creature, sent by God to warn us, miss its way? Might it have knowledge of our death but ignorance of our whereabouts? It came many months before he died: is there a term or date of expiration on its warning, or can it warn us as long beforehand as it chooses? If that is so, the corpse bird might fly through the window and flutter about the curtains at our mother's lying-in bed, for all who are born must die. No, I must shoo the bird out of my mind as my mother's broom and Bethan's coming in shooed it out of the parlour.

There are other signs by which you may know a death. The corpse candle is a light, red, white or blue, which leaves the house of the future dead one at night and processes along the path the coffin will shortly take, the path to the church. A child's light is pasty and juvenile, while that of a grown person burns brighter. And if you chance to be standing near water when the light passes, you may gaze into it and see the dead one's face reflected there. Or you may know when your death is approaching by a little bell that sounds in your ear, the *cloch bach*, like a fore-echo of your passing bell.

Father, did you hear it, the little bell?

But as he lay there, red and shaking, he made only a noise that sounded like *Woolach, woolach.*

All this took place without anyone being ready for it, not myself, nor my family, and not even my father, who was ready for most things and guided the course of the year from lambing to gelding, from gelding to sheepwashing, from sheepwashing to shearing, from shearing to tupping, and from tupping to marking, and yet he, who could oversee all these, could not oversee his own death so far as to take to his bed and call Mr Beddow and die there like a Christian, but instead must rise from the bench, put his half-drunk cup of beer on the table so that it might not be spilt, turn to his wife and say, in a puzzled, almost contrite voice that was quite unlike his usual manner, I do not feel well, my dear, then fall backwards onto the floor with a crash. There he lay, his feet still the wrong side of the bench, while we all rose and my brothers shifted both table and bench so that he could lie in more orderly fashion, and my mother ran about saying, O God, in different tones and loudnesses as if to find which sounded the best. Then she went to my father and addressed him, Husband, husband, but when he said naught in reply, she concluded that he was stifling and cried, Give him air. In a short while, my brothers had carried the table and both benches to the far side of the hall in response to my mother's bidding and were debating quietly with each other whether to take them outside, for the labour was a consolation to them and they imagined they were doing some good by it, but Bethan stopped them and after some discussion between the three it was resolved that Owen would take the best horse and ride for Mr Beddow, who, though no physician, was the most learned man that could be found at such notice.

I had clambered from the far bench before they moved it and was now squatting on the floor by my father's head. I guessed at once that he was dying, and so I set myself to discover the reason of this death, which is not to say the cause of it but how it might reside comformably with all else I knew of this world and of God's ways in it. Sometimes my mother noticed me, and called me to Come away, and Give him air, but then she began again on her trying out of O God, and I was left to myself. Besides the hairs of his beard and on his upper lip, there were others that grew in profusion from his nostrils, and though I must have seen these before, yet they seemed to me now very sad and touching, and I wondered if he had ever seen them himself, and whether he counted them as a disfigurement or an ornament. These hairs stirred, which indicated that he breathed still, but he had to close his eyes and shake the breaths forth with his whole body, and even so the strain of it reddened his face as if he had been chasing a sheep or tossing hay-bales, so that I knew he could not continue long.

Therefore I questioned him, while he was still living to enlighten me.

Q. Father, have you heard the little bell?

What kind of a question is this to ask of one's father at such a moment? In my defence, it must be remembered that I was but six years old and had had no time to think of better. So I asked about the premonitions that I had heard of from my mother's talk over the carding.

Q. Father, have you heard a screech-owl calling outside the window at night as you lay in bed?

Q. Father, have you found any bruises or marks on your body, not caused by any accident you know of?

Q. Father, was there a dog that howled all night, a dog that was neither Geraint nor Pero? I heard it not, but did you hear it?

My father made no answer, being too busy dying. And so I asked my questions many times, while my mother ran about zealously and Griffith stood at the table trying one end of it to see if he could lift it and Bethan fetched my father's cup of beer again, which he would not drink, and so she spilled some of it down his face then took the cup back to the table. But if only I had had time to prepare myself beforehand, I should have asked quite otherwise:

Q. Father, have you thought well on your worldly affairs? Is the settlement of your farm and land in order? Have you remembered all your children, even down to the least of them, whom you call your darling?

It was too late to ask him all this, but whenever I think on his dying, these are the questions I ask in my mind, and sometimes, in my mind, he answers them and calls for Bethan to leave off fussing with the beer or for Griffith to leave off lifting the table and bring him pen and paper. For what was there in my own foolish questions to rouse him to a sense of his last duties? It is no wonder he moved his head from side to side as if vexed with them and began muttering his curious word, *Woolach*.

As to this word, I have asked many, and all agree that it is not to be found in the British tongue. It has somewhat of a Welsh sound to it, which is to be expected from a Briton, and somewhat the look of the English *Wool*, which was his business, though if for some reason he wished to speak of wool in English he marred it sorely with this *-ach*, and besides did not complete his sentence. As a last word it is of no great import or utility. But it is the only answer I had of my father before he left me forever.

Q. Father, have you heard it, the little bell?
A. *Woolach, woolach.*

Chapter XI
A Beatitude for the Disinherited

The Scripture tells us not what mountain Our Lord stood upon to preach his sermon, or what was the weather that day, but I suppose he stood on some rock or cairn, with the disciples clustered just below in one of those flat grassy places that are often found in such eminences, and the mass of the people were at the foot of the mountain, or straggling along the paths to the summit, for it was to the disciples that Our Lord spoke, so that they afterwards could carry the message down the mountain to the people below. His standing there was to be closer to God and to heaven, for we must remember that Moses climbed a mountain to receive the word of God in the form of Ten Commandments, and from such a place you may see the great part of the world stretched out around you, and so God sees it and sends out his word across it, as the shadow of a cloud crosses fields, rivers, villages, woods, lakes &c. Jesus gave to the people that day not Commandments but Blessings, or Beatitudes, and instead of ten, there were nine of them, viz:

Firstly, he blessed the poor in spirit for theirs would be the Kingdom of Heaven.

Secondly, he blessed mourners, for they should be comforted.

Thirdly, he blessed the meek, for they should inherit the earth.

Fourthly, he blessed those that hungered and thirsted for righteousness, for they should be satisfied.

Fifthly, he blessed the merciful, for they should have mercy.

Sixthly, he blessed the pure in heart, for they should see God.

Seventhly, he blessed the peacemakers, for they should be called the children of God.

Eighthly, he blessed those who were persecuted for righteousness' sake, for theirs would be the Kingdom of Heaven.

Ninthly, he blessed his disciples who would be persecuted for righteousness' sake.

So to these Beatitudes, and in a spirit of true meekness, I add a tenth:

Blessed are the disinherited, for they shall inherit–

I have not yet rightly formulated what it is that they shall inherit, but I hope to arrive at it by the end of this chapter, for a blessing I know it to be, only it is long in the explaining. But I will say this, that I have as much of the world as my father now has being dead, which is nothing, and so I am closer to him than my brothers Owen and Griffith ever were, who took to themselves the land and sheep and farm and money, the outhouses and fleeces and horses and dogs and pigs and fowl and peas and barley and all the other vanities that he cast from him with his disdainful cry of *Woolach.* For this *Woolach* I take to mean, Have it all, I want none of it, the dead being notoriously frugal in their earthly needs. It is certain that my mother in her zealousness understood not his *Woolach,* for she continued crying, Give him air! after he had stopped breathing it, as one not knowing that the dead have no need even of this most invisible and insubstantial of benefits.

As for me, the dullness of wit which failed to foresee this death and prompted me to ask the wrong questions stayed with me a few days longer. I felt myself magnified by the greatness of my loss, so that at his funeral women looked at me with a new softness and men clapped me on the shoulder like equals, though they had to reach down to do it, and all affirmed that it was myself they were sorriest for, and that I was the hope of the house and the image of my father. My brothers took refuge as before in hoisting and heaving, for they had a whole coffin to bear now, aided by some other men of the district, and they processed out of the hall and through the passage to the front of the house accordingly and laid my father on the bier in front of the house, while I carried nothing but walked before them as if to announce their arrival. The respectable persons talked in low tones, laughing sometimes in a shamefaced way, while the poor stood in a group of their own, a little to one side, and said nothing. My mother came out last, with Bethan beside her holding the cheese and the purse, and the girl with the platter of white loaves. My mother did not weep and held her face and person with a very proper stillness. She took the purse from Bethan and fumbled forth the pence one by one, pressing them into the rind of the cheese so effectually that they all stayed in place except the last, which she pushed not hard enough, so that it sprung out again and rolled on to the path. Though it was nearest me and one or two looked in my direction, I knew my place better than to stoop and pick it up, for I was not here to fetch and carry like my brothers, or to dispense cheese and coins like my mother, but only to be an image, a hope, and an object of sorrow. Therefore I waited while Bethan and the girl shuffled the burdens in their hands and finally my mother herself bent down, picked up the coin and wiped it on her apron before putting it back into the cheese.

Pray accept this offering, said she to the old man who had established himself in the vanguard of the poor, in memory of my husband.

He bowed to her, taking the cheese in one hand and picking out the coins with the other which he gave to those around him. Thus did a pittance of my father's fortune spend itself before my eyes, but I counted it not, but fixed my gaze on the cheese for I was curious as to how they would cut and apportion it. In this was I disappointed, for the man continued to hold it, while the poor people were given a loaf each, and I saw that they did not intend to eat it there and then.

Fetch the ale, my mother said, whereupon Bethan and the girl returned into the house and presently came out with a tray bearing many small cups of ale, though not enough to go round among so many, and a platter of cakes. While the poor refreshed themselves, Bethan took me by the hand and led me to the coffin to say goodbye to my father. When I gazed in, however, there was none of him visible, only a winding sheet somewhat the shape of him, broad-shouldered and broad-faced, though in other respects smaller than I expected and with a smell of rosemary and some other sickly herb coming out of it. This goodbye seemed even then the least of my omissions but I said it to satisfy her, and then the parish clerk came up and added salt to the rest, which ran down into the base of the coffin.

Then was I blessed by the cold sunshine and the cracked sound of the passing bell, (which was the same note it had when it called worshippers to church on a Sunday, but I minded it not then), and the long walk along the path to the church. I walked behind the coffin and ahead of all the other mourners, and was not to be distracted by yellow butterflies in the hedgerows like broken-off pieces of sunlight, or by thoughts of the corpse candle which must have traced this route a few nights before, leaving perhaps a few drops of wax on the beaten earth of the path, which I did not stoop to look for, or by a fluttering in the branches of a newly green hawthorn tree, which was not the corpse bird, or by a little throbbing inside my right ear which was not a *cloch bach*, cracked or otherwise, and it was my father who was dead and not myself.

We arrived at the churchyard, and the pallbearers laid the bier beside the grave. Mr Beddow was already standing there, and I was surprised to see him, for I thought a man of my father's considerableness should have the rector for his service, but Mr Beddow had been my father's friend and was beholden to him. When all were gathered and standing in silence (the poor, I saw now, had left their cheese behind), Mr Beddow began his prayers. And I was so far blessed that the words did not touch me, nor did I hear the rubbing and rustling of doublets and gowns as the mourners pressed to each other in listening, nor feel a cold wind that had risen up from somewhere.

Blessed are they that mourn for they shall be comforted. As for the disinherited –

I know not when Mr Beddow put aside his prayerbook and began reading from another document he had with him, for there was no change in his voice, which always sounded as if he was conducting a funeral even when he was not. But still most of these words flew over my head, and I only glimpsed them in passing.

In the name of God, *Amen.* I, Evan Evans of the parish of St David, Llangluin, farmer, being in perfect memory, and strong in body, do thus make my last will and testament. *Imprimis,* I do bequeath my soul to God my Creator who gave it, and my body to the grave to be decently buried within the parish church of St David in Merionethshire as my executors shall think fit and agree. I also as for my worldly goods desire that all my personal estate be divided as followeth...

What was any of this to me? I took no heed of *my son Owen Evans* or *my son Griffith Evans* or *my wife Elin Evans,* or of so many other Evanses who were uncles and aunts and cousins I had never seen because they lived in the next valley, a David here, a John there, a Mary and a Susan elsewhere, not to mention those cousins and aunts and uncles who were not Evanses at all but Joneses and Williamses and Prices, nor did I care who had one silver spoon and who two, who had a death's head ring and who five shillings for a ring. I was a little tired by this time, which was something my mother always said of me when I wanted to go elsewhere or do something other than what I was told to do: Oh, he is tired. I was waiting for the coffin to be lowered into the grave and dirt to be cast over it. And so I missed the moment when the looks that were cast at me and the voices that murmured behind me took on a different pity. It was not, poor thing, he is the image and the hope any more, but another poor thing altogether, with nothing of hope in it.

In the days following the funeral I often observed myself breathing and thought what a great quantity of air there was in the world and that I, having inherited no earth or water or livestock, had received all this air instead, which was a great burden upon me, to have to breathe all of it, as if I had been asked to drink up the ocean. It seemed to me then that when my mother had cried, Give him air, the *him* she referred to had not been my father but myself. And therefore when a few days later my brother Griffith said, Go hence, Rhys, you are standing in my field, I, not sure whether he meant it for a jest or no, had nothing to say in reply but, Go hence, Griff, you are breathing my air, which only confirmed him in his opinion that I was distempered in mind, as he told my mother at supper.

Oh, said she, you must not tease him, Griff. But all the same, I wish we knew what to do with the poor child.

Which was a thing nobody ever asked of me before, but she said it all the time now, to Bethan and Owen and Griffith. And I wished to say, but dared not for fear of further insults, Mother, you need do nothing with me, for I have already too much to occupy me in this breathing of air, and also this beating of my heart (for it beat so hard I could scarce keep up with it and was worn out trying). There was nothing else for me to do, for Mr Beddow had turned me away from the schoolroom, where I had thought to learn the grammar and the accidence. (Even Owen and Griffith were there no longer, being busy at all times about the farm.) My mother told me that being turned from school should be a lesson to me to think less vainly of myself, and of my accomplishments. For, your dear father having left you out of his will, said she, everything you have now you owe to me and to your brothers. Nothing in this house or on this land is yours, and therefore you should be grateful for everything we give you, and work hard to pay us back.

One afternoon, Bethan came into the hall where I was sitting by the remains of the fire, using what strength remained from breathing and listening to my heartbeat to scrawl in the ashes with a half-burned stick, for I had heard a little of the accidence in times past from listening to my brothers repeating it, and was trying to remember what I could.

What are you writing? said she.

Have, said I, *hast, hath.*

What is that?

It is the accidence.

Poor lad, said she, sniffing to show she liked the accidence no more than the Fair People or the corpse bird. Are you not sorry for your father's death?

What then? I said. Cannot I go to my father at any time?

How can you go to your father that is dead?

Yes, I can. It is but thrusting a knife into my belly, and then I shall die and go to my father.

O child, no, Bethan said. Your father is gone to heaven, but if you make away with yourself, you will go to hell. You must think upon God continually, and not think such thoughts.

Until that moment, my thoughts had come unbidden, whether of accidence or Xerxes or sheep or nine-men's morris or dogs or hoodman blind or my father's death or breathing. Never had I understood that it was possible to think something at will. How can that be? I said. Do you think upon God continually?

She said, Yes, that I do. Every time I draw my breath I think upon God.

It is rare if it be true, I thought, for I found breathing hard enough on its own without having to think in time to it. Just then my mother and brothers came in, and Bethan told them what I had said, and they affirmed that they also thought upon God continually, which I would never have believed. However, they said so, and I was rebuked. Nevertheless, I remembered how I had surpassed my brothers in Angel and Zeal, and so resolved then and there that I would surpass them also in thinking upon God.

I am come to my Beatitude, as I said I would, only it is a long one, being, as it were, botched together out of several of the others. Blessed are the disinherited that have no sheep or fields or pigs or barley to think upon, for they shall have more space thereby in their minds for God. Being poor, theirs is the Kingdom of Heaven; being mourners, they shall be comforted; being meek, they shall inherit the earth; hungering and thirsting for righteousness, they shall be satisfied. Blessed are the disinherited, for if their fathers on earth have forgot them be assured that their Father in heaven never will.

Chapter XII
The Needle Threaded

My wife is become very cunning, for I never catch her reading my writings, but she sweeps the room pointedly when I am at my desk, or else she comes in from the baker with a pie from the cook's shop or a dish of stewed eels which she puts down before me and makes only the faintest sigh, such as none but a husband would be able to hear, and I am to understand from this that the money for such comestibles came not from my letter to His Majesty of my nose (which has not sold according to its deserts), but from what little earnings she has accrued herself from her ministrations to the neighbours, and what she cannot earn she has borrowed. She will never believe that the King will remember me, as he told me when he laid his sacred hand on my person. She knows that my book has veered from its aim (which is to say her aim), for eight chapters have gone by since last I picked up the appurtenances which were to aid me in the explication of the trade. Never would she understand the necessity of including in a book of tailoring the catechism or the beatitudes or the death and funeral of my father, for having a woman's narrow imagination she understands not that all things are joined to all other things, which is indeed an insight proper to a tailor, whose work is joining things, by his needle and thread, together. I feel her eyes on me now, moving between my page and my appurtenances and my nose, for if she cannot have me write as she will then she will have me the object of her *unguentum*. Therefore I reach at last for the appurtenances, and find an unexpected pleasure in the handling of them after so many chapters.

Having listed in a former place all the necessities for an apprentice tailor, I find I have omitted one, which is to say a bag to put all in. When you are more accomplished (for I write now for the apprentice, not for his mother and father, it being understood by this time that the son is settled in his apprenticeship to a master tailor), you will be able to make such a bag yourself: it is only a pocket unattached to breeches or doublet. For now, you must buy one, or have your mother or some other female person make one for you. This bag or pocket will need a drawstring at the top so you may close it easily to prevent the appurtenances flying out of it, for you must remember that your trade is practised in a high place, not Cader Idris, but still on top of a shopboard, which is high enough, and a most inconvenient summit to clamber down from when all your belongings are flown.

Now it is time to begin your instruction in the art of sewing, and for this purpose you will need a piece of cloth to practise on. Let it be housewife cloth or coarse lawn or some other inexpensive kind that will not offer too much resistance to the needle, and the length of one of your arms. Choose also a needle of medium size and some thread, whatever you have, though linen is best for strength. Now take your place on the shopboard, sitting with legs crossed and the cloth upon your lap.

Observe first this cloth. What is it but a crisscrossing of many threads, the warp that runs downwards and the woof that runs across? Tug at it a little with your hands. It stretches somewhat, which is its nature, but only so far before it resists. There is a strength in it that comes from its multiplicity, for you could break the separate threads with pulling on them, but not this whole. Now lift one side of it and drop it again. Feel how softly it falls, and see how it settles in a kind of wave, like water. What a strange material is this, substantial and formless at once. Only so can it clothe the body, for it must move as the body moves and yet be strong enough to provide protection against cold and heat, air and water. And this material you must make yourself master of, for its nature is always to escape and flow away from you, to have no shape or purpose, and only by binding it with threads can you hold it to your will.

Lay the cloth down again for now: it is time to thread the needle. First break off a good length of thread, and take the end of it in your right hand, holding the needle upright in your left. (If you wish, you may moisten the end of the thread in your mouth before the attempt, to stiffen it.) Approach the end of the thread to the needle and pass it through. This you should do more easily than myself, for you are young and have good eyesight, and yet I confess that I never at any age did it without trepidation. The eye is small and the thread fine, the eyes of your master are on you; each of your hands shakes slightly, no matter how hard you try to hold them steady (which task is so unexpectedly difficult that you surmise now you must spend all your days with each part of the body in subtle oscillation, only you do not notice it, being accustomed), and you move the thread eyeward. When the two cross, you know not at first whether your goal is accomplished, but then you see that needle and thread are still separate. So it continues, and the more your master watches, the harder it is to do, and this is after all not even your work but the minute task you must accomplish before your work can begin. You could be at this all day (for there seems no reason why the two things should ever be in the same place at the same time), and your master would still say nothing, but merely stand at the cutting board watching with one eye sour and the other amused, and you unsure which to believe. Nevertheless, and sooner than you think, the thread end catches the rim of the needle's eye. It does not go through, however, but bends and looks to spring off again, only you prevent it in time by slackening the tension, your whole being now intent on staying the capriciousness of the thread. You succeed at once, or else you fail and do it again, but in any case you succeed sooner or later, for which you must thank God, for only he knows how you accomplished it.

You are now ready to sew, and these are the stitches you must begin with, firstly, the basting stitch, secondly the forward stitch, and thirdly the backstitch. You must learn quickly before your master loses patience, for I see him now drumming his fingers on the cutting board. He can do little work until you are accomplished, unless he has another apprentice or journeyman to help him, and so he is giving up his time to make you perfect in your craft.

As I have been writing the above, I had a piece of cloth on my lap taken from our clothes chest, and have been preparing to work it, my intent being to sew along with this reader of mine (my wife watching all the while, though pretending to be reading a letter from our daughter) to ensure that all my instruction is as clear as I can make it. It is true I have no shopboard here, but I sit crosslegged on my writing stool, which is not over-precarious for a man used to keeping his balance as I am, only it pains my knees as I said before. And when I threaded the needle, I found that, despite my poor eyesight, God enabled me to find the aperture at the first pass, such was my faith, and I see now why our Lord compares the entering of the Kingdom of Heaven to this threading the needle, for only faith will accomplish it. I was to do all the stitches after that, but after my joy at threading the needle, and writing of the master with his one sour eye and his one amused eye, I found myself remembering my old shopboard in Westchester with my master Hugh Jones looking on, for the sour and amused eyes were his.

Rhys, said Mr Jones, this name will not do.

I had not threaded the needle yet, but already I had disappointed him, and with something I could not help. It is my name, sir, said I.

My customers will never pronounce it, not that I expect them to call you by name often, but they may have cause to do it, and they may hear me doing it, and speculate what this uncouth noise is that passes my lips. Rhys. You may wonder why I can say it at all, but the truth is, boy, I was Welsh once myself. Do you know what your name means?

I think it has not a meaning, sir.

It has indeed. A name is a word like any other, and words have meanings. Thread the needle. You may talk and work at the same time.

I waved the needle and thread past one another, and again. He did not mention my failure, but I felt those eyes upon me. Light as I was, I also felt the shopboard sway and wobble under me, which filled me with fear, and made threading the needle harder. It seemed he waited on my reply, so I said, Then it means me, sir.

Not so, said he. There are other Welshman also called Rhys, and if your name signifies you then it signifies them just as much. No, I have looked into this matter of the name Rhys, as I have looked into many matters above and beyond tailoring, and I find it means Arise, and that is the right English of it. Is the needle threaded? Let us see what you can do.

Many times since I have been glad of this name Arise, which has a most happy sound, and I believe Mr Jones was right that it is the meaning of the name I was given. And my ear became so attuned to it that I answered whenever this word was spoken, so that when my master upstairs called his daughter to arise from bed in the morning, I cried out from my shopboard, What is the matter? The very utterance of my name instructs me what I must do, stirring me to activity. For this is how the Lord commonly addresses his prophets, as when he said to Joshua, Arise, go over this Jordan, thou and all this people unto the land which I do give to them. And when the Last Judgement comes, I know that the first word I hear after the blast of the trumpet will be my own name.

Chapter XIII
A First Stitch of Many

If you are come with me so far, I take it you are held securely in place, and must stay bound to the end. You are indentured to your master as all prentices must be, for seven years or whatever was agreed between you. So it was with myself and my first master Mr Eldridge, that I was sent to after my father died, only I was released from my binding by Mr Eldridge's going broke, and then, after an interval of three years in which I returned to my mother in Merionethshire, the indenture was transferred to his father-in-law, Mr Jones. This indenturing is but one of many bindings that hold the world together, from the vows of baptism and confirmation and marriage to the laws of the kingdom, the catechism and the ten commandments, for without them we would all fly asunder. When Our Lord gave to his disciples the power of binding and loosing, he gave them the greatest power on earth, and, by the by, showed once again his understanding of tailoring, which is neither more nor less than the craft of binding and loosing. The loosing, being the cutting part of the craft, we shall come to in due course, but I begin now with binding, that is with sewing things together, and first of all with the basting stitch, which is a means of holding the cloth in place till you have sewn it properly, for, as I said before, cloth will escape if given the chance. You may hold it also with pins, as indeed you should, but a pin has not the subtlety nor the flexibility of a stitch, and will work loose at the first opportunity.

Before you begin your basting, you must mark the line down which your needle will move, and the convenient way to do this is by creasing the cloth. Remember that in this instance you are merely practising the stitches on a single piece, but in true tailoring you are like to be sewing two pieces together. To make the crease, hold the cloth firmly, turn the edge down towards you and press with the thumb-nail and your left forefinger, until it is flat. Do a few inches at a time in this manner until you reach the end. Now when you unfold the cloth you will have a sharp line down which you may sew. Thus by the work of your hands you make an impression upon it which it may not forget. In the same way, my own folding of my legs by sitting crosslegged on the shopboard has made an impression on my knees, so that there are creases in the very bones. I believe the mind too carries such creases, for my second and only true master, Hugh Jones, was so diligent in teaching me that he folded my being into many curious lines, not all of them straight.

Did you baste it first? he would say, give it here (seizing from me the doublet or whatever I was working on and holding it up to the light from the window). See this (showing me how the stitches stretched with the weight of the cloth so that little loops of daylight appeared between them)? Your lining is already loose. How will it be with a month's wear, let alone a year? What do I always tell you?

Baste it, said I.

No, not that, that is what you must do. I asked you what I always tell you.

To make a good beginning, and the end will take care of itself.

That's it, that's my boy. We'll make a tailor of you yet, or both of us will die in the attempt. Only listen to what I say at all times, even when I am not talking about tailoring. Here, take it back and unpick it. (And he would throw the cloth across the room, so that it fluttered like a bird.) Now *baste*, Arise, is a remarkable word. Have you thought that it has three meanings?

No, sir.

As well as its tailoring meaning, it means to beat an unruly person, such as a bad prentice, with a rod, and to pour sauce on a joint of meat while it is roasting. Now what do these things have in common?

I know not, sir.

Think about it, boy. They are all laying one thing on another, the rod on the prentice, the sauce on the meat and the cloth on another piece of cloth. Therefore the word *baste* must mean to lay one thing on another. And I believe the first of its three meanings must be the saucing of the meat, for it is clear that *baste* has the word *paste* behind or beneath it.

This talk of rods frighted me at first, for I remembered how his son-in-law used to beat me when first I went to him as a small boy, and indeed it was some time before I noticed that, however fiercely Mr Jones looked at me with one of his eyes, he was always smiling with the other, and though he talked of beating me, yet he never did so. What mean you, master? said I. How may a word have another behind or beneath it?

He cut out an arc of frieze, his eyes fixed on the material, panting a little as he always did when cutting. Why, said he, as a garment has a lining, all words have another beneath them, as your false name Rhys has your true name Arise beneath it. Keep your eyes on your work, for you may listen and sew at the same time. Have you done your basting? Thread a new needle, then. Have you said your prayers this morning? said he, chuckling a little as he always did when he asked this question.

Yes, sir.

Well, you may say them again presently, in about half an hour I would say. We need your intercession with God.

For my master so esteemed my piety that he would shut me into a small room or closet to say prayers at certain times, asking me to remember himself and his daughter Philippa and his married daughter Eldridge, who had a worse temper even than her husband, and the aforesaid good-for-nothing husband, and the servants. And do not mark anything you hear outside the room, said he, for it is only the visit of a customer, and I would not have you concerned with worldly matters when there is praying to be done. And here I would stay for an hour or so, and he was always in a great humour afterwards, saying my prayers had done him much good.

This, then, is your first stitch of many. Your cloth is basted and held firmly in its place, and in no wise can it escape until you release it, as my master, at the end of conferring with his customer, opened the door to the closet and released me from my prayers.

Chapter XIV
The Needle Plied Forward and Back

What, said Mr Jones, did my son-in-law teach you nothing, Arise? Every piece of cloth has a front and back.

It was a winter morning, the workshop as usual at that time of day filled with sunlight from the great window high on the wall, and also with the smells of logs burning in the hearth and of fresh cloth, stale cloth and cloth warmed by the iron. This same iron had burned the palm of my right hand the day before when I picked it up without taking a rag to muffle the handle in, so that it hurt me every time I took a stitch, a slantwise pain running from the lower knuckle of my forefinger to the heel of the hand. As I did not slow in my stitching for any such inconvenience (which, indeed, I was accustomed to in my apprenticeship, having already made such mistakes many times) the pain grew to be part of the rhythm of my work, along with the snipping of Mr Jones's shears at the cloth and the sound of his voice. As to what he was saying about the front and back of cloth, I knew it well enough, for he was always upbraiding me for sewing on the wrong side, but he was never content that I should know a thing (if indeed I could truly be said to know it when I forgot it every time I came to sew), but I should know the philosophy of it at the same time.

There are some cloths, said Mr Jones (snipping), where this difference is manifest, as satin where one face shines and the other is plain, or a twilled cloth like worsted where the weave shows and feels differently in the two faces, but there are others where the front and the back are identical in warp and woof and pattern and colour, in all their properties, and yet, Arise, to you as a tailor they can never be the same. For the front of the cloth is that which will appear to the world; it will be fair and smooth, or else embellished and embroidered, while the back will hold the raw workings of your stitches or a lining, and the moment the cloth lies upon your lap you must and will know which is which, for unless they are first different in your own mind they will never be so in reality. Such doubleness is a property of everything in the world, and of every person. We are not meant to see the threads and thrums of another's soul, or the puffy plainness of their lining, but our own we feel familiarly rubbing against us whenever we move. In this a garment is like a man or woman; how should it not be, made as it is in our image? Therefore when I teach you to sew, I am teaching you to ape your creator, to make a being like yourself, fair on the outside, rough within, and before you may do so you must sense this difference in the cloth, directing you to bring it into existence. How have you done? Let me see. You call those stitches?

Saying which he took the cloth from across my knees, snipped at the thread with his small scissors and unpicked all my work. There, said he, we are as we were before. You see, Arise, said Mr Jones (biting off a fresh length of thread and threading a needle with it), just as cloth has a front and back, or an outside and inside, so also it has a forward and backward. And we ourselves have a direction as well as an inside and outside; we move forward, beginning in infancy and growing to youth, maturity and, if we are spared, to old age. The needle moves forward, both under and over the cloth, piercing outside and inside alike. Here, take the needle and try again. Make the surface stitches of the same length and those on the underside half the size or less of the upper stitches. No, do not let it pucker; smooth the seam between the left thumb and forefinger as you go. How is your hand, boy? Well, it is only pain, and what is pain to such as us? Next time remember it is the cloth that should be ironed and not the tailor. There, your seam is made. Now take a couple of stitches in place to finish it off. Think, boy, if this piece of broadcloth were your life, it would be over now, and these two stitches you take in place would bury you and tamp down the earth on your grave, one, two. Now for the backstitch.

But when he showed me this same backstitch (not for the first time, for I was slow of learning), I found myself more confused than ever.

Your needle must move both forward and back, for, after going forward underneath, you bring the needle back on top and make a stitch in the reverse direction. Thus you proceed, now this way, now that, until you have a fair line of stitches to be used for seams that will be strained in the wearing.

But master, said I, if the forward stitch is like my life, what is the backstitch like?

He took the cloth from me and held it up in the light from the window. Well, said he, making the curious distortion of the jaws, which I had learned signified a smile, if your life is like this backstitch of yours, then it is miserably badly sewn. But tell me, Arise, do you think we live only forwards, from birth to death?

Certainly, master.

Then what is remembering, eh? Is that not a sort of stitch taken in the reverse direction from the rest of your life?

What mean you?

Sit still, boy. A good apprentice crosses his legs on the shopboard and then forgets them for the rest of the day. You will have no need of them till you are a master. Very well, Arise, tell me, where are you?

In your workshop, master. On the shopboard. In Westchester, said I, not knowing which of these answers he wanted.

And where will you be tomorrow?

The same.

And where were you yesterday?

The same also.

Very good. Here, take your cloth. I have uprooted your brier-patch, and all is prepared for your next attempt. Now, we may consider these days of yours, which are all the same, as being like so many small plain stitches, one after the other. Well, start sewing.

Yes, master.

But Sunday, say, that is an ornamental stitch, made with coloured thread. You will not be sitting on the shopboard then.

No, master.

You will go to church, and then, I dare say, play football with the other lads of the parish. What, you do not play football? What do you do then?

I pray, master. And read the Bible.

Arise, you are not one of these Puritan fellows, are you? They that call themselves the godly and would have a sermon last all day, and anyone who falls asleep before the end burned in hell? Good. What do you pray for?

Wisdom, master.

That is something, I suppose. It is not a bad answer. And these stitches run ever forward, six weekday stitches and a Sunday stitch. But the backstitch, instead of taking you onward to tomorrow, takes you backward to yesterday. Or last week or last year, for, the thread of thought being such a subtle one, you may make the backstitch as long as you like without any entanglement or puckering. What are you now, Arise, fourteen? Well, where were you, say, on this day four years ago?

Over there, master.

Meaning across the road, with my son-in-law? And what he can have taught you I have no notion, for you arrived knowing less than nothing. It is no wonder he went broke. In any case, Arise, with this thread of the mind, you can at any time be back in his workshop, and this backstitch we call memory.

I do not want to be there, master, I said.

No? Where do you want to be, then? For you may be anywhere.

Maes-y-Llan.

The true name of it is Maes y Llan Cader Idris, this last part being the mountain nearby, which name I shall explain fully in another place.

Maes... I do not think I have heard...? Ah, it was where you lived, was it not? After you left my son-in-law, and before you came here.

Chapter XV
Prayer's Efficacy Proven in the High Places

The sheep ran from my approach, for I complained aloud, asking that the Lord God of Israel hear my prayer, and give me wisdom. It was a fierce day, with clouds rushing across the sky and a cold wind tearing at my doublet. I left the river, where the witch's house was, (but the witch was not standing outside her house that day, and so I had no need of my pin), and began climbing the path. All this time my breath was coming harder and louder, so that I had much ado to continue my prayer, yet I did so, Lord, give me wisdom, hurting my feet on stones, sliding on mud and scratched by gorse, until I reached a place called Bwlch Rhiw Credire, where the mountains on each side were higher than I was, but the path was now very narrow and there was a great drop on one side of me, with tufts of heather and bushes projecting out of it. I pressed myself as close as I could to the wall of mountain on my left, but the wind kept pushing me back, half turning me and almost lifting me off my feet. There were spatterings in it, too, and a grey cloak of rain was spread over Cader Idris which now loomed before me, a great chair fit for God himself to sit on. Then I reached a place where the path turned and I no longer had the protecting mountain on my left, but the drop on that side was even sheerer than the one on my right. To walk on I would have to traverse a path not more than a foot wide between the two abysses, and the wind now seemed to come from all directions at once, so that I rocked first one way and then the other. Down to my right as I swayed, I saw dark rocks and a small silver pool that seemed as deep again as the distance to it

This name also shall be explained in another place.

was far. To the left, on the other hand, the ground, though just as remote, was soft and green and grazed by sheep. I was inclined to go home again, but reflected on why I had come here, and that the Lord having brought me so far would not grant me a second occasion. Therefore I stepped out further on to the most exposed part of the path where the wind almost carried me over the edge, making me pray still more fervently: O Lord, give me wisdom. A few more steps, and the rain began in earnest, but I no longer cared for comfort, only for my next step and keeping my balance. The path was muddy in the middle and mossy at the edges, and I stepped in the middle, fearing the deep mud less than the slippery moss. O Lord, I prayed, give thy servant wisdom, as also dryness and windlessness and solid ground beneath my feet, for these in my terror seemed a part of wisdom. A dark grey object about the size and shape of a horse passed me on the right hand, and another followed it directly. Cader Idris had vanished, and far from being wise I no longer knew where I was or in which direction I was walking. I slipped and slid to my right, putting a hand to the mud to keep myself from falling. O Lord, remember thy servant Rhys, who has come to this high place in great peril of his life. Give him wisdom.

I asked for wisdom because it was what Solomon asked for. He was the son of David, and king after him, and being a younger son was no bar to his inheritance, for the Lord favoured him over his brother. But not being satisfied he went to a high place, and the Lord God appeared to him in a dream, and Solomon spoke to him and asked him a favour. It was not riches or a kingdom, for he had a kingdom already, nor was it a beautiful woman: he asked for wisdom. And the Lord was well pleased, saying that if Solomon had asked him for riches and power and women he would not have given him anything, but because he asked for wisdom, he should have that and all the rest besides.

The horselike things passing by my shoulder were clouds, for I had reached a height more frequented by ethereal bodies than earthly ones. Having prayed so hard, I felt easier in my mind now, and my feet no longer slipped, though the clouds rushed past still faster and thicker than before, making me dizzy. So I walked on for another hundred yards, lightly and without fear, until the mists and rain began to disperse and I saw the path ahead of me, broader at last and sheltered between welcoming rocks. It was only now that I looked down and saw that I was walking in the empty air, hundreds of feet above the valley floor.

I had not so much leapt or flown from the earth as forgot it, as if remaining there had proved too irksome a labour for me to persist in. I walked rather than flew, for my feet still kept their earthly habits, relieved from the fear of toe-stubbings, ankle-twistings and mud-slitherings, but they carried me not, for it was God who carried me, as he carries his angels. Looking down I beheld the backs of ravens flying beneath me, and far below that the green earth lined with stone walls and glinting rivers and dotted with white moving beings that must be sheep. This world, I thought, is only where my feet chanced to be anchored, and will be again, but it is nothing to me, nor am I as much part of it as I am of the air, that is, of heaven, where my father is.

Chapter XVI
The Sun a Servant of God, and Must Leap to His Bidding

Glassy sunlight struck down over my shoulder, there were the smells of smoking logs, fresh cloth, stale cloth and cloth warmed by the iron, a sharp pain running slantwise across the palm of my hand. It hurt most when I stitched, therefore I had just taken a stitch. I pulled the thread through, the whistling it made so fine I felt it inside my head, and was readying my fingers to take another one when Mr Jones caught me by the wrist. Now, Arise, said he, as I have often told you, you may talk and work at the same time, but there is no use in stitching if you are not going to think about it. I believe you would carry on sewing if I took the cloth away from you, and never notice the difference. You are still caught up in the backstitch you took just now, and I do not wonder. Flying?

What, master?

You flew through the air, above the fields and farms of this Maes-y-Llan or whatever its name was, like a witch or sorcerer? And alighted afterwards unharmed?

I rubbed my eyes and forehead with the unburned hand, not that they ached, but I had an uncomfortable sensation that they were not there at all, and wished to confirm their solidity. It was not flying, I said, or I did not think of it so. And I am no witch, master. I prayed to God that he would give me wisdom and he answered my prayer by, by carrying me. Which was not the answer I had expected, but a very comforting one.

Hm, said he. You are a curious lad. You never mentioned such a thing till today. Did you tell your mother and father about it?

My father is dead, sir.

Yes, boy, I know that. I mean your stepfather.

I had no stepfather then, master. That is to say, I did, but he was dead too, by that time. When my father died and I was sent out to be apprenticed to your, to Mr Eldridge, my mother married again, and moved to Maes-y-Llan, which was four miles off from our old farm at Llangluin. But my new stepfather died soon after, so that when I came back from Mr Eldridge, my mother was alone on the farm, my brothers being back at Llangluin.

And now she is married a third time, in Wrexham? She must be a fair woman, this mother of yours.

She is very zealous, sir.

He looked somewhat puzzled at this, but after a little began walking up and down the workshop, having seemingly forgot my instruction in sewing for the moment. Now many men, he said (not looking at me, but sometimes at the floor and sometimes upwards at the sunny window), many men, not having my knowledge of human nature, would laugh at you for a thing like this, Arise, or else they would call you evil names and seek to bring you before the law for it, saying you must be in league with the devil. But I know you well enough, though I have not known you long. You are a wretched needleman, but you are no liar, and I never knew such a boy for praying and Scripture. And I have heard other stories of this kind. But you have forgot your sewing. Here, take it up again where you left off.

He handed me the cloth, but continued looking up out of the window, so I did not start yet, waiting for him to speak again.

Tell me, Arise, why were you seeking wisdom in the first place?

Because I have nothing else, sir. When my father died... but any man may have wisdom, if God chooses to grant it to him. And for that reason I think on God continually, and ask him for wisdom.

And has he granted it, would you say?

I looked up from the cloth in my lap to see if Mr Jones was laughing at me, but his eyes were still turned to the window.

I think he means to.

And how do you know that, eh?

Well, master, it is because he made the sun rise and play when I asked it of him.

Then Mr Jones did something I never saw him do before or since, for, though heavy, he was on his feet all day and never looked to rest. He took the high-backed chair from the corner behind the cutting-board, carried it over to the shopboard and sat down, his eyes now being on a level with my legs, so that I had to bow my head to address him. There he waited, saying nothing, but when I looked questioningly at him he nodded to show me that I might continue.

It was of Bethan I heard it first, said I, when I was very small at Llangluin, and she was carding before the barn door. My mother said she was minded to be up early on the morrow, being May Eve, to gather may dew, for she had heard that any woman who washed her face in it would be beautiful ever after.

Hugh Jones nodded again.

And Bethan said she had never heard such vanity. What do you want to be beautiful for, said she, a married woman like yourself? And I thought that was the end of it but then Bethan said that if my mother were to wait till Whitsun and then go and pray in the hills, then she could understand it, for anyone who went there before dawn on Whit Sunday might see the sun rise and play, and God would grant their prayers. But, she told my mother, I suppose you would ask for some vanity like fair skin, or eyes, or hair, and so God would never permit the sun to play for such as you.

Rise and play, Hugh Jones said. What did she mean?

I knew not, nor did I ask her then. But later, when I was living at Maes-y-Llan, I was watching the sun setting one evening and I recalled that it would be Whit Sunday the next day. And I had a great urge to go out on the hills and see it play at dawn, for I thought then what a great body it was, and how mighty must be God's power to keep it in its course, day after day till the end of all things. And what God did he could undo when it pleased him, for did he not cause the sun and moon to stand still when the Israelites were slaying their enemies? And Job also says that the Lord commandeth the sun and it riseth not. Therefore I understood that the sun is God's servant and must obey his command, and if it was God's will that it should play at its rising on Whit Sunday, then it would do so, and I resolved to see its playing and utter my prayer.

To this end I left my bed while it was yet night and went to a hill called Gole Ronnw. I climbed in the dark, lighting my way with a lantern that showed the rocks in front of me but did not touch the gulfs of darkness into which I might fall at any time, until at last I reached a rock near the summit, extinguished my lantern and sat there to wait, watching the sky change from grey to blue to purple and orange, while the birds woke and sang on the hill below me. The sun first showed itself according to its custom as a blob of fire in the east, and lifted itself further till it rested there with its lower rim on the ground. Then when I had grown to expect a day like any other, the Lord commanded it to play, and I saw the sun turn around like a wheel, first slowly then faster, sending forth shreds and ribbons of fire and rising up the sky, skipping, like one on a holiday.

This name also shall be explained hereafter.

Skipping? Mr Jones said.

Or dancing, or fluttering. I know not what to call it, but I fell down upon my knees, lifting up my eyes, hands and heart unto God and cried, O Lord most high, that hath made all things for thy glory, give me grace, wisdom and understanding, that I may glorify thee as this instrument doth now before all the world.

Chapter XVII
The Dreadful Dead Man Pointed At

You call yourself a Welshman, yet you know nothing of Merlin or Taliesin? (Hugh Jones was in a Welsh mood that morning, for his Welshness came and went, a consequence of his living so many years in Westchester.)

I never heard the names till now. Who are they?

They are long dead, Mr Jones said, but they were prophets. What do you know of prophecy, eh?

There are many prophets in the Bible, I told him, as Elijah and Ezekiel and Amos and others.

And what did they do? Carry on with your seam, there is no need to look up.

They told of the wrath of God directed at his people Israel, for the people could never do right without a prophet to interpret the Lord for them.

Indeed they did, Arise, but as usual you miss the point. A prophet does not tell the wrath of God, he foretells it, for a prophet, properly speaking, is a man who can say what is to come. Have you not heard of the Dreadful Dead Man?

Is he a ghost?

No, not a ghost, Arise. This dead man is not truly a dead man, but is signified as such in the prophecy, for it is delivered in language the mass of men cannot understand. Merlin tells us that there shall come a Dreadful Dead Man, and he shall have the crown and shall set England on the right way and put out all the heresies.

His deeds will not be so dreadful as his person, then.

Hugh Jones put down his shears and tested their edge with his thumb. These need sharpening, Arise, said he. Do it tomorrow morning, before I begin my work. Dreadful Dead Man, hm. I have asked myself often who such a one might be. The Prince of Wales, Prince Charles, he is not dreadful, nor is he dead. Then again, we must not forget the Chicken of the

Eagle. For Taliesin tells us this Chicken will rise up and take the place of the White King, whoever he may be.

After that, I sewed on in silence for some time, and Mr Jones continued to cut, muttering a little under his breath about the bluntness of the shears. But when Philippa came in with our morning draught, he wiped his brow with his shirt sleeve (for any exertion, even the cutting of cloth, would make him sweat), swallowed some of his ale and made one of his distortions of the lower face, indicating that he was content enough. Tell me, Arise, are you still praying for wisdom?

Every day, master.

And if God grants it to you, will you recognize his gift? Will you know wisdom when you see it? For myself I should be glad if God gave you the wisdom to be a good tailor, for there is no better profession. But I suppose you mean something else by it.

I cannot say what I mean, master.

I know, I know, Mr Jones continued, his mouth full of bread, you were never intended for a tailor, and should have been a sheepfarmer, if your father had not forgot you in his will. But a sheepfarmer does naught but farm sheep, whereas a tailor, now... Have you thought, Arise, what a fine thing is a seam? A seam is the rightful emblem of our order, for on the left side of it is one thing, and on the right is something else, and the seam unites them both. And now that I think of it, when I have seen banners and coats of arms in the Guildhall or the church, almost all of them have had a seam running down the middle, with different devices on each side, or several seams, across and down, as if the heralds that painted them had really wished to be tailors all along. Yes, tailoring, Arise, is the only trade for a thinking man, for when you are sewing your seam, you are but doing with your needle what your mind does in cogitation. On the left side of your mind, as it were, is some thought of sheep, or God, or your esteemed mother, who sounds to my ears such a fine woman, and on the right is something that may be half a universe away, such as Merlin or Taliesin or the Chicken of the Eagle, and in between is yourself on the shopboard in Westchester, plying the needle, and joining one to the other. And as with tailoring, so with thinking: the more you do it the better you will do it, till no one will be able to tell that Maes-y-Llan and the Chicken of the Eagle were not joined together by God at the creation of the world, for the seam will be so tightly sewn and so well turned and ironed in place that it cannot be seen. Talking of seams, have you finished the one I gave you to do?

Here, master.

It is not straight, said he. And this part is too slack and will come undone with wear. No need to iron it in, Arise, you must unpick it and start again.

Chapter XVIII
The Tailor's Workshop Illustrated

I have wearied of trying to keep the book from my wife's eyes, for our tenement is so small that she can always have occasion to stand behind me and read it over my shoulder, or if I move my stool and desk to the wall to avoid it, then she takes a paper as she passes and reads it. When I forbid her to do it, she only says that disobeying and contradiction are not the same thing, and when I remind her also that she promised to obey me as all wives do in the marriage service, she says she has obeyed me on many occasions and will do so on many more, but she never promised to obey on all, nor did she promise not to disobey. After a few weeks of these doings I find I can no longer remember why I wished to keep the book to myself in the first place. In truth, it pleases me to have a reader with whom I can talk about it as I write it, a thing I never had before. I wonder why she did not do as much with my earlier books, but when I ask her, she says the matter of those did not touch her so nearly, for she never cared who was King or Protector as long as there was food on the table.

I like this Hugh Jones, says she.

He was my dear master, say I, and taught me many things, not least the right meaning of my name, without which I would not be the man I am now.

It was from him that you learned most of tailoring? Then you could write the whole book in that fashion, as a dialogue between Mr Jones and yourself. I believe that style is much favoured nowadays. Set it out with the names of the speakers in the left margin, or rather, instead of Mr Jones you write *Dominus*, and instead of Mr Evans you write *Ephebus* and then *Ephebus* may say, Pray tell me, *Dominus*, how I may best proceed with the making of a gore for a lady's gown, and *Dominus* will reply,

First, *Ephebus*, you must cut the cloth on the bias, like so. Though now I remember to have heard that in their speech they should call each other *Domine* and *Ephebe*.

This being the grammar, or perhaps the accidence.

I care not for this notion. Who are these persons, *Dominus* and *Ephebus*, or *Domine* and *Ephebe*?

It is Latin, and is as much as to say Master and Pupil.

And how, Mrs Evans, do you know so much of the fashions in writing of books? You are a woman, and it is not your business to read.

Well, says she, and looks abashed for once, twisting the end of her kerchief between thumb and forefinger, you forget, husband, that I have made it my business to learn as much as I can of the apothecary's and physician's arts. And sometimes when I am out visiting or buying some necessity, I stop in Paul's Yard and look at the physic books there. Mrs Lowndes is my friend and lets me spend some time reading the stock when business is bad.

Does her husband know of this?

She makes a shrugging gesture with her hands. I like this Hugh Jones, she says again, but I like not the discussion of prophecy. He should keep to tailoring.

It is very well to say that. You should tell him, only I suppose he is dead these twenty years or more. All who were acquainted with Mr Jones knew that he could not talk of tailoring for five minutes together without talking of something else into the bargain. His understanding of tailoring was woven together with his understanding of prophecy and history and languages and many other matters, as linsey-wolsey or grogram are woven from cloth of different kinds. He was a very ingenious man in all things, and this conversation I have reported is just as it took place.

You could use him further, she says, to explain all you need to of the tailoring trade.

I had thought to use woodcuts, say I.

With a woodcut I need do no more than leave a space in my text of sufficient size for the craftsman's work to appear there, and could then write: There is the stitch – study it well, reader (or *Ephebe*) and endeavour to copy it as perfectly as you may. For there is nothing like a woodcut for showing the true grain and hatching of the world. Why I could have myself in a woodcut sitting on the shopboard, needle raised aloft and Hugh Jones, stout and roughbearded in front of me, standing so as to show either his sour eye (so that my reader, misled by his profile, pities me for having such an evil-eyed master) or the other way about (which exposes me to the terrible one). There would be a gown stretching on the rail, with a heavy weight hanging at the skirt, a hell stuffed full of cabbage clearly and incriminatingly visible beneath the shopboard, a pair of shears in my master's hand, a pattern and a couple of yards of cloth before him on the cutting board, an iron heating in front of the fire, the light of Westchester falling through the window on the scene, and perhaps even the door opening and Mrs Windrush come for the gown. There are her billowing skirts and one of her small feet showing, and my master (or *Dominus*) is saying, Arise, it is time you were at your prayers again.

What? says my wife, do you know the cost of a single woodcut?

Chapter XIX
An Instructive Dialogue Between *Dominus* and *Ephebus*

The writing of dialogues, I find, is much the same as a catechism, with this difference only, that it is the younger and more ignorant of the two speakers who first asks the questions, and the elder and more learned who answers them. My wife having thoroughly instructed me in the style, I am persuaded for her sake to attempt it, and to think no more of woodcuts until I have done so, though I still cherish a resolution to visit Mr Lowndes in his shop at Paul's Yard and ask the cost of them, for a tailoring book illustrated with woodcuts would be a handsome thing, and I doubt not it would please the public. So I commence my dialogue, having always in mind my woodcut of the tailor's workshop, so that my *Dominus* is a stout man with his two eyes different and a rough beard, while my *Ephebus* is a small but well-favoured youth whose own eyes are turned heavenward at all times.

Eph. *Domine*, you have spoken much of seams, and I long to try my hand at them. Pray tell me, how may I go about making one?

Dom. Why, *Ephebe*, the making of a seam is but the stitching of one piece of cloth to another, without which no tailoring can be done. And you may contrive one with ease, by first laying your two pieces together with the edges touching. Now before you begin stitching the seam together, be sure first to pin it and afterwards to baste, else your pieces will come adrift. What do I always tell you, *Ephebe*?

Eph. Take care of the beginning and the end will take care of itself.

Dom. Very good. It is a curious word, this *seam.* You will notice, *Ephebe,* that it has the same sound as the word that means to resemble, but the spelling is different. However I cannot think that this other seem is the word behind or beneath it, for there is no similarity of meaning. No, *Ephebe*, the word behind *seam* is *semen*, which is to say the seed of generation, for you must think of the two pieces of cloth as mating, the one with the other.

Eph. What mean you, *Domine*? I never heard this word *semen* before.

Dom. And you a reader of the Bible, *Ephebe*! What think you that it signifies when it tells us that Onan spilled his seed on the ground?

Eph. I know not, *Domine.*

Dom. How old are you?

Eph. Sixteen, *Domine.*

Dom. It is remarkable. And you know nothing of...? And have you never wondered why I, when Mrs Windrush, and you, in the closet? Never mind.

(This dialogue will need botching, for I feel my cheeks redden as I write it, and I remember now that this *Dominus* of mine was by no means the purest in his language or in his thoughts, and he would instruct me in many matters other than tailoring, not all of which were fit for a young man's ears, or any Christian person's: What, he would say, you know not which part of your person is your *todger-pin*? And yet I must defend him, in part, for his use of such a word, which he only mentioned because he was teaching me the importance of pinning, and could not resist his usual inquiries into words and their relations.)

The handle of a scythe, which projects out sideways; and is used by vulgar persons to signify the privitie of a man.

Dom. And you should know further, *Ephebe*, for you will need to one day, that the corresponding part of a woman is called her *whib-bob* and this too is a curious word, for you will note its resemblance to whip, and to bobbin, the latter being, as you know, the spool or reel on which thread is wound. Now I have made investigations into this word also, and I find–

The privitie of a woman.

But I can write no more of this, and must remember to burn this page before my wife comes back from her physicking, for she would die of shame if she read it, and keeping any of my pages from her eyes is beyond my skill. Meanwhile I will try the dialogue again, remembering that this *Dominus* is not Mr Jones and *Ephebus* is not myself at sixteen, but the two of them are figments expressly created for the better instruction of the reader. Thus I proceed with the making of a seam.

Dom. The making of a seam is but the stitching of one piece of cloth to another, which you may contrive thus. Lay the first piece on top of the second with the edges touching. Now you must first pin one to the other, and then baste them well, without for a moment pausing to consider the meanings of the words or what lies beneath them, their underpinnings as it were, for you have no time to do it and Mrs Windrush is waiting for her new gown. Is it well basted, *Ephebe*?

Eph. Yes, *Domine*.

Dom. Then you may begin the stitching. For a simple seam, a running stitch is sufficient, but as this seam is like to undergo some strain, we must use a backstitch. Thus will the sleeve of her gown remain secure. Sew carefully along the line I have marked out for you, for it is the sign of a good tailor to keep to the line. What do I always tell you, *Ephebe*?

Eph. Take care of the beginning...

Dom. No, not that one. Mark your line –

Eph. Mark your line and stick to it.

Dom. Good, for everything in the world has a line that it must move along, whether we can see it or not. And this is what Merlin referred to in his prophecies when he said that six of the Boar's descendants should hold the sceptre after it, and next after them would rise up the German Worm. For we speak of a line of kings, or of any family, do we not? – a line that stretches from the past into the future, and it was the genius of Merlin that he could see along the length of that line.

Eph. Tell me, *Domine*, who is this German Worm?

Dom. I know not, *Ephebe*, but Merlin tells us that the White Dragon shall rise up and summon a daughter of Germany, and that the German Worm shall be crowned and the Prince of Brass buried. The North Wind shall rise against him, snatching away the flowers which the West Wind has caused to bloom. I have thought much on these words, and I recommend you to do likewise, only you may sew and think at the same time.

It was when Mr Jones was at his most Welsh that he talked of Merlin and Taliesin, and his voice changed when he did so, acquiring a grave resonance unlike his usual tone. And he liked most to talk of death, plague, war, fire and earthquakes, all of which were imminent as foretold by his prophets, and I heard him with a shudder that made my body turn cold.

Eph. Pray tell me further, *Domine*, what date these prophets have set for the aforesaid cataclysms?

Dom. Well, now, let me see, *Ephebe*, the golden number being nine, the moon also having changed on Low Sunday Eve, there is a prophesy of Taliesin that announces a woe in Britain in the year 1623, and moreover it bids us beware of a fire upon the land the second Thursday after Midsummer Day.

Eph. But, *Domine*, this year you speak of, 1623, is the present year, and it is Midsummer Day next week.

Dom. Indeed, *Ephebe*, and I should not be surprised if the Day of Judgement itself should come to pass on that very Thursday I mentioned. That may be the meaning of this prophecy.

He sighed contentedly at these words, and as if to say he was satisfied that the world should so end. And when I asked him what was the use of my continuing to baste and sew and to learn new stitches and patterns that I would never need after that Thursday, he replied that a man must work and what would God think of us if we arrived at the Judgement Seat having passed our last ten days in idleness? Only, he added, we shall need your prayers more than ever now, Arise, and I think you had better go to the closet presently. For we should not face our maker without having made the best of our lives, yours and mine.

As I knelt in the closet, I could hardly move my lips to say the prayers, and it was as much as I could do to keep my eyes closed. There were always two smells fighting for predominance in this closet, the stale wood of the worm-eaten panelling and the stale cloth of the cabbage that was kept there, for Hugh Jones had been in the trade so long that his workshop was like to be overwhelmed by unused stuff, and so he put out the older and more unsuitable snippets in the same closet where he put me for praying. And on this day, which was a hot one, I felt the two smells would smother me. And indeed, I know not how I endured the next ten days, or the nights either, for I did not sleep much, but Mr Jones spoke no more of judgement and continued in good

He was in an English mood that day, and gave little heed to prophecy.

spirits, as if not expecting his destruction imminently. And when the said Thursday came, he asked me what ailed me.

Eph. The Day of Judgement, *Domine.*
Dom. The Day of?
Eph. Judgement. You said it was prophesied for this day by Taliesin and some other persons.
Dom. Did I? Oh yes, I believe I did.
Eph. Shall I go to the closet and pray, *Domine*?
Dom. Not today, *Ephebe*, for Mrs Windrush is not expected. As for the Day of Judgement, we shall continue sewing quietly, and see what transpires.

In the course of that sewing, my fear exhausted itself and became tedium. When I had finished the doublet I was working on, Mr Jones told me there was no further work for that day, and I might go and pray or read the Bible or whatever I would, but instead I walked around the town, it being no later than four o'clock, and walked along the Rows, both upper and lower, and the market at the cross where there was a great stall of pigs' heads and feet, and another of fish, and a boy came there bearing a salmon as I looked. How useless it was to kill those pigs and that fish so shortly before their creator was to appear! I went up close to the fish and marvelled at the wet silver of his scales and the red gape of his gills and the shining gold-and-black buttons of his eyes, and his existence on this earth seemed so tenuous and unlikely that I was sure I could put my hand through him if I chose. (Just then the boy asked me if I wanted to buy, and I shook my head and moved away.) The smooth, blue-grey sky, portending a storm, was pressing on my head, pinning me to the street, and I felt that presently either my head would break, or else the sky would, to reveal the Creator sitting in Judgement above it. And so I walked on, scarce able to breathe, my head aching, while my fear became tedium and my tedium became impatience, and I felt angry with God for not bringing about the Judgement earlier in the day. Nothing had caught fire yet, no one had so much as drawn a sword, the great black and white houses were still leaning over me in their worldly pomp, and even the storm had not broken. And I understood at last what I had inwardly known all along, that the day was not today, and so Mr Jones's prophets were wrong, as he had known also, with the English part of his mind.

But perhaps they were not wholly wrong, only Mr Jones had not the skill to interpret them. For if the Judgement Day was this Thursday following Midsummer Day of 1623, then what was to become of his Dreadful Dead Man and his Boars and his German Worm, and all the lines of kings whose prophecies he expounded in the more Welsh of his moods? No, I thought, there may be other Judgements and other cataclysms on this day that neither Hugh Jones nor myself knows of, and the prophecy may refer to those, for the world is a great place, and I have seen little of it as yet. So I thought and walked, and my mind grew clear and tremulously joyful, as it did sometimes in those days, for what reason I understood not.

But I cannot think a dialogue such as the foregoing is the best way of expounding a seam.

Chapter XX
Britain's History Briefly Related Between Two Woodcuts

I would have this woodcut, in any case. A young man wearing a broad brimmed felt hat stands on the bank of a wide slow river where a boy is fishing. Before them is a building of new brick with a pointed roof and a chimney half detached from it like a buttress, the whole surrounded by a curved skirt of wall such as might enclose the lands of some great lord. The river and the building together suffice to show the locality of the scene, but I should have a caption for the illustration, for all the best books do so, and it should read: Islington, the Water House. For the boy is fishing in the New River, which gives of its waters to the great city beneath, and behind those walls, though the woodcut cannot show as much, lie the engines that convey the water through a system of pipes contrived from the hollow trunks of trees. This man is a traveller, as we can tell by the knapsack on his back and the stick in his hand with which he points to the view, for he stands on an eminence with the north-west prospect of London spread before him. The gloomy bulk of the Cathedral of St Paul with its low square tower and long nave presides over the city with a congregation of spires around it: St Mary Colechurch, St Mildred, St Bartholomew, St Mary Woolnoth, St Stephen Walbrook, St Mary Somerset, St Mary Botolph, All Hallows the Great, All Hallows the Less, All Hallows on the Wall, the French Church, St Andrew Undershaft, Blackfriars, with as many other churches as the artist may be able to fit in between the pointed roofs of the houses. At such a distance the houses seem to touch each other; only the shining lines of King Street, Fleet Street and Thames Street will be seen, as if too narrow for any to walk or ride on. For distance erases the forms of men and women, so that the people, horses and wagons that throng those thoroughfares shall be invisible. The River Thames shall lie behind, and, though it is at all times choked with barges, wherries and the traffic of the watermen ferrying passengers from one district to another, none of it will be seen from here, unless the artist can suggest its presence by a cunningly placed flash of sunlight (though this is not easily depicted in a woodcut). But he will show great houses and public buildings, the Palace of Westminster and those of Whitehall and Greenwich, the Guildhall, the Tower, the Royal Exchange *&c &c*, with their own space around them, and a smattering of trees as intricate as moss, though he cannot show their greenness, nor the blue or grey of the smoke which hangs over the prospect. Yet there shall be a general haze in the direction of the city to signify smoke and distance both.

I would have this illustration as my seam, for just as a garment is made up of front and back and sleeves or skirts and other pieces and embellishments which must be joined one to another by sewing of seams, so a book may have numerous parts which need joining, and I feel the need of laying this chapter end to end with the last and pushing the needle into the space between. Thus will I make a seam of my own for the present chapter, on the one side Westchester, where I served my apprenticeship, and on the other London, where I first worked as a journeyman and have passed most of the rest of my life.

The young man in the woodcut is myself, for I was now grown and the time of my indenture was expired. Mr Jones would have had me stay but my heart was for London, and besides while he was still arguing it with me I went to church and heard a minister preach on the text Arise up, my fair one and come away, and I understood it to be directed at me. So

This text is from the Song of Solomon which is dear to my heart on account of that King having been granted wisdom by God, *qv*.

my master gave me the brass thimble and the shears and yardstick which I still have and which are on the desk in front of me as I write these words. The yard especially I treasure, for it is the symbol of a mastership I never had except in Mr Jones's fancy. We'll make a tailor of you yet, said he, or die in the attempt. I know not whether he made a tailor of me after all; I am but half of one, it seems to me, and the other half prophet or author or what have you, and it matters not now for Mr Jones is long dead anyway. This seam-margin of mine I shall call Coventry, for it was there I first went on leaving Westchester and stayed there a quarter of a year, working as a journeyman. I was detained by an old chronicle that I found in my master's house that showed the whole history of Britain and Ireland from the time of Noah's Flood to that of William the Conqueror, so that I could not leave till I had read it all. Whenever my master left the shop on any business I would read as much of it as I could, forgetting hems and buttonholes, and I spent some of my earnings on candles for the night, so I could stay up while the rest of the household was in bed, reading more of the history of our nation in the cold shadowy room with the mice running around my feet and the moths a-flutter in the air around my candle. Though it was five hundred pages long I read it all, and got most of it by heart.

Thus I learned that my race, the Britons, lived in these islands before the English came, or even the Romans before them, and this word Briton is formed from Brutus, a prince of Troy who left his city when it was destroyed by the Greeks and travelled with a band of followers through many countries of Europe but eventually found his way here, where they joined with the inhabitants they found there and became one people. And Joseph of Arimathea came here and preached the Gospel before there was a Church of Christ at Rome, and he lies buried at Glastonbury. And besides him Thomas the Apostle was sent here about the same time to preach Christ to us. Therefore it was not a hard thing for Lucius, King of the Britons, to establish the Christian faith in this kingdom, thus becoming the first Christian King in the world. In due course our people grew weak and divided amongst themselves, and Satan stirred up enemies against them: the Saxons, Danes, Normans and all the nations round about fought to destroy them, till they drove the Britons into Wales, and at last Edward the First secretly sent his queen to Caernarvon, where the first English Prince of Wales was born, and the Britons submitted to him and became slaves. The English destroyed their ancient records, intending to extinguish their language and nullify the prophecies written in it. But the Britons, through God's providence, preserved their language and as much of their writings as they needed. Then Henry VII, a British prince, came to the throne with those prophecies as his guide, united York and Lancaster, redeemed Wales, and was the means to bring England and Scotland under one head. Thus far God has fulfilled our prophecies. Therefore it is time for you Englishmen to consider it (and not henceforth to scorn the Welsh) that you may as Britons partake of the blessing with us, for surely the Saxon race shall vanish as our prophecies prove.

This history, being an old book, went no further than Henry VII, and when I reached the last page, notwithstanding the word FINIS, I still wished to carry on reading, for it seemed to me that no book whose subject was time could conclude until God brought time itself to an end. Therefore I turned the page, and found that there were some blank pages there, yellowish with age and yellower still in the light of my candle. Someone should have continued writing in this book, I thought, for history did not end with Henry VII, but we have had other monarchs since. And I supposed that the last page would treat of our present King, after which there would be no more room, only the board and cracked leather of the book. The second volume has still to

This was King Charles Steward, his father King James Steward having died four years earlier.

be written or perhaps there would be no second volume.

I should have two woodcuts, I think, for this chapter, as a seam has two flaps (or arms, or wings, for I know not what to call them and it is too late to ask Hugh Jones). For the first woodcut I described is really part of the second piece of the garment, and it should have a companion for the first piece, which should match it almost exactly: a young man with hat, stick and knapsack (myself) a river, wall and edifice (the Water House), a distant prospect covered in smoke and haze (London). This was the vision I saw in a dream months before the day I first stood there, on the night after I went to church and heard the minister preach on the Song of Solomon. Never had I visited Islington or London before, or been further into England than Westchester, and yet I saw the scene in every detail and felt it too, and this was the first inkling I had of my prophetic powers, for while the Lord had carried me through the air and made the sun play before me, he had never yet shown me a vision of what was to come. And yet all was not as it was to be when I stood there later in reality, and it may be that my prophetic gift was not yet fully formed, for when my dreaming eyes followed the line of my stick towards the south-west horizon, I saw, not the great cathedral crouching above its congregation of spires, nor the houses and parks and palaces I had seen before, but all was blackened and burned with a haze of dirty smoke rising above it, and nothing remained of London but a few stone walls.

This has not come to pass in my lifetime.

Chapter XXI
A Spleen Proof Against Spleenwort and a Melancholy Untouched by Melancholy Thistle

As I was writing my last chapter, there comes a knock at the door, and my wife, being busy about some cleaning, goes to answer it. Then there is a commotion, and I understand that my son Owen has arrived. When he has untangled himself from his mother, he comes over to greet me at my desk by the fire, and I rise awkwardly. Neither of us will look directly at the other, for the last time we met we quarrelled, and indeed the three or four times before that, and so we embrace, which is easier than standing apart, for then our eyes need not meet.

Come in, son, say I, wondering what I mean by it since he is in already. Take some ale, or some small beer. Be seated.

He thanks me, and fetches drink for us all. I have the day off, says he.

So I would think. How does your master?

Well. Every man is altering his cloak to a coat. I have learned much of coats.

He is sitting on a stool that is too low for him and his knees take up most of the space between us. My wife stands just behind him, unable to decide whether to sit with him or busy herself about making him still more welcome.

I will fetch a dish of tripe from the cook's, she says, or some cheesecake. What will you have, Owen?

Nothing, thank you, mother.

But you must have something. What have you eaten today?

A piece of cheese to my dinner, I thank you.

You are not fasting?

No, mother.

Well, I will fetch something later. You will stay with us to supper in any case?

Owen shrugs at this, being accustomed to speaking more with his shoulders than his voice.

Your father is writing a book, says my wife

Owen shrugs again.

No, says she, it is not one of his former books. This is a book of real use and value, which we believe will sell plentifully. It is to be a book of tailoring, all the crafts and skills of it, stitches and pinking and pressing and I know not what. It would be a useful book for you, Owen. You could do worse than study it, and then you would please Mr Greenhaugh.

I shall never please Mr Greenhaugh, Owen says with that scowl his fine-boned face wears most of the time. I do not wish to please Mr Greenhaugh, and Mr Greenhaugh does not wish to be pleased by me. Father, how does your nose?

As you see, I tell him, though he is not looking at it. I feel a strange begrudgement at my son's asking after my nose, as if he were trying to make me beholden to him by his concern for that organ. The King cured it with his touch, I say, and seeing my wife open her mouth to speak, I continue quickly, also your mother ministered to it most kindly with her ointments. But it was already cured by then.

Is there anything, dear son, says my wife hopefully, that I can mollify in you? Any warts or ill humours? Did you come to us seeking any special alleviation?

He shakes his head, saying, My ill humour is my own, mother. Pray do not take it from me for it is all I have. (And smiles despite himself at having framed so melancholy a definition of his character.) Tell me about this book of yours, father, says he. Where did you find the matter?

In my life, say I. This book shall contain all I know of tailoring.

Yes, father, but, says he, and pauses, unsure how to proceed. Do you know enough of tailoring for a whole book? It is not –

Tailoring, I tell him, is a fine craft and one you would do well to apply yourself to. It is a worthy occupation for any man. The first tailor was Adam –

Enough, husband, says my wife. He can read this in your book.

They will need tailors, I know, Owen says, in the New World. And whatever a man's trade is, he should strive to do it well, for industry may be a token that he is of the elect. But it is hard to do it here, where all my labour goes to clothe the damned. Father, you have not worked since the King was restored, you do not know what it is like in the city now. Satins and velvets –

You should thank God that your customers are wealthy enough to give you a living.

He puts down his mug, gets up and kicks the stool over. No, I do him an injustice; he cannot be said to have kicked it, but it was involved with his legs, and though he seemed to have freed himself in his rising, it fell over the moment after. He had intended to stride up and down, I think, though there is little scope for such activity in this room. Now, seeing the stool lying at his feet, he looks at it in some puzzlement and, if not rage, then at least a sense of hurt, as if feeling it has betrayed him. Finally he picks it up by one leg, sets it upright and sits on it again, resting his head on his hands and his elbows on his knees.

This is spleen, says my wife, and a little melancholy. I have the thing for it. And she goes to her chest and commences taking out jars and pots. This stuff, says she, holding up a flask and sniffing, is extract of spleenwort, with oil of melancholy thistle. Or I think it is. It smelt not so last time I used it. When was that, husband?

How should I know?

It was to cure an ill humour of yours, when no one would print your *Voice from Heaven*. It was the year of the eclipse, was it not, that they called Black Monday? And I thought then it smelt somewhat of cloves, but greener. Smell it, says she, holding the pot under my nose.

I would turn away but she pushes the flask after me and I can nowise escape it. It is useless to hold my breath, for I wish to speak, and I cannot do that without breathing. My authority is nothing in this house. I can forbid my wife to do the great things, but she does the little things before I can think of them to stop her. I cannot issue an edict against waving of tinctures under my nose. It is wrong, I tell her. You must not think to cure a man's feelings or his inner being with, with... sour milk. Sour milk and tomcat, with a trace of, yes, liquorice. It is the worst thing I ever smelt. Where did you get this potion?

Are you sure? says she, snatching it away as if I had been trying to take it from her and sniffing it again. That does not sound like melancholy thistle. Either it has gone off or it was something else all along. Surely the eclipse could not have soured it? I am sure this was the stuff. Still, I trust your nose, or I did before it was diseased. Perhaps it is solomon's seal.

Solomon's seal? This is strange. I have writ somewhat of Solomon in my book. What is the use of his seal?

I know not, says my wife with a sigh. I must have bought it for something, that is, if I did buy it.

Mother, put it away, my son says. I am not ill. I am only yearning to go to America. This country is finished. There is nothing here for a godly man, not now the Commonwealth is ended.

Commonwealth? say I, godly? You know naught of this godly Commonwealth.

I grew up in it, says he.

Yes, but you know not how it began.

Indeed I do. I have heard much of its beginnings from the minister and from the elders of our congregation. Before the Parliament rose up, the Church was full of Popery and wickedness. The Archbishop was an idolater who put rails before the communion table and would have us call it an altar. And the King put out a book called the Book of Sports that incited the populace to lewd pursuits on the Sabbath, archery and football and maypole dancing.

That was King James, not King Charles.

James did it first, and then Charles did it after. Besides, they were father and son, says he, his face hot.

I open my mouth to reply, but catch his eye and think better of it. And so we sit here, staring at each other in silence, while my wife recommences her rooting in the chest, in search of some medicine that will cure both of us.

Chapter XXII
The Struggle with the Angel

It was cold in Blackfriars Church, and, the morning outside being overcast, the light within was unclean and cobwebby. At the other end of my pew were an elderly man and wife I could not recall seeing before. They looked sidelong at me and I looked sidelong at them; I still knew almost no one in the congregation, and believed my place in the pew was not fully secure. It could be, thought I, that I have been suffered to retain it these four years because the churchwardens have overlooked me, and soon their error will be brought to their attention and they will move me elsewhere. Or it could be that the pew really belongs this couple, who have been away all this time and are now come to reclaim what is theirs. I supposed they were Puritans, which would make them the less disposed to be charitable to a interloper at the other end of their pew. I fixed my eyes on the King's arms displayed on a blue shield on the wall of the church and imagined myself in Maes-y-Llan, on a sunny day by the river, a reverie that was only disturbed by the unaccustomed voice of the preacher, who had mounted to the pulpit meanwhile. It was a younger voice than Dr Gouge's and had a hoarseness, not as of one suffering from a sore throat, but ingrained in it by nature. I peered into the grey light, and made out a pale man, a stranger, one of the new godly sort. The text was of Jacob, how he arrived at the ford Jabbok with his two wives, and his two womenservants, and his eleven sons, and sent them over with all his possessions, while he remained on the near side alone. My mind still dwelling on the river at Maes-y-Llan, which was no more than a foot deep and almost narrow enough to leap across, I pictured this river as no wider, a seam in the earth. It had much the same name as Jacob himself, or, as Hugh Jones would have said, the name Jacob lay beneath it, and so I thought it was as if the man had come to a thin line in his own being that he might not cross without great change and commotion. His wives and womenservants and sons could cross easily, the ford not bearing any of their names, but Jacob must remain behind and wait.

And a man came and wrestled with him until the breaking of the day. And when it was daybreak day, the man who wrestled with Jacob saw that he prevailed not, and touched the hollow of Jacob's thigh so that the sinew shrank.

Wrestlers have many tricky holds and trips, but I never heard of one that could shrink a sinew with a touch. When Jacob felt his leg weaken he must have known that he was not struggling with a common man, but one who could destroy him whenever he chose. This was an angel, (though the Scripture does not say it), but disguised in an earthly form, not having wings or wearing the fine linen of its kind. But God had suffered Jacob to defeat it by holding it off till daybreak, and the price he had paid was a halting in the leg which he would carry with him the rest of his life.

The angel now thought only of escaping back to heaven, the time for his struggle being elapsed, and said, Let me go, for the day breaketh.

And Jacob, knowing now what creature he had hold of, was determined to have the reward of his victory:

I will not let thee go, except thou bless me.

What is thy name?

Jacob.

Thus was Jacob renamed, and the name Israel signified his new being as Arise signifies mine.

Thy name shall be no more called Jacob, but Israel: for like a prince hast thou power with God and with men, and has prevailed.

Then Jacob asked his name in return, and the other would not give it, but he blessed Jacob, as he had asked.

You know, brethren, said the strange preacher with the hoarse voice, how men put forth all their strength in wrestling, so that suddenly one prevails.

When we men reckon with God, we do so not by the strength of our limbs but by prayer, for we cannot prevail with God except by prayer. And just as the wrestler delights in his struggle, so God delights to have us strive with him by prayer, and is willing to be overcome with our prayers if we so wrestle with him, and the prayer that God delights in is not a multitude of words, nor does God care whether it is fine elegant words, but the desire of a heart, expressed with faith, fervency and all the strength put to it, in a moment, as men do when they wrestle, and unto such as wrestle with him so he gives his most excellent gifts.

He seemed a puny fellow to talk as one who knew the ways of wrestlers. Nevertheless, I understood at once as I heard him that he had been sent that day, angel-like, to impart a message to myself, that my own struggle was impending.

I left the church, walking alone with my head cast down, remembering a dream I had had the other night, a dream that was no more than a voice speaking these words:

Get thee to the Root.

What was the Root, and how was I to go there?

When I came to my chamber I fell upon my knees, and began to pray. So hard did I struggle that I was soon out of breath and not able to utter a word, but I prayed on in my mind for about two hours, until I began to be weary, and cold, for I had no fire. I got up then, and stretched out my legs, which were sore from remaining so long in the same position, then went and lay down on my bed, hardly able to remember what it was I had been praying for. I was about to fall asleep when a voice spoke, close to my ear:

Go to your Book.

It was sharp and shrill, but not a woman's voice, or a man's either. It spoke not harshly, but like one giving a command that must be obeyed at once. So I arose and I got up and walked to the table where I found my Bible lying open, though I had not left it so, and sat down and read in it. The text was this:

Wherefore he saith, Awake thou that sleepest, and arise from the dead, and Christ shall give thee light.

And Arise from the dead, said I. God is calling my name, and I must have this light he promises. Immediately upon this the Scriptures came all of a sudden into my mind, as if I had learned them by heart, with another understanding of them than I had before, for before I looked on them as a history of things that passed in other countries pertaining to other persons, but now I saw them as a mystery to be opened at this time, and belonging to us.

Chapter XXIII
The Letter A Made Manifest

As I sat on the shopboard and sewed, I began to reflect on the state of the kingdom. Many, like myself, knew that all was not well in the land. Nevertheless, I should be cautious about how I spoke of it, and to whom. People would not take it kindly of me to speak of the King and of a judgement to come suddenly upon him and the court and the nation. I would lose work by it. It could not be denied that my sudden understanding of Scripture came from God, but I was no minister. If I told everyone of the visions I had seen, I would come to trouble, and perhaps lose my life. I kept my eyes on the to-ing and fro-ing of the needle, feeling my master watching me. My neck and back ached, and my eyes also, from the effort of not moving them. Sometimes, far away, I heard Mr Broad clear his throat as if he would speak, but seeing me, as he supposed, so intent upon my work, and not knowing me well enough for friendly converse, he was silent again. He stood almost behind me, at the cutting board and I was facing away, with the light of the window falling over my shoulder on to the cloth. In front of me was the end of the board, somewhat more than a foot and less than a yard of empty wood, but I did not let my eyes stray even so far. I had been too much alone in my room during my hours away from the workshop, had spoken to too few people and brooded too much on matters of court and policy that were none of my business. These thoughts were not for such as myself. It was not healthy to have them. I was no prophet, but a tailor.

How is it that we know when someone is in the room? Mr Broad had been there all along, but I do not mean him. How did I know, after an hour of stiffnecked sewing and downcast eyes, that some other person stood beside me? I heard nothing nor felt nor saw anything but I knew that space at the end of the shopboard a little beyond my vision was changed, that it was filled with what it had not held before, a presence. And so, having no choice but to do so, I looked up.

It was A from the hornbook, the first of created beings. In form he was a young man of my own age, slim and beardless, standing upright, his feet a few inches from my right knee, yet I felt that in reality he was flying across some space between stars and planets, for his robes endlessly flowed and fluttered, though the air in the closed workshop was still. This, I thought, is an angel, and I must remember everything about him for I may never see another in my lifetime. For one thing I must endeavour to understand the weave and cut of his heavenly linen, in case I ever see Mr Jones again and he asks it of me. Also I must establish whether or not he has wings. But neither of these things could I be sure of: the white of his skin and the white of his linen were perfectly matched as to both hue and texture, and both seemed to move in the ethereal wind of his flight. At his back this fluttering of his person seemed more pronounced and to extend at times far out beyond his shoulders, but whether it were proper to characterize these flickering projections as wings I could not tell. His face and hands, legs, arms, and feet were formed like my own, but they too moved with the rest of him. Either the bleach that had been used on the linen was so fine or its whiteness reflected all the light in the room, or, as I thought, there was some light inside the angel that caused it to burn, not with the yellow or red of common fire but with the white of certain stars, though closer and more brilliant than they. This made it harder still to inventorize the angel and his garments, for I could hardly bear to look at him. The only understanding I could come to was a strange sentence that formed itself in my head at that moment: an angel is a man woven by God.

The eyes were of the same colour as the rest, but more so, for when he looked at me, which he did without any movement of the head, I beheld their radiance as greater by far than the rest of him. He had a mouth also, which I figured to myself as a vent or placket in the material, neither closed nor altogether open but in both states at once. It will speak to me, thought I, and I will not be able to bear the sound of its voice. Or it will move to threaten me. And yet, for all its fluttering, the angel could not be said to move at all; it remained standing, its feet somewhat apart, its left hand stretched forward towards me, its right held high above its head, and longer far than the other. Looking up among the roof beams, I saw that this great arm was sharp-edged and ended in a point as fine as my needle. It was a flaming sword.

Have I made known to thee by several infallible ways my will and given thee light, and made known unto thee what is to come upon this nation, and wilt not thou declare it to them? If thou do it not, though they die, yet will I require their blood at thy hands. Thou, therefore, gird up thy loins and Arise and speak unto them all that I command thee. Be not dismayed at their faces lest I consume thee before them.

A fear seized my limbs and made my heart beat in my ears, and I turned away from the vision to my master to try to tell him of it, but no words came, and he continued placidly cutting out the bodice for the gown I was sewing. At last he sensed my trouble and looked up questioningly but the angel was invisible to him, having come for me alone. So I turned back and found the apparition unchanged yet ever-changing, the flickering sword held high, the eyes fixed on me but seeing everything.

I swept the heavy material from my knees, put down my needle and jumped from the shopboard. I must go at once, said I, I have business. I knew not of it this morning, or I should have... I must go.

And I departed the place, leaving Mr Broad staring after me and the angel still standing on the shopboard. Then I went to my house, looking at every moment for fire from heaven to fall upon me and thrust me into Hell for rebelling against God in neglecting his work, and hurried up the stairs to my room. I pulled up my stool and sat at my table, where the Bible lay beside pen, ink and paper. I took up the pen and began to write.

Chapter XXIV
The Domestic Air Unsweetened by Pepperwort and Mithridate Mustard

My son Owen came here this morning – again, for he spends more time away from his work than he spends at it, it seems to me. He looked somewhat agitated and would not sit down for long but paced about the room. When I asked what ailed him, he said that the Lord was exercising his patience with a cold, but, says he, it is the gentlest and most cherishing of reproofs.

He should have known, however, that it is dangerous to make such an excuse in this house. A cold? says my wife, why said you not so before? I shall see to that.

Her bustling disturbs my train of thought, for I am doing my best to expound to him my understanding of the divine right of kings, and he sitting still at last, very assured and comfortable in the ministrations of his mother, having been brought up to such salving and dosing and infusing from infancy.

The Church of England is the true and only Church, and the English are God's chosen people, as are the Welsh, who were of the True Church before the English were, and King Charles Steward is God's anointed, which is proven by his very name.

Is this the second King Charles, or the first? He that parades in St James's Park with his mistress before the eyes of the multitude, or he that married a Papist?

It is true, say I, that Her Majesty the Queen Mother, being French, caused much discontent throughout the nation when she came here, with building of a Popish chapel and hearing mass there, among bells and incense and stage machinery. These were wrongs, and I warned against them. The bishops lived in luxury, and were become temporal lords more than spiritual. And because the King was ill-advised, men said there should be no King. Because the Church was ill-led, men say there should be no bishops. But there were worse evils than these. There were those who would overthrow the kingdom and the Church because they said God willed it. There were those in the Church who claimed to be ministers though they wore black cloaks instead of holy vestments, and refused to bow the knee before God's altar.

We do not refuse to bow, Owen says, but we do it inwardly. We bow the knee of the heart.

My wife takes the kettle from the fire and pours some water into a bowl where she has mixed some tinctures. It gives off a smell of boiled greens, strong waters and spice, and I feel my own passages clearing, though I knew not that anything ailed me.

Whoever heard of a heart having a knee? If you come before the King or some great lord, do you bow the knee of the heart, or the knee of the leg?

I bow nothing before any man.

That is because you have never come before the King or any lord. Believe me, if you had, you would recognize greatness and would bow. In the King especially there is a majesty that comes from his being imbued with God.

Owen must be silent perforce now, for he is breathing the infusion my wife has prepared for him, with an apron of hers over his head, and I may continue unchecked.

You begin by calling yourselves godly and others not so. You end by warring against all those you call ungodly, King and Church and all.

He emerges at this, his cheeks pink and an angry look in his eyes.

Someone should have shown that fool Charles what he was at before it was too late, he says. I believe Mr Prynne tried to.

This is desperate talk, Owen, say I. Wife, what is in that remedy of yours? He will get himself hanged, drawn and quartered, and be damned into the bargain.

Only some pepperwort and a little mithridate mustard, says she. I gave you the same last winter when you had a cold, and it did not make you talk more dangerously than usual.

I would have done it myself, Owen says, only I was not there, not being born yet. It makes me mad. And now I must go to America to have any life at all. Father, have you any money?

You know we have not, Owen, my wife says. Breathe the mustard again, for I see it is making your nose run, and that is good.

Stay away from the bowl, Owen.

But it is useless to tell him. He returns to it and puts the apron back over his head. At least this way he is not uttering treacherous blasphemies, only little sniffling and coughing sounds. While he is thus prevented from speaking, I continue my expounding of his errors.

Owen, his late Majesty was badly advised, as even your own faction confessed before war and politics clouded their judgement. And being called on by God to explain these errors, I wrote him a letter myself, as you would know if you had read my writings. My words were to this purpose, that two deadly enemies were seeking to ruin the kingdom. The Papists whispered that the Queen would prevail and bring the King to their religion, so that all the people must become Papists now or risk being burned at the stake when he came to be converted. And the Puritans said we must stand up against Popery now or be undone.

Owen surfaces from the apron at this, and makes some splutterings as of one who would like to speak but has no air inside him to do it with. Puritans, says he finally.

I know you are of their faction, my wife says, taking back the apron from him. This is the way of the young nowadays, they will be always against their parents.

Mother, says Owen, I was the only boy among my fellows whose parents did not allow him to fast with the others. When they asked if I was of the elect or the damned, I did not even know the answer, and then they said I was damned, and laughed at me for it. And they laughed at me still more when they learned who my father was.

They did so because they feared me, I say.

Well, says my wife, these same boys that laughed at you are Puritans no longer.

Some of them are. The best, and as for the others, we care not for them, says he, his eyes and nose streaming.

Husband, give him your cloth.

What, wife, the one with my stitches in it?

Why, you have finished the stitchings, have you not?

I know not, for I may practise some more as I come to write of them. I cannot tell what I will write before I write it.

In any case, my wife says, it needs washing. But I think it will do for Owen, since we have nothing else, and I can wash it afterwards.

You cannot tell what you will write, says my son, and yet you claim to know the whole of God's will before he performs it.

How? What washing is this? I have done nothing with this cloth but stitch on it. It is not soiled.

Everything is soiled, my wife says, by the mere being in the world. And therefore everything must be taken down to the pump and washed, your cloth as well as everything else. (For this is another mania of my wife's, to waste water on cleaning things, herself included.) Look, says she, there is coal dust on it.

She goes to the desk and takes up my cloth to show me. There are the stitches as I wrote of them, the basting and the forward stitch and the backstitch. It is true that the cloth looks somewhat smutty, but now that I look round the room, everything in it looks somewhat smutty also. For all my wife's cleanliness, a thin layer of soot forms on walls and floor, desk and stools faster than she can clean it off. Even the paper I write on has black smudges on it which are not from the ink.

There is coal dust on everything, wife. You would not have one thing cleaner than the room it is in?

But she has already passed the cloth on to my son, who blows his nose in it and wipes his eyes. Thank you, mother, says he. I feel the better for our talk.

What, is this a talk? I thought it was an evacuation of the organs, I say, looking with sadness on my defiled needlework.

And I acknowledge that you mean well, father, Owen says. It is something that you know the Bible and can quote it with the best. Only you are not saved, and so it is not enough. I need ten pounds to go to America, and I have it not. What shall I do?

Do, Owen? Why, stay here, of course. This is London, the greatest city in the world. What could you want with a savage country where there is no King or Parliament or law or books? You may do anything here, write books yourself, have an audience with the King or with great lords, with the speaker of the Parliament, whoever you wish, and tell them your thoughts and your grievances.

Alas, says he. Why should the King listen to me? He will cast us out of the church. We are as nothing to him.

The King listened to me, Owen. Or indeed, if he did not listen, still was I suffered to present my petition to him. And yet what am I but a humble tailor?

Chapter XXV
A King Displayed in his Regality for the Edification of Youth

The river was full of small boats, some with sails, others with oars, female boats and male ones, chasing and skirting around each other like dancers. We were almost arrived, and I beheld the towers and ramparts of Greenwich Palace, a cluster of warlike fortifications and peaceful houses, their chimneys smoking, and trees rising behind them. The east wind blew off the water into my face, and I clutched the Bible in my left hand, not daring to open it, for whenever I did so, God's words leapt out at me glowing and sharp-edged, words that had existed in the book since he dictated them, but meant, as I now knew, for my eyes alone.

My son, you talk of godliness: do you know what it is to carry God's message?

I disembarked at Margaret's Bridge, paid the waterman and turned left along the road to enter the Palace. Several men in ruffs and cloaks passed me, talking and laughing, as I stood beneath the windows of the Hall, and I made a movement to stop them and ask the whereabouts of the King, but they ignored me. I climbed the steps to the hall and, finding the door open, walked into an echoing wooden space, like a church. A group of guards was standing just inside the door, and seeing me, one of them came over. He wore a ruff and bonnet and carried a halberd, but he was a young man, slouching and sarcastic-looking rather than overbearing. Not being sure how to address a royal guard. Sir, said I (and as soon regretted it, seeing that after all this was only a common soldier), Sergeant, can you tell me where the King is to be found?

Who?

His Majesty the King.

The other guards had come over now to see what the matter was, and they stared down at me with my Bible under my arm.

What will you do with the King?

I have a message from God for him.

The men laughed among themselves, looking at each other to confirm their laughter, as men do in a group.

When did God speak to you? the first man asked.

Therefore I told them how I was called, starting with my childhood and the time when I flew above the mountains at Bwlch Rhiw Credire, and then later when I saw the sun dancing on Whit Sunday at Gole Ronnw, and how I had been summoned by God to bring this message, who had sent one of his Angels to threaten me if I delivered it not. The men no longer mocked me but seemed to hang on my words. I told them that I was necessitated to come here with this writing to His Majesty, and I gave them the writing to look upon.

Welsh, are you? one of the men said, a fellow with some grey in his beard.

I am a Briton by nation. My name is Arise, son of –

Give that here, the slouching man said, and took the paper out of my hand roughly. It was not sealed, merely folded, and the man read it aloud to the others in a flat voice. They repeated certain words under their breath.

Papists... Puritans... a lost man... church government... confusion... upside-down.

Do you intend to teach the King what he shall do? the older man asked. He has his Bishops, Council and Doctors, who are both wise and learned, to consult with about such things. The King will take no notice of an unlearned man like you.

Though the King will not regard it, I must deliver it into his own hand.

Very well, the first guard said, you may do it. The King is shooting in the garden, but I promise you that you will not hear of it any more, for he will receive it as a petition, but when it is looked upon, it will be thrown away.

I made my way to the garden, and stood under the leafless trees with other petitioners, and a few guards. On the other side of the gravel, in a roped-off area of muddy grass, a number of gentlemen were taking their turns to shoot at a target that was none too distant. I did not recognize the King among them, having never seen his likeness except on coins of the realm. All I saw was a huddle of men in dark cloaks, hats and ruffs with neatly trimmed beards and long hair. Sometimes a flash of bright silk was visible as they swept back their cloaks to shoot. From the way the bows were handled, I knew the men were aware that they were watched, pretending to be absorbed in their craft, and talking quietly to each other without ever once looking up at the petitioners across the path.

Which is the King? I asked.

Yon little fellow, a woman said.

His Majesty was a head shorter than anyone there, and slightly built, yet there was a power in him. He did not strut, but held his body upright, walking with a slight stiffness or awkwardness. He talked less than the others, and when it was his turn to shoot, took less time to aim the bow, raising it without hurry, but directly, not stopping to laugh and joke with the others waiting their turn, as most did. There was some applause after the shot, as there was in every case, but no more than for the courtiers. The arrow had hit the target, but I could not tell from here whether it was in the gold or not.

This, my son, was your King. And just as you must venerate myself, who am the father of your body, and God who is the father of the universe, so also must you venerate the King, who is the father of the nation.

The party made their way to the gravel path, the King leading. He stopped before us, and the guard beckoned to each of us in turn to come forward. I was among the last. As I passed, the guard whispered to me, Say nothing. Bow, present your letter to His Majesty, bow again, and step back.

I nodded, thinking, I will speak, however. The Lord will move me to some utterance.

The King was standing on the gravel, his friends behind him; I had to step over the rope to approach, and the guard stayed close by his side. When we reached the edge of the path, the guard whispered, Bow! and I obeyed him. The King was about the same height as myself, or an inch shorter. I could see now that his legs were somewhat crooked, though he stood straight upon them. Under his cloak, he wore a suit of cinnamon satin which caught the sunlight like no cloth I had seen. His ruff was not the largest, but perfectly white and cunningly made, with many folds and complexities, not angel clothing, but an earthly miracle of cutting and starching and pressing. He stood with his head on one side, looking at me with his serious brown eyes as a sparrow does when it expects some bread.

I handed him the letter, my heart loud in my ears. The Lord did not move me to say anything.

Th-thank you, said he, his voice light and hesitant. We continued to look at each other for a moment, then the King turned away to hand my letter to a man behind him, who held all the others.

This, my son, was the man your Commonwealth put to death.

Bow! the guard whispered again.

Chapter XXVI
God's Message Unheeded in the Halls of Greatness

The porter led me up the great stairway to the door of the private room. When I entered, the Earl was sitting in front of the fire, his head in his hands. I went and stood before him, waiting for him to acknowledge my presence. You are Mr Evans, said he, and you are...?

A tailor, my lord.

He smiled as if I had meant it in jest, but perhaps it was not a smile after all, for it seemed to hurt him in the performance of it, and perhaps it did hurt, for his narrow, bony face was much disfigured by the scars of smallpox. This earl was a slight man, dressed in black velvet with a small ruff, lace cuffs and pearl buttons on his doublet. I could not see any stitches at all, and marvelled at the workmanship.

That was what Jeffers told me, said he, but I was reluctant to believe him. He is not an easy man to get past – you must have rare powers of persuasion. You are a tailor, and you are come to see me, to give me news that affects the safety and stability of the kingdom or words to that effect. This knowledge has come to you and not to me although you are a tailor and I am the Earl of Essex.

His voice was excessively gentle, as if trying not to cause offence by his speech.

My lord, it has been granted to me to see visions and receive revelations from God.

Has it? said he. I wonder what that is like. I would give much to see a vision or receive a revelation from God. It would make up for certain checks and discomforts I have in my life, and perhaps also for some things I have seen that I wish I had not seen. Yet you do not look a particularly holy man.

I have been visited, my lord, by an angel as I sat at my shopboard working, and God has spoken to me in my dreams, and through the words of Scripture. I have seen the kingdom at war, with bloody battles in English fields, one neighbour against another. I have seen the King overthrown by a party that is to execute judgement upon the court for its errors and corruptions. And I see you, my lord.

Myself?

When the kingdom is shaken, some will fall, while others will rise. None will rise higher or more swiftly than the Earl of Essex. I have seen you, my Lord, riding at the head of a great army. You will be General of all England.

This earl was not a sort of man to laugh readily, but he made a coughing now that was the nearest he could get to it. Oh, I like that, said he when he was able to speak again, You do very well to tell me. You have given me great pleasure. General of all England. I must find something for you. Wait a moment.

He went over to the desk in the corner, unlocked a drawer and took out a small bag of soft red leather, which he fumbled inside. Take this, said he, as a gift, a little Jacobus.

He pressed something heavy into my palm, and I looked down and saw the head of King James Steward, in gold, with letters round it: *Rex, D.G, Fid. Def.*

No, my lord, said I, I have no need of your gold. I did not come here for money, but to tell you of your destiny, and your duty.

I handed the Jacobus back, and the Earl, without looking at it, took it and slipped it back into the bag. Honest man, eh? he said, I knew there must be one somewhere. Come and meet my guests. I would like them to hear what you have told me.

In the banqueting chamber the guests had finished eating, and were toying with some swans' feathers which had been used along with the head, neck and beak to decorate a swan of spun sugar. Now the remains of both the real bird and the sugar one were heaped like a fox kill on an oval pewter dish in the centre of the long table. Some guests were still drinking toasts to each other, springing up and sitting down again at intervals, which made it hard for the Earl to gain their attention. The gowns of the ladies were of satin and cunningly made so that there seemed to be too much material in the lower half and not enough in the upper.

Tell them, the Earl said in a high, strangled voice. Go on, Evans. Tell them, what you told me.

Who is he? a lady asked.

This is Mr Evans, a tailor. And a prophet. (At which those who were not laughing before did so now, and the others asked them what was the matter, which caused some confusion in the explaining.) Tell them, Evans. Hush, ladies and gentlemen, I pray you.

So I said again, disconcerted by all their eyes upon me, and still more by the single eye of the swan staring up at me from its catastrophe of feathers, that I had come to tell my Lord the Earl of Essex that he was to be General of all England, that there was a judgement to come upon the nation suddenly, and that he should be the man to lead the army that executed this judgement.

There was much noise at this. Someone asked who the Earl would be fighting against, and when I replied the King, the laughter became uneasy, and most fell silent.

Send him to Brooke! one cried suddenly.

Indeed, said Essex, the man you want, Evans, is my Lord Brooke. He is fitter for such a purpose than I am.

Can this be true, my lord? I asked. I never heard of Lord Brooke before. And I am assured in my visions and messages from God that you are the man who will be General of all England.

I did not know your thoughts ran that way, Essex, said a plump man at the far end of the table.

They do not, the Earl said. I brought this fellow into the room to amuse us with his cleverness. And now I thank him. Mr Evans, you have given me much merriment today. But you should know that I am a man that does not meddle with the court, (here laughter broke out), nor yet with the other party.

Therefore I cannot be their General. As my Lord Ashurst has said (and he put an arm round my shoulders) you must go to Lord Brooke, and tell him all you have told me. You will find him in Holborn.

And as I started to protest, he continued, No, I see dinner is finished, and my guests will not miss me for a few more minutes. I will come with you as far as St Clement's Well, to see you on your way.

Having parted from His Lordship at St Clement's Well, I made my way to Brooke House and waited all afternoon in the cold by the stables in the courtyard, watching the door Lord Brooke would emerge from, if indeed it was the right one. I was almost sure it was. Once the door behind me opened, the one that led to the street, but it was only a servant in blue livery, returning from some errand. He pushed past me as if to indicate that I was standing in the way, even though there was plenty of room to pass me on either side. In the stables, a couple of grooms were sweeping and mending tackle, talking all the while, and seeming not to notice me. There was nowhere to sit, so I walked up and down on the cobbles, following always the same path, a tight loop some five yards long. I gazed at the lifeless windows of the house, tried to guess which was Lord Brooke's closet or parlour, and repeated verses from the Bible under my breath.

On the last of my perambulations I turned and saw two men standing watching me. Before I could decide which of these was the man I must speak to, one of them approached me. What are you doing here, fellow? said he. He had a country accent and I guessed he was one of Brooke's servants.

I come from the Earl of Essex, at his prompting to see my Lord –

What do you want?

I explained about the rending of the kingdom and of the pressing danger to His Majesty, and about the angel that had visited me, and how the Earl of Essex (and not my Lord Brooke) was to be General of all England, and that I was here because the Earl had said my visions must be mistaken, but that they could not be because they were of God, but that nevertheless –

Then you are of our party? the man said, low and fast.

What party is that?

You are for the true Church, and against bishops and popery? You are of the godly?

Firstly, said I, the true Church is the Church of England. God will make use of your party as a scourge to his Church for a time, yet your end will be miserable. This I have foreseen...

So I continued with my other points but before I had got further than *Seventhly* I found I could no longer see the countrylike man's face very clearly, and understood that it was getting dark. This man had interrupted and argued fiercely for a while, but he had stopped now, silenced by my mastery of Scripture.

Where is my Lord Brooke? said I.

He has gone some time since.

I should not be here, I told him. It was the Earl of Essex I had to speak to, but I let him put me aside for this Brooke, even though I know not who he is or what fate God has stored up for him. I should go back to Essex House, but it is too late now, and in any case the Earl will not listen to me. Still, it makes no difference. All that I say will come to pass, whether men listen to me or not.

Chapter XXVII
A Prophet Returned to his Own Country

The corn was already yellow, and swifts were chasing the midges above the brown water of the Gwenfro as I crossed the old wooden footbridge. I could smell roasting malt from the kilns nearby. Before me was the church with its tower of golden stone, too grand for a town of this size, and beyond it were the Shire Hall, the High Cross and the High Street, with Town Hill rising to the left. The streets were still busy at this hour, with many wagons and horses. The June fair was due to start soon, and the town was full of traders, animals and farmers. It was not a great city, but a clump of stone and dirt in the midst of the soft yellow and green of the fields. In the distance, where the sun would set after its midsummer loitering, were the folds and ridges of high moorland that marked the beginning of the wild country, still black and dead-looking at this time of the year. Somewhere over there was my true home. I had never lived in Wrexham for more than a few months, after my mother was new-married there for the third time.

I knocked at the door of one of the fine houses at the High Street end of Hope Street, and a girl I knew not answered it. Though little taller than myself, she contrived to look down at me, taking in the dust and caked mud on my shoes and breeches. What business have you here? said she.

I told her I was Mrs Beynon's son, and that I had come home, that is, I had come to the place where she was, though my true home was where my brothers lived in Merionethshire, having walked from London where I now dwelt, and that I had urgent news for my family which was given me of God, though I could not speak of it here.

Hearing this, the girl looked down at me again. Who did you say you were? she asked.

And I, not liking to be catechised by her: My name is Arise Evans.

And she: My mistress has a son Owen and a son Griffith in Merionethshire, but I never heard of any other sons. What was it again?

Arise, said I, and I have been admitted to greater houses than this, and by less insolent persons than you are. When I was in London –

Oh, said she. You are from London?

Indeed I am, and I have spoken with the King and with the Earl of Essex and my Lord Brooke (which I said hurriedly, having forgot that I never spoke with this Brooke) concerning a great cataclysm that is to come upon us all, yourself included, being a judgment upon us for the sins of the nation, as I can prove by Scripture.

Well, said she, you should have said you were a minister, though I never saw one so badly dressed. I will fetch my mistress.

My mother was now advanced in years, yet she still had somewhat of zeal in the clearness of her eyes and the flutteringness of her hands as she walked about the room, for any little or great thing could discommode her most prettily. And so she walked in her parlour saying, What is to be done with him? and her friends watched her face and the flutterings of her fingers. They were great men of the town, and the quietest of those present was her own husband, who cast an anxious look upon each of the others in turn and then back upon his wife, as one who knew his answer would avail nothing. And my mother, likewise, looked not upon him, but on the other men. What is to be done with him? said she again.

All this time I was striving to expound my prophecies, but they heard me not. Mother, said I, I have come all the way from London, and not to eat your food or to sleep in your sheets, though, God knows, I am entitled to it. (I could smell a joint of lamb roasting in the kitchen.) I have travelled on foot and by cart to come and see you. I have slept beside the road when it was not raining, and otherwise begged my accommodation.

That, she said, I can see. Rhys, there was no need.

I must do what God tells me. I have received news, of God, that is of the most urgent kind. No, mother, do not interrupt me, I beg you. I speak to you now, not as your son, but as God's messenger.

Oh, Mr Trevor, said she, what is to be done?

This What is to be done? was the question she had asked after my father's death and my own disinheritance, and just as I had then I thought it now most impertinent, for she should have said it to me, not about me, the disposing of myself being the least pressing problem before her. She talked round and over and through me, and so did Mr Trevor and my stepfather, and the other men there, until I began to doubt the words that came from my mouth, not their meaning but that I was uttering them at all. They stood in a knot in the centre of the room, and talked low, but I heard them anyway. He speaks high treason, they said, and if you suffer him to go abroad he shall be taken and imprisoned, if not die for it.

This is no treason, I said, for it is to save the King that I speak.

Still they continued their conference, not looking at me.

He has raised the matter of God. He seems to know his Scripture. We must do nothing until he has first been examined by a minister. I say not that he speaks truth – that would be preposterous – but if he brings in Scripture, then we risk exceeding our authority.

There is no authority but God, said I.

What will a minister tell us, they continued, that we know not already? A man may quote from Scripture for treasonous purposes.

Nevertheless, they said, a minister should be called, or several ministers, for they may not agree and safety must be ensured in all respects.

There is no safety, said I, when God is angered.

If need be, their voices continued, you must keep him in by force, mistress, for he is in the flower of his youth, and his blood boils in his veins, and his great strength has brought him to this frenzy. Now shut him up in a chamber, and keep him from sleep, and from all manner of sustenance to make him weak, and he will come to himself again.

God will not suffer you, said I, to imprison his messenger and stifle his message.

By all means, they said, but let us call a minister first. Or several ministers.

Chapter XXVIII
Heaven's Blessing Conferred in Rainbow Vapours, and Is Found Delectable

I might lie on the bed, but I might not sleep. If I closed my eyes, my mother's friend shouted at me, and if I did not open them again at once the friend would come and shake me until I did. I found it hard to lie down without closing my eyes, so I spent much of the time walking up and down the room. The friend sat on the stool in the middle, his arms folded and his head bowed, seeming asleep himself. I walked quickly, feeling the roughness of the floorboards against my bare feet; if I dropped my pace for a moment, I would perceive my weariness, and it would be impossible to walk again. The friend nodded, then opened his eyes. That is good, said he. As fast as you can. I would see you walk. Walk for me, Rhys.

My name is Arise.

Walk for me, Rhys. There is much walking to do before morning.

I wished to stop now that I knew the friend desired me to walk, but I dared not. If I stopped, I would faint and fall down and the friend would shout at me. I was cold in my shirt and drawers, for the friends had taken my clothes away when they locked me in this room, but I was glad of it, for the cold helped me to stay awake, and to walk. It was a summer coolness, easy enough to shake off with a little exercise.

You must walk to weaken yourself, Rhys, for only when you are weak will you come to yourself again.

The friend stopped to take a sip from the cup of ale on the floor beside the stool. He had not yet touched the white bread and cheese next to it.

Thirsty, Rhys? Have some water. You will die if you do not drink.

Water will make me ill, said I. Already you have taken my clothes. If I drink water in the cold it will chill me, and then I shall die indeed. Give me some of that ale, or some small beer.

Later. You must not touch such things until you are cured.

I am not mad.

I was angry at myself for talking to the friend, and above all for asking him for something. He gained satisfaction from refusing my requests, for my clothes, for my Bible, for food, for the chance to sleep. Mr Trevor was a lean man in his forties with a long, pale face and a shy smile.

Your father and mother are troubled about you.

My father is not troubled about anything any more.

I would say your stepfather and your mother. A son must be dutiful to his father and mother, Rhys, as we read in the Scriptures. Honour thy father –

Will you bandy Scripture with me? I said. My mother has brought the most able ministers in these parts to confer with me, thinking they will be a means to make me alter my opinions. But they found such power in me that they could not contradict, saying that I am in the Hand of God endued with such knowledge and understanding of Scripture, and having so much reason that no reasonable man can with any reason contradict me in what I affirm.

No one is contradicting you, Rhys, the man told me. What you say may very well be true, and in any case your parents and friends are not such as can understand it. It is only that you must not say it. If we suffer you to go abroad you will be taken and imprisoned, if not die for it, and bring shame to us, for you speak high treason.

How can that be? said I. It is for the King that I say these things, to defend him from his enemies, and from the certainty of death, for they will kill –

Mr Trevor was not listening to me, but had started to hum, at first under his breath, then louder, to blot out my words from his mind. Seeing that I had stopped my pacing and was staring at him, he blushed a little and turned to his bread and cheese, which he pretended to be busy with, breaking off little pieces with his fingers and squeezing and rolling them before putting them into his mouth.

A little after dawn on the second day, there was a knock, and another friend of my mother's arrived to relieve him. They muttered in the doorway, keeping the door between them and myself, though I could hear pretty well.

If he sleeps, shake him. Say nothing. He is cunning and will try to persuade you. Do not listen to him. If he seems too lively, call for help. Geoffrey will be nearby, and Mrs Beynon has promised to give you anything you need.

The new friend came into the room. He was tall, thin and altogether hairless, so that I could not tell how old he was. He looked like a vigorous and manly infant. He stared hard to impress himself upon me, then looked away.

I waited to be sure that the other had gone before speaking. Friend, said I, I am hungry and thirsty. I have not eaten for a day and a night. Will you bring me something for breakfast?

The man sat on the stool, looking at the floor.

My mouth is dry. At least bring me something to drink.

The man's eyes slid in the direction of the water pitcher by the bed, then back again.

May I talk to my mother? I am her youngest son, and she cannot be content to see me treated like this.

The man sighed like one weary of conversation, and I returned to looking out of the window.

The second day of my imprisonment was harder than the first, for I no longer had the strength to walk up and down the room. I felt faint now when I stood, and wished to vomit, although there was nothing in my stomach. The day being hot, the lack of clothes was not so uncomfortable, but my drowsiness was the more distressing. I lay on the edge of sleep, but was continually awoken again by the bald man, who shook me fiercely but said nothing. So it went on, sleep and shaking, sleep and shaking, till the angry face seemed to be ever present above me. It had a large round lump on the brow that looked like a sprouting horn, and the sight of it was an irritation to me, for I desired it either to be in the centre, like the horn of a unicorn, or to have a balancing one on the other side. I tried to tell the man this, but my words sounded confused even to me. Then I sought to prevent the face from returning by pulling the bedcurtain across. But the man snatched the curtain back, and we tugged it back and forth until it ripped.

This provoked him to speech. If you do not behave yourself better, said he, I shall call the others. He sounded peevish, which made me guilty, for it was not his fault he was so ugly.

The third guard was fat and cheerful of face and so more pleasing to look upon. Enough of that, said he when I rolled over and tried to sleep, and laughed, but he was as rough with his shaking as the others. I had grown weary of pleading for beer by now, and had drunk all the water in my pitcher, uneasy at first because of its strange tang, but relieved that at least with long standing it had become lukewarm so that I would not take cold from it. I asked for more, but the guard refused.

It grew dark. The guards were changed. A new pitcher of water was brought, and a candle for the friend, which filled the air full of the rancid smell of tallow. I plotted inwardly to eat the candle when his back was turned, but he did not turn his back. I used the chamber pot, and prayed, and recited passages of Scripture, but the friend (who, I saw now, was the bald one again), would not suffer me to speak them aloud, so I uttered them in my mind.

When dawn came, I was lying on the bed, unmoving, dreaming some of the time with my eyes open, cunningly, so that the friend did not even know I was doing it, but this kind of dreaming exhausted me as much as wakefulness; I got no refreshment out of it, only a certain pleasure from the victory. There was a burning all through my body, and my limbs were almost too heavy to lift.

They were talking in the doorway again. The bald man said they should get a physician to me, but Mr Trevor replied, What would a physician say? He would say he needs food, feed him, or he is short of sleep, let him sleep. And that would defeat our goal, for it would strengthen him again, and that would restore in him the courage of raving. Do you not notice how silent he is become since he has grown weaker?

But now my faith was roused again, and in my mind I sent forth a great cry: O Lord, thou seest thy servant in the hands of his enemies and thine, in great distress of body for want of food and sleep. Sustain him, Lord, lest he perish, leaving thy work undone.

No sooner had I framed this prayer than I knew God had heard it. Something in the room changed. The window was open and it looked to be a fine sunny day like the last ones. A breeze had arisen, and it smelt sweet with none of the foul odours that haunted the town when the wind was in the wrong direction, the smells of the Beast Market, the tannery and the privies. It made me think of the aromas in Essex House while I waited for the Earl to appear, gravy, hot sugar, white bread, the smells of eatables that had no coarseness about them. And as I breathed this delicate air, the kindness in the light grew more tangible. I wondered to see so much dust outside the window, filaments rising and falling there, and becoming, as I watched, more intricate and luminous. They were a marketplace of shining motes, coming and going, joining and separating, passing specks of fire to each other. No, it was not dust but a mist rising. Nor was it yellow any more, but a rainbow of shifting colours. It gathered together and became a cloud more or less round, its edges boiling and swimming, about three times the size of a man's head.

The discussion outside the door must have become graver, for one of the friends pulled it to, leaving me alone for the time being. Now the cloud began to nudge in at the window, courteously as if it wished not to disturb me. Inside it was still brighter, the colours varying faster than my eye could follow, and, though it made no sound, I felt the air full of power, like a storm. The smells were stronger than ever, making me pleasantly aware of my hunger as before a good dinner. The cloud continued to roll and slide towards me until it was directly over my head, then lowered itself until I was inside, breathing it.

It was warm and thick with a sweetness as of honey and a strength and restoring power like strong red wine. As well as gravy, bread and sugar, I could taste strawberries, and a savour of oysters or anchovies. While the cloud held me, I saw nothing but its muffling brightness, and I no longer felt I was in the room in my mother's house in Wrexham, but in heaven. It remained in place a quarter of an hour, then departed out at the window and ascended out of my sight.

Mr Trevor and the bald man were continuing their converse in the passage, and, being alone for once and, strengthened by the heavenly sustenance I had received, I rose and walked about the chamber, thinking how I might proceed. These friends of my mother's, it seemed to me, held an unholy power over her, that they might keep me prisoner in her own house, and herself unable to prevent it. The tall, pale one especially, Mr Trevor, had a look of the infernal about him. Remembering their whispers in the middle of the parlour, I recalled that they had looked at me strangely, holding me with their eyes as if to look inside my soul, to bewitch me as they had bewitched her. And I knew now that my mother, being old, had forgotten her own advice: Rhys, she would say, if you go past the witch's house, forget not to take a pin with you, for a witch cannot harm you if you draw her blood. But now she had allowed the witches into her house and let them keep every drop of their blood.

Then I raged, for I was now without a pin for almost the only time in my life; I was in my shirt and drawers in a chamber bare apart from the bed and the stool. Many a time had I cursed the ubiquity of pins in the tailoring trade, for I could never remember how many I had put into the cloth before basting it, and so there was always one left behind when I commenced to sew, upon which Hugh Jones, would cry, What, Arise, pricked your thumb? Suck it then, suck it well, for this is an ash-coloured frieze, not a blood-coloured one. And he would say also that a pin being of brass and not of steel like a needle, the metal was apt to become corrupted with poisonous matter. It is called verdigris, said he, on account of its colour, which is between green and grey. And because of this, you must keep your pins dry, taking even more care of them than your needles. Nevertheless, there is always a little on every pin, and so often do you prick yourself and suck the blood afterwards, Arise, that I fear your life cannot be long. But take comfort, at least, that you have found this pin, for it is better that you should be pricked than the customer when he tries it on.

I went over to the window. The men carried no swords or knives that I could take from them, and I did not relish the thought of trying to bite one of them. Brooding thus, I ran the tips of my fingers across the sill, not knowing what I was doing and felt a hardness there. Looking down I saw something sparkling. It was a sliver of glass, much smaller than a pin, which must have been there for years, from the time the glass was first put into the window. I picked it up. It was almost too small to hold, but I found I could grip it between finger and thumb so that the end of it projected, invisibly. I needed but a single drop of blood.

The door opened and Mr Trevor came in. He walked up to me and seemed about to say something, at the same time raising his hand to my shoulder, perhaps to lead me back to the bed. At that moment, I raised my own hand with its sliver of sharpness and touched him near the third knuckle of his index finger. He screamed and jumped back, clutching the place, but not before I had seen a red drop well up.

How did you do that? said he. Madman!

I took a step towards him and he retreated till he was standing with his back to the door, opening and closing his mouth. I raised my hand again, as if to strike with an imaginary dagger, and saw him flinch away. I have you now, I said. The Lord has delivered you into my hands. I have drawn your blood.

Mr Trevor wrenched himself away from the door and lurched forward, pushing me so that I staggered for a moment. Then he opened the door and fled through it. The bald man at the end of the passage turned round to see his friend running towards him. Mr Trevor pushed past him, crying, He will kill me!

Then he was gone down the stairs, the other looking after him in amazement. I leant against the doorjamb panting and smiling to myself, a man in his shirt and drawers in the daytime, holding a weapon I could not see.

Chapter XXIX
A Worldly Dialogue, Yet Not Devoid of Spiritual Utility

Through the open door I could see that the church was almost full, but many were standing around in front of it, talking in the sunshine, or sitting on the steps of the High Cross, or wandering bridle in hand looking for a boy to take their horse to one of the inns, or strolling between the stalls that had arisen along the High Street and the narrower streets round it, browsing among the knives and cups, the shoes and fire-irons, not to buy, but to have the feeling in their hands of something they could own if they chose to. I was half-walking, half-running between the stalls, with Mistress Maud after me.

Mr Evans, Mr Evans, said she, are you coming to sermon today?

Yes, mistress.

Then you should come this way. Come with me, Mr Evans, or you will never get in. It will be starting presently. Come on, she said, and reached for my hand, but I turned to a stall with horse tackle on it, and pretended to be examining a martingale.

Do you not long to hear Mr Cradock?

Certainly, in time.

I never heard him before. There is no one like Mr Cradock for a sermon, they say. Or have you heard better in London?

I have heard Dr Gouge, said I.

No! What was he like? I should so love to hear Dr Gouge preach. They say he is a saint.

Yes, Gouge is well enough, very well indeed. I hear him every Sunday, and sometimes at the Wednesday lectures. He is wise and speaks well. Where are your parents, mistress?

They are just over there, see them? Think not of them, they do not mind me talking to you.

She was wearing a white linen waistcoat and apron with a red petticoat, a plain neckerchief and coif and a black felt hat. Her hair, under the coif, was black and fine, and her skin was white, of the shiny kind that tends to break into moles, and indeed there was one beneath the corner of her jaw that I noticed when she turned to indicate her parents. Apart from that, she looked like any other maid, though smaller than most.

But to hear Dr Gouge every week, or more than every week, said she. It must be such a happiness to live in London.

It is, said I and tailed off, for I could think what it was, and realized that I had merely confirmed her statement, when I had intended to qualify or even deny it.

You are a holy man yourself, they say. Will you study for the ministry?

I am a tailor, mistress, I said, and walked on, thinking to have put her in her place, though I suppose it was but putting myself in mine.

I know, but you are no mere tailor, are you? I mean you are a holy tailor, she said, following me still, her voice coming from behind my right shoulder.

Holy? What is holy?

I have heard you know the Scripture better than any, and that is why I thought you should study for the ministry.

You know nothing of ministers or the ministry, I told her. And no more do I. Now let me alone.

You are troubled, she said. I have watched you many times in church when you did not see me, and I could tell that you were troubled about something. Will you tell me what it is? What can be so serious that it disturbs the peace of a man who lives in London?

London is nothing, I said. I have business, God's business, and I may not do it.

God's business? So you are seeking to become a minister.

I may not talk of it, mistress. I have promised my mother that I will say nothing of it to anybody.

But I am not anybody at all, and besides I can keep a secret.

I made to walk on again, but she ran after me, clutching at my sleeve. We had formed an obstacle now in the width of the High Street, and customers had to go round us to reach the stalls.

If it is God's business, you must speak of it, she said. God's commandment is more potent than any other, and you must obey it whether your mother wills it or no.

Honour thy father and mother, I said. That is God's commandment, too. I am being broken in half by the power of God, pulled one way and the other by two commandments of equal force.

Tell me what God commands you to do, then, said she, and let me advise you. Even I know that God would not give you a command you could not obey, or command you to commit a sin.

Very well then. I am a prophet. I have seen how this kingdom will come to ruin.

A prophet! I never met a prophet before. A prophet must be even greater than a minister. It should be yourself preaching and not Mr Cradock.

But I cannot, said I and leaned against the stall we stood beside.

Well, she said, Jonah refused to prophesy, and God caused him to be swallowed –

By a fish, yes, what of it?

I think a prophet should be able to do anything, since God has asked it of him. If you have promised your mother not to speak and God commands you to prophesy, then you must prophesy without speaking. After all, anyone can deliver a sermon. Mr Cradock and Dr Gouge can deliver a sermon, but I never heard either of them was a prophet.

I laughed and made to move on again, but I was closer to the stall behind me than I had thought, which turned out to be cluttered with dishes of most unnecessary shapes and sizes. One of the greatest was standing on its rim by some contrivance of the stallholder, and my hand caught it and knocked it over, causing it to settle ringingly on the table.

Watch yourself, goodman, the stallholder said. You'll smash my plate into a thousand pieces.

Chapter XXX
The Nation's Shattering Emblematically Prefigured

Walter Cradock leant over the pulpit as if about to fall from it, and half his congregation were afraid for him, while the other half were afraid of him, for his pocked face was so terrible and his presence so lordly that they thought he was about to expose their sins then and there, before the whole church. But he neither shouted nor threatened; his voice was no more than a whisper, and yet by some quality of the church or of his own lungs, all heard him as distinctly as if the whisper was in each person's ear. None slept when Cradock was preaching. The young men looked at the maids, and the maids looked back (for this was a church, after all), but half-forgetfully, their minds being on salvation, and on the sins of the time. Cradock was speaking of the Book of Sports, for the condemning of which he had already served a year's suspension but he was not afraid on that account. For, said he, if those to whom the Lord has confided his message will not deliver it, then how shall the Lord speak? And how shall the voice of righteousness be heard above the clamour of the wicked?

I sat with my mother and stepfather in our pew, the platter across my knees. Every now and then, my mother glanced at it and then at me. I would not meet her gaze, but instead looked across the aisle to where Mistress Maud was seated with her own family. My mother noticed this, and tried to catch my eye again, but again I would not look in her direction.

And so, Cradock continued, the King and the great of this nation would have us whirl round a maypole, saying that no harm comes of it and that tradition exacts it. But what is this maypole but an idol? That it is no harmless object we may see by its uselessness, for a pump or a hitching post or even a pillory has a purpose, and this has none. That it is no good and serious thing we may see by its gaudiness, for it is like an immodest woman with its coloured ribbons.

I shifted the platter from one knee to the other. It was oval and heavy, glazed in white, and had cost me ninepence; Maud had tried to cheapen it, but I would not let her.

For no man can see the future, Cradock said, but I ask you all, with the King and the Court being come to such a pass, what is to become of the nation? With the nobles and the gentry being as they are and doing as they do, what is to become of the nation? With papists and idolaters welcomed among our great persons, what is to become of the nation? With such swearing and drunkenness in public places, what is to become of the nation? With gaming and dancing on the sabbath, what is to become of the nation? This is what I ask, and no man can tell the answer, but God knows it and will answer it. What is to become of the nation?

His voice grew deeper and more sorrowful, till at the last question he seemed about to weep. He gripped the rim of the pulpit and stared out across the pews, shaking slightly with the force of his grip. At such moments he was known to remain silent for five minutes at a time, holding the congregation as he held the pulpit, refusing them the relief of his concluding prayer. It was said that the life went out of him at such times, and it was as if they were being stared at by a corpse. And in that silence, many were seized with fear or sorrow or a sudden melting happiness. Afterwards they would stand together in little knots outside the church comparing their experiences and marvelling that so much seemed to have transpired in those moments.

This silence of Cradock's had but lately started when I stood up in the pew. Most did not remark it, their eyes fixed on his face, their minds searching their souls for the answer to his question. But Cradock himself slowly became aware that a stirring was happening just below his gaze. A doubt crept into the eyes, which wavered slightly, trying to look down without any seeing it. It was not uncommon for a member of the congregation to rise at such a moment. When others preached, some, having heard what they came to hear, would leave before the concluding prayers and make their way to a second church to find another sermon or comelier maids. But it seldom happened when Cradock was preaching, and I saw the fear in his expression, for if one left, others might follow.

I climbed on to the pew and lifted the platter above my head. A beam of light from one of the windows struck the rim and leapt up in a spark as if the plate had caught fire, then died at once as I swayed out of its reach. The plate was heavy; people in the pew behind and in several of the pews in front (for they had all turned to look at me now) shrank away, and some started to edge from the pews, nudging and whispering to their neighbours.

Thus, I shouted, thus. Thus! (already flinching and turning away).

It seemed as though the platter left me of its own accord, and moved slowly through the air, travelling slantwise, catching other beams as it flew across the corner of the next two pews and then lost its hold on the air and dropped to the stone floor of the aisle, where it became a multitude.

Inside the glaze it was a dull brown, and the fragments twinkled as they spun through the dimness, turning from white to brown to white again. The din endured long, for each piece rang on the stones as it landed, and many rebounded to land again somewhere else. When it had finished, the particles were scattered up and down the aisle for about ten feet each way, and over the pews on either side. People were picking them out of their hair and clothing.

Thus, I shouted, shall England, Scotland and Ireland come to ruin!

I said no more at that time, having promised my mother to be silent.

Chapter XXXI
A Promise Not to Be Retracted

Tell me, mistress, I said, should a prophet have a wife? We were walking in the town fields of Wrexham between the pleached quickset hedges, live hawthorn and blackthorn stems woven together, the hawthorn in leaf, the blackthorn in flower, and when I looked down at her, she being one of very few grown persons I have ever been able to look down at, and saw her dark eyes look back at me with that expression I thought of as *knowing*, I found a certain wonderment in myself that I had not thought to feel in such a place and with such a person. She had helped me in this business of the platter, which had so prospered that the people of Wrexham talked of nothing else afterwards, and I believe it is still talked of there to this day. So I thought that a wife might, after all, not be entirely a hindrance.

How should I know? said she. You are the one with the Bible at command.

We walked every day when it was not raining, the idea having come from her, and she had persuaded my mother it was for the good of my health. I will care for him, she said. My conversation is such that he will worry no more about kingdoms and prophecies, for he cannot talk about such things with a maid. And this more than the air of the place or the good it would do me to exercise my limbs persuaded my mother to consent to it. And so we walked among the hawthorn and blackthorn and those small yellow flowers they call lent-lilies in the fields that are called in Welsh *maes y dre*, and they are a maze indeed, a mingle-mangle of narrow strips grazed by sheep or cattle or planted with sprouting corn. Others were about, too, that morning, for it was a favoured place for the people, especially lovers. Where the hedges were low enough we would see another couple many yards off, and not know whether they were approaching us because of the confusion of the paths; sometimes they would be walking off to the right, then to the left, and yet the next moment we would be face to face on the path itself. Then there would be touching of hats and murmuring of good morning, and much crisscrossing of gazes, and if this had been a dance we would have changed partners there, but as it was we changed places on the path and went on as before.

The prophet Isaiah was married, I said. He married a prophetess, and she conceived and bore him a son called Maher-shalal-hash-baz. But this was at the instruction of the Lord who expressly wished he should have a son of that name. I cannot say if his wife was a prophetess because she foresaw the future or merely because she was married to a prophet. The prophet Hosea was also directed by God to marry, and in this case his wife was a harlot. No, mistress, protest not, for this is the word of God, and I must say it. When you are with me, it is as if you were in church, for you listen to preachers expounding this word there.

It is dark in church, she muttered.

Well, I am not looking at you, I said and looked at her despite myself and found she was blushing.

What of the other prophets?

I know little of them, for the Bible is more taken up with their words than with their lives. The whole purpose of a prophet is to prophesy, and whatever life he may have is as nothing compared with this duty. The patriarchs, on the other hand, were married, else they could not have been patriarchs, for fathering the people was the task God had assigned to them. But what are we to make of the prophets and of the wives they chose when they had wives? A prophetess and a –

We know not, said Maud, that the others were not married. And no doubt they were married to respectable women, and that is why the Bible does not tell us of them, because there was nothing to tell.

That is very possible. But then it behoves us to ask why, in the absence of any clear direction from God either for or against it, a prophet should marry.

For the same reasons as other men.

And what reasons are those?

She stopped, as if she could not answer the question while walking. Love, said she finally, and because it is what people do.

What people do?

When people are of an age to marry, then they, for the most part, marry. The maids do. The men marry also, but for them the age is different, being in general older.

What people do, I said, is a bad guide, and especially for one who is called to prophesy. But you have said nothing of the getting of children.

I do not – she said, but the next sound she made proved not to be a word at all but a sort of gulp.

I have mentioned the son of Isaiah, whose name was Maher-shalal-hash-baz. The prophet Hosea also had offspring by this harlot of his, a son called Jezreel and a daughter called Lo-ruhamma and a son called Lo-ammi, and each of these names had a meaning, just as my own name has. The meaning of Jezreel –

Mr Evans, she said (we were walking again now), will you return to London soon?

I must. I have done all that I may do here. I have sought to persuade my mother and brothers, and my countrymen. Now I must go back among the great men and try to make them hear me, so they will understand the storm that is coming.

And then it can be prevented?

Nothing can prevent it – I have come to know that this past year or so. If it could be prevented my prophecies would be false. I am not called to prevent it, only to make men understand it. And I must continue in this task even though I fail.

She seemed about to ask me another question, but none came and so we walked on, saying nothing. After a while we arrived at a turn in the path, where the hedges were higher, putting us for the moment out of sight of the other couples in the fields. I was aware of a curious feeling I have occasionally, which indicates that God is about to make his will known to me. I felt it for the first time when I flew over Bwlch Rhiw Credire, and most recently when the cloud of many colours entered into my bedroom window and fed me. At such times, I move through the world and do not touch it; I do not even touch the walls of my own being. The first time I felt this sensation I was flying indeed, but even when I walk and talk and go about my business I feel like one borne up by the air. This is strange, I thought. What I am about here is but trivial, some might even call it worldly, though there is no worldliness in my mind. What has God to say to me here?

We both stopped as if by agreement and she looked at me, her mouth slightly open. I took her hand.

You love me, do you not, mistress?

That is an unseemly question.

But you do, do you not?

She nodded.

I thought so. This is a hard dilemma for a man of my calling.

I let go of her hand and walked up and down, looking at the ground. This kink in the path was like a green room with no ceiling, the hedge walls about the same height as myself. I examined each of the walls in turn, face to face with the foliage, occasionally breaking off one of the small leaves. I knew not why God was telling me to look at the leaves, but it seemed to me at that time that they demanded my most serious scrutiny.

It is true that you love me with more tender love than ever my mother did. That I have seen and felt, and human beings are enjoined to love one another. This great love, then, must be of God, so that it would be a sin in me to spurn or deny it. Granted all this, it must be that I am permitted to marry, and indeed a wife, and, shall we say, children, may be a help to me in my work. The Lord Jesus, though he did not himself marry, yet he forbade divorce except by reason of the wife's fornication, saying, *What God hath joined together, let not man put asunder.* And when his disciples said that it was not therefore good for a man to marry, he told them that all men could not receive this saying. And St Paul said further that it was better to marry than to burn. So then, I said (seeing she was about to walk on), so then –

I threw the leaf of the moment to the ground and turned to her.

Will you be my wife, mistress, yea or nay?

She said nothing.

Yea or nay, mistress? Yea or nay?

Shall we live in London? said she.

We shall.

And you will preach?

I shall prophesy.

Well, said she, that is as much as preaching, and in some respects better.

Then, being directed by God to kiss her on the lips, I found them soft in texture like a plum or a cherry. They had no taste at all that I could tell.

Yea, said she then, when she was free to talk once more.

Then, I said, if you will be my wife, you must consider two things. First, you must never contradict me, but follow me whithersoever I go to do this great work of God.

Never contradict you?

All the world contradicts me, but the things I say are of God, therefore they must not be contradicted. And so if I have a wife there is one person who will believe all that I say, even though the world denies it. Promise me.

I promise.

Second, you must not enjoy me these three years, for now I must go to London and there be put in prison, where I shall remain three years.

In prison? Three years? What – ?

I let fall her hands. For I see the mind of God, I told her. The three days my mother detained me in a chamber of her house signify three years imprisonment that I shall suffer under my spiritual mother, the nation. There shall you come unto me and be a means to have me out, and then shall we enjoy one another.

Chapter XXXII
Woe Unto Them That Be Not of This House

The new chapel at Somerset House was not finished yet but had scaffolding round it and pieces of white marble, planks and builders' tools lying about outside while the mass was being held in the old one next to it, with the Queen and all her followers inside. A solemn music came from thence, such as I loved to hear at church in my childhood, for it is not only Papists who raise music to the Lord. I smiled at the porter as I went by his lodge but he called to me to stop, and when I continued, going so far as to open the main door, he rushed out by a back way and laid hands on me, closing the door again.

What do you come here for?

I have a letter to one of your priests.

We will have no more of your letters, the man said.

It can do no harm. It is only a friendly warning. Let me go in, and I will give it to one who understands what to make of it.

No more letters, the man said again. He was a veiny old person, and stood so close that I could smell his breath, which was strangely sweet, as if he had been eating sugar or honey.

Well, then, friend, will you take it from me, and pass it to the right man?

No, the porter said again, showing me the shape of the word with his lips as if I could not hear what it was for myself, and exposing me still more to the senile honey of his breath.

I will wait till they come out.

You will go hence, and away, and return no more.

Again he said those words *go hence* and *no more* in a miming sort of way, as one does to a young child.

I have done nothing, I said, trying to sound meek and offended, though it was far from my true feelings.

No, and will do nothing, neither. Go hence.

I went off a little way to the courtyard in front of the chapel. The porter stood on the steps and watched me, but made no further movement, and after a while went back into his lodge. There was a seat not far away with a clear view of the door, and a young man sitting on it, so I sat down next to him.

We shall have rain presently, he said.

I was not surprised at his words but at his speaking at all, for he seemed sullen and self-absorbed, and spoke as if reciting them by rote. So we shall, I doubt, I replied.

Are you a London man?

I have my abode here, and my work, but I am a Briton by nation.

A Briton? What is that?

What you would call a Welshman.

I met a Welshman once, the young man said. He was a few years younger than me, apprentice age, with a thin body that he kept arranging into different configurations on the oak seat. He spoke like a Londoner, and in a high, unformed voice.

You have met another now.

The young man said nothing. We sat thus for about ten minutes, the young man continuing to rearrange himself and fiddling with the laces that held his doublet to his breeches, which could never be tight or loose enough for his satisfaction, while I looked at the door, imagining what I would do when it opened.

The new chapel, said I, is almost finished. It will be very fine, I suppose. Have you seen it, the engines and such?

He looked at me suspiciously.

I have heard, I said, that there will be a machine to exhibit the sacrament, very beautifully ornamented with archangels, cherubim and seraphim, singing and playing on instruments among clouds and rays of sun, and that the whole will be hidden behind curtains as in a theatre, to be unveiled and set going during the mass, as the Lord's supper is called by those of the Queen's religion.

I know nothing of this, said he, and I wonder you do.

They say, I continued, that there will be paintings and golden chalices and embroidered vestments for the priests. Though I have heard also that there are many who do not relish such ornamentation, and will be much provoked by it.

He sniffed and returned to his laces.

How long will it be before they come out of the chapel?

The young man looked up and I saw some expression cross his face quickly, though I could not be sure what it was. They are gone out the back way through the garden already, he said quietly.

My hand was already in my doublet, feeling for the letter. I stood up and ran towards the steps, with the young man after me. He shouted something which I, in my haste, could not make out, and the porter emerged again from his lodge and made to bar my way. I reached the door first, turning the heavy iron latch and pushing it open a foot or so. As the porter grasped my waist I threw the letter as far as I could into the darkness inside. It would be some time before they found it: it might be lodged in a pew or at the back of a hassock, there to be discovered by the chaplain or the Queen herself, as God directed.

The porter released his grip on my waist and stood there with hands on hips, saying nothing, but looking at me reproachfully. I walked down the steps, brushing by the young man, who made no move to stop me. I felt giddy with my success, and also a little empty, for though I had finished what I came to do, the occasion required something more of me. Therefore I turned and faced the white façade, which stared brighter than ever in the gloom of the day, and raised my hands to it.

Woe be unto them that be not of this house shortly!

This was what God commanded me to say,

though I was not sure then what it meant.

The young man smiled at me in a puzzled way as I went past and continued to stand on the same spot for some minutes afterwards. It was not until I reached the corner of the Strand that I became aware that he was running after me, and crying out again, as well as he could with the exertion.

Stop, stop! Papists! cried he.

By now I was got into the press of people; it was difficult to move above a walking pace, and the man's cries mingled with the noise of traffic and the voices of the crowd. I thought at first I had left him for good, but after a while his voice came to me again above the rest, Papists! Then there was a thickening in the crowd that made it difficult to walk, and in a short time I was stopped altogether, as if the whole of the Strand had wrapped itself round me. I caught the eye of a woman pressed against my right shoulder, but she immediately looked away, and so did a large-bellied man directly in front of me. None of them offered me any violence, but without holding me they nevertheless pressed so tight that I could not move.

The young man came up then, and the crowd moved back to let him confront me. So we stood breathing a little while before either of us could speak.

That man has said if we are not all Papists within a little time, we shall be destroyed.

The crowd murmured.

What did I say?

The young man cleared his throat. You said – he cleared his throat once more – you said, Woe be unto to them that be not of this house shortly, meaning the Queen's Chapel.

Friend, you err, I told him, for I did not mean the Chapel but this house of my body and of my faith and judgement.

How is your body a house? the man said. A house is a house.

Is he a Papist or is he not? the woman against my right shoulder asked.

I am no Papist, said I.

Why did he say he was then?

A house is a house, the young man said again, like one reasoning out the meaning of a sermon to himself, and the Queen's Chapel is the Queen's Chapel.

But the people had started to drift away, and the man himself seemed to have lost the thread of what he wanted to say. He was still standing there in the street when last I looked back.

Chapter XXXIII
The Law's Greatness Humbled by a Law Still Greater

The Secretary, Sir Francis Windebank, was of too high standing to do his own writing, but had a secretary of his own, who sat beside him at the table with pen and ink, already writing busily although nothing had yet come to pass. There were other men around the table who wrote from time to time, but none of them spoke. I stood across the table from them, my back to the door. The sun shone into my eyes through the windows opposite, which were greater and higher even than those in Hugh Jones's workshop. I read again through the papers I had brought with me, though I knew every word by heart. The two guards who had escorted me from the prison saluted and stood back, one each side of the door. Over to the right, standing next to the unlit fire, was the young man from the Queen's Chapel, accompanied by the beadle and two constables. The Secretary's secretary wrote faster, showing no sign of stopping, while the Secretary himself had a stack of papers before him and was picking up each of them in turn, reading a little, then putting it down again. I saw my own handwriting there. Sir Francis, however did not look at me and said nothing for so long that I thought he had forgot me. He was a handsome, dark-complexioned man, some fifty years of age, his hair and beard thick and grey and his expression stern. I thought he looked more like a soldier than an administrator.

You are Mr Evans? said he, looking up.

Yes, sir.

Well then, Mr Evans, you know, I take it, that I was called for especially from the country to come and investigate your case?

No, sir.

A case, it seems to me, that a Justice of the Peace could deal with very well. Now what is it, Mr Evans, that makes your case too high for a Justice of the Peace?

I know not, sir.

You know not? That surprises me. Well, bring forth the witness.

The young man from Somerset House was led forward from the fireside, contorting his body more than usual in an attempt to look neither at myself nor at the Secretary.

Administer the oath, Mr Clerk.

Wait, said I.

The Secretary looked at me from under his eyebrows. Mr Evans, said he, I have heard a little of you, and I understand a little more from these, your writings. I have a feeling that you are going to be impertinent. Do not be impertinent, Mr Evans.

Sir, I wish only to save the court's time. Honest friend, I said, turning to the young man, there is no need of you here. I shall not defile your conscience by taking any oath against me. I am the man that wrote those writings, and I do willingly and joyfully own them.

The young man looked at me, and then at Sir Francis

Wait a while, Mr Gilbert. There is also a matter of some wine that was not paid for, in which I believe you are a witness.

Sir, said I, I was passing the Mitre Tavern at Strand Bridge a few days since, when this young man, Mr Gilbert, came running after me. Friend, he said, I have been looking for you.

You had seen him before?

Yes, sir, when I went to the Queen's Chapel with that letter you have before you. I believe this Mr Gilbert is a sort of spy or guard there.

Gilbert tried to speak, but Sir Francis forestalled him – Strike that from the record, Mr Clerk. Mr Evans, we will tolerate no insinuations or calumnies from you. Pray continue.

He asked me to go into the tavern and accept a pint of wine, for he said I had got him into trouble and he desired some conference with me.

And you accepted his invitation?

We went upstairs, sir, to a private room, and there the young man left me, which I was puzzled at, but he said he would go to the bar, where he had a friend who would be sure to give him good wine.

And he returned presently with this wine?

No, sir, but after a little time a boy came, bearing a tray with a bottle of sack and two glasses. So I sat and drank it, and waited for Mr Gilbert to return. The bottle was not above half full when the door opened and he returned, bringing a great company of constables with him, armed with swords, and a beadle at their head carrying a staff. There is the man, said Mr Gilbert, and the beadle told me to pay for my wine and go with him.

And did you pay?

No, sir. I raised my glass to each of them in turn, and drank to them. I called for no wine, I told them, neither will I pay for any wine here. Then I spoke to the young man, Mr Gilbert. I am sorry for you, said I, that you are so like Judas in this thing. If you had told the truth, I would have taken you for my best friend, but you have lied and betrayed me, and now as it is, I am the gladdest of you all.

I see, I see. And Mr Gilbert, I suppose, will swear to the contrary.

Yes, sir, Gilbert said. I was never –

You were never in the employ of the Queen's Chapel or the Mitre Tavern, and you did not encounter Mr Evans in the Strand or invite him to drink with you in a private room and so on. Yes, yes, I see. But this case is not about wine, is it? They would not summon me from the country to try a case about a bottle of sack in a tavern.

He put his head in his hands and groaned.

Administer the oath, Mr Clerk.

When Gilbert and the officers had given evidence and were dismissed, Sir Francis sat a long time in silence before speaking to me again, so that I almost thought he had forgotten what he was about. The sun had risen a little so that it did not hurt my eyes any more. It was set to be a fair day. Finally, he sighed and roused himself

Now to the real case. You are a prophet, sir, I believe?

Yes, sir. The Lord has seen fit to speak through me on several occasions.

Of what station in life are you?

Sir, I believe you know what station I am of, so there is no need to answer it.

Humour me in this a little, Mr Evans. What is your station or calling?

I am a tailor, sir. But my father owned a considerable portion of land, and was respected by all, only I did not inherit any of it when he died.

What land was this?

It was in Wales, sir, in the parish of Llangluin.

So you stood to inherit a part of Wales, one of the unpronounceable parts. But instead you are a tailor. Why should God speak to you, a tailor? He does not speak to me.

Indeed, sir, he speaks to everybody, but not everyone will hear him.

Have a care, Mr Evans.

St Paul was a tent-maker, sir, and Our Lord himself wrought with wood in a carpenter's workshop.

So I believe. And you call yourself, what is it? Arise Evans. What sort of name is that?

It is the name God calls me by, sir, when he speaks to me, so it should be good enough for yourself.

Again! the Secretary said, drawing in air through his teeth. It seems a canting, puritanical name to me. Are you one of the godly?

I believe in God and try to fulfil his commandments.

I mean, are you a Puritan? A follower of Mr Prynne? One of those who rail against the bishops and against His Majesty the King, and would have us strip all the fair paintings and statues out of our churches? One who mutinies over taxes and castigates his betters for their so-called vices and their so-called idolatry?

I am a loyal subject of His Majesty, I said. I believe God chose him to lead our people, only he has permitted himself to be led.

For that alone, you deserve to be locked up, and you will be, I promise you.

I am already locked up, I told him. I am happy in my prison, and with your permission, sir, I would like to stay there a little longer. I have a fair chamber to myself where I can read and write.

You will find it very different when you are sent from this place. No chamber to yourself then. You will be in the dungeons with the common felons. Mr Clerk, why was the prisoner granted a chamber to himself?

I know not, sir.

Well, who does know? (Sir Francis looked round the room, but no one would meet his eye.) They give him a chamber to himself, and they call me in from the country. For a tailor! Depend upon it, Mr Clerk, there is some business here that I know not of. Whatever it is they want me to do, I will not do it. Only it is not easy not to do it, when one does not know what it is. Give me your pen. It seems I am not to have a pen. I am only a Secretary, after all.

He took the pen from the clerk and made to write something, then stopped, chewing the end of it, till the strands of feather were wet and bedraggled and the hollow shaft was broken. The clerk took another pen from a box in front of him and sharpened it with a pocket knife. Sir Francis removed the pen from his mouth and looked at it. On the face of it, he said quietly, this is the simplest of cases. A man of no account, trespassing on the Queen's property, and making a nuisance of himself with impertinent messages. Repeating your impertinence in the court, nay even proud of it. I could fine you for that, even imprison you for a time. Public nuisance, disturbing the peace, stealing some wine from the Mitre Tavern. But if that was all, they would not have brought me from the country and given you a room in the jail. Do you have friends in the Court, fellow?

Which court, sir?

His Majesty's Court?

No, sir.

Of course, they may want me to make an example of you, show I can be strong. Your offence could well be construed as blasphemy or even treason. They may want your ears, or worse. But in that case, a room of your own? Think, who is offended here?

I have offended no one, sir.

This Windebank was said to have Catholic sympathies, and some years afterwards was forced to flee the country for it.

Silence, fellow. You have indeed offended many, the Queen's Majesty above all. And there are those who would rejoice at that, perhaps, and would be glad to see me punish you, because that would confirm them in their mutterings against me. Who told you to do this, fellow?

God, sir.

No, who told you really?

I made no answer.

On the other hand, said he... Read the indictment, Mr Clerk.

All of it, sir?

No, no, not all of it. The part where he shouted out as he was leaving the chapel.

And that the said Rees Evans or Rice Evans or Arise Evans did shout certain words on leaving the said Chapel, these words being writ hereunder, Woe be unto them that be not of this house shortly.

There, do you hear that? Woe be unto them that be not of this house shortly! What did you mean by that, Evans?

I have already explained it, sir.

Explained it? I heard you not.

I explained it to the young man, sir, Mr Gilbert, when he ran after me in the street.

Then you have not explained it to the Court. You meant woe unto all those that are not of the Roman Catholic faith, did you not?

No, sir.

And if I do not punish you for that, they will have me. They will have me one way or the other, anyhow. I am not clever enough for them, Mr Evans, and yet I always thought myself a learned man.

Sir, it is not true.

You would give me the lie, would you, impudent tailor? You are their tool, and it gives you the confidence to defy me and to defy this court.

It is not true that I meant the Roman Catholic faith. I meant –

Sir, you do not yet know who I am, or what I am capable of. But I shall make you know me, before you and I part.

I believe we shall be better acquainted, I said. For you are the King's Secretary, and I am God's Secretary.

The sun rose further in the silence that followed.

Then it was if I had not spoken, for Sir Francis did not reply, and his mood seemed to change. He was no longer angry or doubtful, but murmured to his clerk, conferring over the details of the indictment. When he addressed me again, it was in a brisk voice, with no feeling in it.

Rees Evans or Rice Evans or Arise Evans, this court finds you guilty of causing a public nuisance in the precincts or vicinity of Her Majesty the Queen's Royal Palace at Somerset House, on the seventh day of the month of August *anno domini* one thousand six hundred and thirty-five, and of causing a breach of the peace in the vicinity of the Strand on the same date. And this court also finds you guilty of fraud in that on the eleventh day of August *anno domini* one thousand six hundred and thirty-five, you did enter within the precincts of the Mitre Tavern in the Strand, and there did command or order to be brought to you in a private room a bottle of wine, to the value of one shilling and sixpence, and there did consume the contents of the same, without intent to pay for the same goods. And this court also finds that you have uttered oaths or sentences or imprecations of a blasphemous nature and having a tendency to subvert the good order of this kingdom. And this court finds further that you have written or caused to be written documents of a blasphemous nature and having a tendency to subvert the good order of this kingdom. Therefore by virtue of the authority vested in me by the King's Majesty, I now pronounce sentence. You will be taken from this place unto the Gatehouse Prison in the City of Westminster, and there kept a close prisoner at His Majesty's pleasure while further investigations are made into the causes of your actions. None shall be permitted to come and speak with you in that time, and any that so enquire shall be taken and likewise detained until their motives are made certain. Neither shall you be allowed pen and ink or any writing materials.

May I have my Bible, sir?

He conferred again with the clerk.

This court grants you the comfort of Holy Scripture, said he, but no other written or printed materials shall be allowed. When all investigations are made, then this court shall pass its full sentence. Do you have anything further to say to the court before you are removed hence?

I will be imprisoned three years, Mr Secretary, for so it has been revealed to me, and then I shall be released. And I would desire you to read these words I have written,

I held out my sheaf of papers.

Do I have to take these? (He looked round the court, but there was no one to answer his question, so he took the papers gloomily, holding them at arms' length.) Mr Clerk, let it be noted that I have received these papers at the prisoner's request, and shall investigate them at my leisure. More words, Mr Evans? You are indeed a writer. You will not do so much writing in the place you are going now.

Chapter XXXIV
Arise the House of Charles

It was a glorious day, about two in the afternoon, and I was sitting with my elder brother Owen on the bank of the river, which was making a great commotion as it does in summer when the waters are low, so that, for all its narrowness, I could hardly hear myself speak. This river, I said, I have bathed in and fished in, and helped to wash the sheep in. But it is a curious thing, Owen, that I have forgot its name. What is it called, pray?

It is called the Dysynni, Owen said, and his voice rang out above the sound of the water, so that it seemed to come not from his throat but from all the fields and hills round about.

I remembered then my old master, Hugh Jones, and how he had always said that every word had another behind or beneath it. And with a sort of flash that might have been the sun striking one of the wavelets my eyes were fixed upon, I realized what word lay beneath that familiar name.

The river, said I, is not only before us but all around us and over our heads, for its right name is not Dysynni but DAY SUNNY, and the meaning of that is A SUNNY DAY.

The letter Y being often pronounced in Welsh like a U in English.

Owen said nothing to this, but merely smiled as if he had known it all along. But my mind was now seized with a fever, and I could not help myself but must think frantically and talk as frantically as I thought, so that I knew not which came first, the words or the notions, nor could I tell whether I was speaking in English or Welsh, for the two seemed to me one and the same, a language containing all the words in the world, and in which every meaning was perfectly signified.

This place, said I, where our mother has her farm, is called Maes-y-Llan, is it not? And that is on account of the church that is in the field. And look, Owen, there it is, though I never noticed before that you could see it from this part of the riverbank. (For the church rose up before my eyes the moment I thought about it, and all the people of the neighbourhood going into it for a service, nodding to each other and raising their hats.) But that is only the short form of its name for it takes the rest from the great hill which is nearby (and which I saw now closer than it should have been from this position, a grim chair-shaped eminence bathed in a clear yellow light like that of the hornbook). This, said I, is the highest hill in the kingdom, nay, in the world, and its name is Cader Idris, which it gives also to the parish, whose full name is Maes y Llan Cader Idris. But I never thought when I lived here what Cader Idris means, not knowing then that every word has another one beneath it. I see now that *Cader* is the same word as *Codi* only its form has been clouded over as often befalls the peak itself. But what of *Idris*? It is not *Idris* at all but *y dŷ ruse. Y dŷ* is THE HOUSE, but I understand not ruse, which should mean BURN or CHAR. Is this mountain truly a HOUSE ON FIRE? I turned to Owen, who only smiled again, but I heard the voice that came from everywhere:

Signifying CHURCH IN FIELD.

Signifying ARISE.

The U being pronounced somewhat like an I as in Idris.

☞ ARISE, THE HOUSE OF CHAR.

Then I looked at the mountain again and apprehended its form, which was not a mere chair but a throne; and besides that it was also a crown and a great house, or rather a castle, and all three of these things, throne and crown and castle, were the emblems of kingship. The mountain was the throne and the throne was the King; it was the crown and the crown was the King; it was the house and the castle and both of these were the King, and the King was the father and the father's name was CHAR, which signified a burning, and the name of the burning was CHARLES. It was God who had raised the mountains, saying unto them ARISE, for without God's word nothing can stand, but I understood now that this raising of mountains happened not once at the creation of the world, but continued happening always, for just as the word of God made the sun rise and set every day, so his word also was necessary to hold the mountains aloft, and if once he ceased to utter it then would they fall back to the earth again. It was my own name he raised them with, his word being ARISE, and the greatest of all his mountains was the crown, the throne, the castle and the burning father he called CHARLES. He did this not now only, on this sunny day, but every day and forever, for the HOUSE OF CHARLES was a lineage, father and son and father and son unto the last generation.

Owen, I said, I have travelled to Westchester and Coventry and London in search of wisdom, yet I find it was here all the time, in Merionethshire. The King is here, and the kingdom, and the war and rebellion which are coming, and the redemption and peace which shall come after them. God has writ them in the hills and fields and waters of our own country, along with their names as in a hornbook. There is Gole Ronnw, where I saw the sun rise and play, and the meaning of that is THEY WILL GIVE LIGHT. And there is Bwlch Rhiw Credire, where I flew through the air, and that means BELIEVE, ASCEND THE GAP. I did not know how to read them formerly, never having learned the grammar and the accidence.

I turned to Owen expecting to see him smile again, but of a sudden he was gone. As I lifted up my eyes, the sun by degrees became dark, so that the stars appeared about it, at which darkness the sheep in the fields round about cried and ran to seek shelter in the holes of the rocks beneath THEY WILL GIVE LIGHT, as they do in those parts when a darkness comes before a storm, and all the light of heaven was taken away, so that it became dark as pitch. Then there appeared a great bonfire, and people making merry about it. After a while, I spied a little white cloud breaking forth in the north-east above ARISE THE HOUSE OF CHARLES. Then the blue of the sky appeared again and on it I saw the King's arms as they appeared upon a blue background in Blackfriars Church, and they rode upon the heavens very terribly, towards the south-west, and a flood of waters gushed out of the rocks, and as the light appeared I saw that the bonfire and the merrymakers were gone, and as I was upon the bridge intending to cross the river to my house, I awoke.

I was sitting on my chair in my room in the Gatehouse, the Bible across my knees, the plate and cup from my last meal at my feet. I closed the book, got up and walked to the window. In the room opposite mine a man was staring back – it was too far to see his face, only a blankness above a pair of broad shoulders and a white patch that might be a ruff. Another privileged prisoner like myself, for the higher the room, the further from the dungeons and the better treatment we received. No doubt I was the only tailor ever to be imprisoned this high. This room was inside a gate, being part of the original Gatehouse of the Abbey of Westminster, while the building I saw across the courtyard was one of those that had been added later. As I watched, the gate below me must have opened, which I could not see or hear, but a little cluster of people entered into the silent space. I watched till they were gone into the other buildings, then returned to my chair and my Bible.

I wished I might stay here forever. I never was more prophetic in all my life.

Chapter XXXV
Martyrdom's Privations Delineated to an Unfilial Sceptic

Owen is still hoarse from his cold, but he has refused the further ministrations of his mother, for, says he, God wishing to correct and discipline him by this ailment, it was wrong of him to accept treatment in the first place. Now, after Sunday dinner, he snorts and rumbles between his words, with, it seems to me, a degree of pleasure in the manifestation of his suffering.

The days, hem, the days of, hrgh, of saints and heroes are gone, father, says he. Had I been born, hem, earlier, I might have done something brave for the cause.

Now what nonsense is this, Owen? How could you have been born earlier? (I have sworn to my wife that I will not lose my temper with him this time, for she says he needs a good talk with his father, but this latest sally of his is very provoking, and I turn to appeal to her, but only then recall that I saw her go out the door on one of her errands a few minutes since. Owen crouches on the stool, his elbows on his knees and his chin on the palms of his hands and stares into the fire.)

You were born in time, father, says he, and you did nothing with the opportunity God gave you. You could have, hrugh, fought for the Parliament, or stood up, hurr, and spoken against Papism, but instead –

But I have explained that, Owen. I prophesied as God instructed me. God has given no such instructions to you, and therefore you should content yourself with being a good prentice, and, in due course, with the life of a husband, father and tailor. Now my *Book of the Needle* –

Prophesied, says he. A true prophet would have warned of the excesses of the priests, and of the court party.

I did so.

From what I have heard from my friends in the, hem, church, you spent the years of the Commonwealth as a paid agent of the same party and prophesying every year that the King would be restored.

Well, say I, he has been restored, has he not? And that in itself is proof that God commanded his victory.

He did so, hruff, as a punishment to the godly for their lack of faith. In just the same way as he is punishing me for not speaking out more by this, hurgh, this affliction of the voice. And I joyfully accept his punishment, says he, (though his looks are surlier than ever), but I wish I had lived, as you did, in an age where the right way of action was clearer to see, and then I would have been inspired to speak out, as the great martyrs of our church were inspired. Yea, though I were to be tortured and, hurr, hanged for it. Or have my ears cropped in the pillory. And instead I have a prenticeship with Mr Greenhaugh and a cold.

I am sitting at my desk, the latest chapter of *The Book of the Needle* in front of me, which I was working on when Owen arrived this morning. My fingers are tracing the words as he talks, and with one eye I read them again: Dysynni, Maes y Llan, Cader Idris, Gole Ronnw, Bwlch Rhiw Credire. I know I have strayed from my tailoring matter in these last few chapters, but I was seized with just the very urge that Owen mentioned, only in my case I must write instead of speaking, and I could not help but tell the story of my prophecy.

You should read some of my book, Owen, I say. Then you would understand somewhat of the age that is lately gone, which your Presbyterian friends have so misrepresented to you. For I lived though it, and you did not. And I was punished for speaking out as you so rashly desire to be.

What? Your ears were not cropped as Mr Prynne's were, and Mr Burton's, and Dr Bastwick's. I know you were imprisoned, but that was not for, I mean, hem, it was over –

A tavern bill? That is what your friends have told you, I dare say. That was only a trick that was used to put me in prison. It was my speaking out that had caused offence, and so I was first kept a close prisoner in the Gatehouse, and afterwards, when none came to ask for me and they saw that I was part of no conspiracy, I was locked in the dungeon with the common felons. Would that be enough suffering for you, Owen? To be shut in the dark with no windows or skylights for the sun to enter through by day or the moon and stars by night?

Hrmph.

It is true, some of the prisoners had candles or lanterns which they had purchased from the guards or brought in with them, and which they watched over very jealously in whatever part of the floor they had claimed, sheltering the light with their bodies. But having no candle of my own I could not read my Bible, and saw only the shadows of persons as a greater dark against the dark, when they were moving from one part of the dungeon to another. Besides which, Owen, there was in that place every kind of uncleanness that comes from persons living together in a closed space with no fresh air or water, and worst of all was the channel down the middle of the hall, which served as a sewer, and which, by reason of the darkness, I put my hand in once or twice during the first few days in the course of my crawlings-about, and the hand seemed to burn afterwards as if I had put it into hot water. It attracted rats, mice, cockroaches, lice, fleas and every sort of vermin. And in that place were men and women both, so that I heard there, though I thank God I could not see them, things I never heard before, unclean language and cryings-out and lewd laughter, and the sound of unbuttonings and undoings and then a sort of rhythmic quietness which none ought ever to hear unless he is himself the cause of it.

You, hrr, you should not –

I should not talk about such things? Well, it is you who yearn for martydom, and you should not yearn for what you cannot understand. It was not only husbands and wives that disported themselves so, for common women of the street came there, and sold themselves to any that had the means to pay them, and so I would be pestered at any time of the day or night by a female voice asking me if I had any of this and if I wanted any of that, which I deigned not to answer until she went to ply her wares to the next portion of darkness.

My son's gaze is lost in the flames.

You talk of Dr Bastwick, Owen. He was in the prison at the same time I was.

At this name he sits up and turns towards me. Did you meet him, father? I wish I had known Dr Bastwick.

No, for he was one of the great prisoners in the private apartments, the upstairs gentry as we called them in our dungeon. But he wrote to me.

Dr Bastwick wrote to you? You never told me this before. If I had only known that when I was a boy, father, how my fellows, ahmph, would have admired me for it. Not that I would have felt any false pride, but still. What did he want of you?

One of the guards came to me with a letter from him to ask what I was committed for. For, said this man, he has heard you are a fellow religionist of his, and says that if he can be of service to you he will. I had not heard of him and asked what kind of a man he was, and the guard replied that he was a physician, very learned and spent all day writing, and that he had his wife and two children in the room with him, and could send his wife to ask for my liberty if I wished it. But when I asked what he was in prison for, the guard said, scourging of bishops.

This, says Owen, was a great man.

I told the guard to tell this Dr Bastwick that I had never scourged a bishop. I had accosted one or two, in the King's Palace at Greenwich, but it was only to save them from the wrath of such as he was, for I would not have them attacked. I was no fellow religionist of his, but all I was here for was telling the King of the destruction that was to come upon the kingdom. And, I continued, if Dr Bastwick hears this and still wishes to help me, then will I receive his help. And the guard went away into the darkness and returned no more.

Ah, said Owen, had I been you, I would have visited Dr Bastwick and basked in his saintliness.

You know nothing of saintliness, Owen, if you think this was a saint. I was more of one myself, suffering as I did.

But Owen does not seem to hear me. He rocks backwards and forwards, his cheeks flushed, his eyes shining in the firelight.

Chapter XXXVI
The Hard Times in the Book Trade Lamented

This morning, upon opening the door, I perceive autumn is come. There are no trees hereabouts, so I cannot see the leaves turning, and the air smells as always of the Fleet Ditch, which runs at the bottom of Long Alley and is composed of some five parts sewage, four parts water, and for the other parts I know not what they are. I also smell coal smoke, which is present both summer and winter: it is not clean like the log fires of my childhood, but a choking, dirty odour, as if the earth itself were burning, or the stones and bricks of the houses, yet I should miss it if I ever left this town. But, though there is nothing in the appearance of the place to indicate autumn, the air is colder and drier than of late, and the sunlight, penetrating through the gaps between roofs and pentices, has a softness born of distance. Thus I muse on the time of year and the end of this preposterous wet summer so ill-suited to celebrate the restoration of our King, and by the time I come to myself again I find my feet have taken me of their own accord on my usual walk to Paul's Yard, and I am standing outside the White Lion, which is the house of my publisher, Mr Lowndes.

Many other persons have stopped at the stallboards to glance through the wares, and as the fat man in front of me puts down the book he has been looking at, shrugs and moves away to the shop next door, I take his place and pick up the book: *A Compendious View, or Cosmographical and Geographical Description of the Whole World, with More Plain General Rules Touching the Use of the Globe Than Have Yet Been Published, Wherein is Shown the Situation of the Several Countries and Islands, Their Particular Governments, Manners, Commodities and Religions. Also a Chronology of the*

Most Eminent Persons and Things That Have Been Since the Creation to This Present, Wherein You Have a Brief of the Things That Were Taught, Spoke, Done and Suffered by Jesus Christ Throughout the Gospel. The Which is Not Only Pleasant and Delightful but Very Useful and Profitable for All, but Chiefly for Those Who Want Either Time to Read or Money to Buy Many Books. Now there is a fine title, and a book I might buy if I had the means, for though most of it be familiar to me, yet I doubt not there are some countries and islands I have not read of yet. At the back is a most cunning map, but a wind springs up at the very moment I unfold it, flapping it about so that I cannot examine it with any dignity, but must stuff it back inside the cover as best I can, and put the book down, as one disappointed with the World, and move on to other matters. *Here is Advice to a Daughter, in Opposition to the Advice to a Son Previously Published,* but this is not such a subject as I wish to read of at present. Here is *An Abridgement of the Works of the Most Learned Polydore Virgil, Being a History of the Inventors and Original Beginning of all Antiquities, Arts, Mysteries, Sciences, Ordinances, Orders, Rites and Ceremonies, Both Civil and Religious, Also of All Sects and Schisms*. This I might learn from, for I never heard of Polydore Virgil before, but I have had overmuch of Sects and Schisms in my life. Therefore I put it down and pick up another, which I find to be *The Beast That Was, & Is Not, & Yet Is, Looked Upon, Or the Bo-Peeping Beast Pointed At, Or He That Hideth Himself Hunted Because of Whom Truth Complaineth and Is Spoken to by Pope and Prelate, by Presbyter, by Independent, by Quaker, by Baptist, Together with Truth's Several Answers to Them All. Also a Description of the Beast. Also the Coming Forth and Progress of the Beast Hitherto. With a True Reproof to W.S, a Quaker, Who, in His Book Called The Lying Spirit in the Mouth of the False Prophet, Endeavours to Make Men Believe That He Had Answered H.H. His Book called The Doctrine of the Light Within the Natural Man Leading to Eternal Life Examined by*

Scripture Light. This, it seems to me, is a true product of the age that is lately gone, a time so contentious that an author might lose his temper in the midst of writing a title. What he means by it I am not yet sure, however, and I am wondering whether this book can be read without first reading the books of W.S. and H.H, whoever they may be, when a woman's voice sounds in my ear.

Will you buy, Mr Evans?

She must bend to address me, for she is tall, not merely in comparison with myself, but absolutely. Her face is long and pale and mild in expression, though her nature is not so, as can be heard by the sharpness in her voice.

I come not to buy, mistress, only to better myself.

And you will better yourself at my expense, I suppose. Look what you have done with my book of the world. (Saying which, she waves the book in my face and makes a great business of unfolding the map and folding it up again.) There is a tear in the paper. I could charge you for that.

It was there already.

She snorts, and puts the book back on the stallboard.

Mrs Lowndes, you will not presume to tell me how to fold and unfold? Me, a tailor?

A tailor, are you? And when did you last work at tailoring? I thought you were a prophet, or a divine, or some kind of scribbler. Here, give me that (snatching *The Beast That Was, & Is Not, & Yet Is* out of my hand and putting it beside the World).

I have observed that Mrs Lowndes cares not for authors, though her living, through her husband's living, depends upon them. I am thinking of framing my next retort around some such accusation, for it is surely a weak point, when another thought crosses my mind. Besides, I say, I have heard that you think nothing of letting my wife browse through your stock and read whatever she likes without buying anything. Is this not bettering herself at your expense?

Your wife is my friend, and I feel sorry for her, being married to such a one as you. I help her as best I can, for I know you cannot keep her, and so she must live by her wits. You should be ashamed of yourself to make her live so.

She does not think it.

How do you know? Have you asked her?

The notion of asking my wife such a thing would make me laugh, only there are too many utterances crowding in my gullet to find room for laughter. When my wife wishes, I say, and What my wife wants, and The thoughts and the, the feelings of my wife, and, In any case, I am not here for –

Give me the book.

What?

The book, give it back, for I see you are fingering it again.

Indeed, I discover with consternation that my hands have crept back on to the stallboard and found the *Beast That Was*, and I am riffling through its pages as if I were reading it, though I had no thought of doing so, or of anything else. I close it with a snap and present it to her once more.

You will not buy it? says she.

What, buy that? It is canting Puritanism, I say, (somewhat blindly for I have not yet made sense of the title, and so cannot tell what it is). Such things do not sell in this new age. You should tell your husband, or rather he should tell you. In fact I shall tell him myself when I speak to him, for I am here to see him, the master of the house. Upon business.

I walk round her and push past the other customers into the interior of the shop. There is a still greater press of people inside, taking down books and pamphlets from the shelves, but Mr Lowndes appears unconcerned with them, even those that look ready to buy. My wife will attend to you, he tells them when they approach, even though his wife is still outside the shop attending to the customers there. He is a good deal older than her, and smiles much in an absent-minded way, panting a little, as a dog does. Why, Mr Evans, says he, what brings you here?

My book, Mr Lowndes.

Come into the back of the shop, says he, and we will take a morning draught together.

He leads me into a small parlour where a good fire is burning. It is homely enough apart from the boxes of books and chapbooks on the floor, so many that it is hard to steer between them to the stool by the hearth. Presently a boy comes with the ale. Now, says Mr Lowndes, smiling, what book is this?

I told you of it before, the one my wife would have me write.

He cocks his head as if he has not heard me, but this is only a mannerism of his, meaning he does not understand, or recollect.

The book about sewing. My wife says that the rage today is for all things mechanical and industrial and that a book instructing the young and their parents in the arts of cutting and pressing and needlework will go very well, as tending to enlarge the prosperity of the nation.

This is unlike you, Mr Evans. I know not what to say. Would you buy a book of sewing?

I cannot buy anything, Mr Lowndes, for I am broke. And besides, I know how to sew. This is for those persons who do not.

Well, I know nothing of sewing. But I believe it is only pushing of a needle into some cloth, and who would want to read of that? There is no fire in it, Mr Evans, no excitement. And it is not the matter you are known for.

Then I must be known for something else henceforth. The old days are over.

Indeed they are, Mr Evans, indeed they are, and I very much fear to the detriment of the book trade. The public will not read as they did formerly. For in the time of the Protector and afterwards, men bought books in order to understand what was happening and what they were to do. The buying of books was a sort of thinking to them, and they needed to think then, because all was confusion and chaos. But now no one thinks any more, and I am left with all this unsold stock. Look at this.

So saying he takes a book from one of the boxes and reads its title: *An Anti-Brekekekex-Coax-Coax, or A Throat-Hapse for the Frogs and Toads that Lately Crept Abroad, Croaking Against the Common Prayerbook and Episcopacy, and the Copy of a Letter from a Very Reverend Churchman, in Answer to a Young Man Who Desired his Judgement Upon This Case, viz, Whether Every Minister of the Church of England Be Bound in Conscience to Read: With Another Letter From a Convinced Associator That a While Boggled at the Common Prayer to a Brother of the Same Association Not Yet Convinced, Together with the Above-Said Reverend Parson's Brief and Candid Censure Thereupon.* But lately published, Mr Evans, and I have not a hope of selling it.

Now there is a book I should be glad to read, for its author sounds like a sensible man. Only I cannot buy it, being broke.

And those who are not broke will not buy it. Who would wish to read it now that the Prayerbook is accepted and the Church of England affirmed? It is old news. Or look at this one: *An Account of the Last Hours of the Late Renowned Oliver, Lord Protector, Wherein You Have His Frame of Spirit Expressed in His Dying Words Upon His Death Bed, Together With His Last Prayer a Little Before His Death, Who Died at Westminster The Third of September 1658, Drawn Up and Published By One Who Was an Eye- and Ear-Witness of the Most Part of It.* This one I dare not sell for fear of the officers of the law, for none may publish the Protector's words nowadays, truthfully witnessed though they be. As for the other stuff, the Puritan arguments against baptism and for fasting, or the other way about, I leave them on the shelves and the stallboards for the time being, at the lowest price I can afford, in the hope they will sell before someone comes to close me down for having them. But a book of sewing... Why do you not stick to your old matter of prognostication?

I have done with that. And besides there is no call for it now that all I wrote has come to pass.

Mr Lilly thinks not so, says he (putting the Protector back in the box). He continues to work on his new almanac. Mr Lilly gets great credit for the success of his predictions in the past and everyone wishes to test the new ones. People will always take pleasure in horoscopes, comets and hieroglyphic writings. They like their hair to stand on end. (He scratches the back of his neck in sympathy with his words.) Now there was no better prognosticator than you, Mr Evans, except it may be Mr Lilly, but I think you were even better than he. And just at this time, when I had hoped for a new volume of prognostication from you, you tell me you are writing a book of sewing.

Mr Lilly was wrong about everything. He thought the Chicken of the Eagle was my Lord General Cromwell, when it was clear to any man of judgement that it could be none other than His Majesty King Charles Steward.

The Chicken of the –? Oh, I think I recall, it is one of those learned prognostications. Mr Lilly wrote of this Chicken, did he not, in his *Merlinus Anglicus Junior*?

Mr Lilly is a good-humoured man, a ready man for telling of stories round the alehouse fire, but he is no Merlin, Junior or Senior, and he knows no more of the Chicken of the Eagle than you do. Why, he is not even a Briton – what should he know of Merlin? May I recommend you, Mr Lowndes, to read Pugh's *British and Outlandish Prophecies*? There you will find all you need to know of the Chicken of the Eagle, and the White King and the Dreadful Dead Man.

He shakes his head. This is my gist, Mr Evans. This is why you must write prophecies. Who knows more of them than you? Why, if Mr Lilly –

Mr Lilly was a thorough Puritan, for all he may say now, and all the burden of his prophecy was that the Protector should rule and the country prosper under him. None were more amazed than Mr Lilly when my Lord General ups and dies with his rule hardly begun.

That is by the by, Mr Evans. He made money out of his books, and so may you from yours if you will only stick to what you do well.

This is very vexing, Mr Lowndes. I am well begun on the book and cannot change it now. And I hoped to ask your advice on woodcuts, and perhaps to beg you for a few shillings on account.

He sighs and shakes his head, still smiling. Woodcuts! What happened to this Mr Satterthwaite of yours who was wont to support you?

Mr Satterthwaite is a chimera of the past. He vanished in the light of the present day. I have some hopes that the King will remember me, for so he promised when I spoke with him in St James's Park, but I know not when.

These are hard times in the book trade. Woodcuts! A few shillings! Would that I had them. It may be that a book of sewing will sell. I will not deny the possibility. It may be that the public will recover its taste for religious controversies. (His smile is still sweeter and sadder than before.) Which of us can foresee the future, Mr Evans?

I can, sir.

You can? Oh I see, with your prophecies and so forth. I do not mean that, says he. I do not mean that at all. I mean in the sense of knowing what is to happen, which is not the same thing.

Chapter XXXVII
The Raw Edge Finished

My colloquy with Mr Lowndes having but left me the more persuaded that I should follow my wife's counsel in keeping to my matter of tailoring, I think today to say something of the raw edge. I have neglected to explain fully the properties of cloth in leaving this edge unfinished, and this is very unbecoming to one of my family, both my mother and my great-aunt (or whatever she was) Bethan, having been accomplished weavers. For it is the skill of the weaver to finish the cloth so that the edges of it are, as it were, sealed, with no loose strands or thrums extending out of it, as Mr Jones, my *Dominus* or master, explained to me.

Dom. You see, *Ephebe*, a finished piece of cloth is a perfect thing, as the body of a man is perfected and finished by his skin, which holds the blood and organs inside him. And this finishing we call a selvedge, which is to say a self-edge or edge of itself. Just as your own self has an edge, which is your skin, so the self of a piece of cloth has an edge also. And what happens, *Ephebe*, if you cut the edge of yourself?

Eph. I bleed, *Domine*.

Dom. That's right, my boy. If you cut yourself you bleed because your edge is raw and you are no longer finished. Now the unlearned may think that finishing and ending are the same thing, and that nothing can follow after a thing is finished, but a tailor knows that in cloth finishing is only a beginning and what is finished can soon be unfinished again. This unfinishing of cloth we do every time we cut it, for a cut edge is a raw one, and will bleed, which is to say unravel. What must we do with a raw edge, my boy?

Eph. Finish it, *Domine*.

Dom. Indeed we must, if it is in some part of the garment where its bleeding will show or where it must take a strain, for the raw edge weakens it. And to finish a raw edge, we proceed thus –

Eph. *Domine*?

Dom. What is it, *Ephebe*?

Eph. You said the body of a man is finished and perfected by his skin. What of a woman? Is her body perfected also?

Dom. Why, *Ephebe*, you should know that a woman is unfinished as to the body. Her edge is raw and she... What do you know of women, *Ephebe*?

Eph. Nothing, *Domine*.

Dom. Good, my boy, that is as it should be. But at any rate God made women unfinished and having a raw edge, which makes them somewhat liable to unravelling, and ever since then they have sought the most splendid and perfect of clothing in the hope of compensating for their imperfection. This we call hiding the raw edge; it is something all tailors must do, and it pays handsomely.

Therefore, reader, I pass on to you this advice of Mr Jones that when an edge is raw it should be finished to prevent the bleeding or unravelling of its threads, though I confess it was a weakness of my master that he could never explain a simple thing simply, but must always be making of it into a point of philosophy, and yet I loved him for it, and continued to pray for him when Mrs Windrush visited for her fittings, and for Mrs Windrush also, in her unfinished condition, though I hardly knew her, being most often confined to the closet when she called.

But this talk of bleeding makes me uncomfortable, for I recall my conversation with Owen the other day and his dreaming of martyrdom and having his ears cropped in the pillory. I was writing then of my time in the Gatehouse, which lasted, as I had foreseen, for three years, and then my wife came to visit me. She held a candle before her face so that, my eyes being accustomed by this time to darkness, I saw her only as a small woman with a candleflame where her head should be, and it was so long since I had married her, and we had known each other so little that she would have seemed strange to me even in her regular form.

Husband, said she, have you heard what was done upon Mr Prynne, Mr Burton and Dr Bastwick?

I have heard something of it.

She put her hands up to her face, with the candle in them, which I perceived mainly as a fluttering in the general luminosity of that region, and her voice shook. It was terrible, said she, and yet it was not. It was like a festival, for as they came along King Street, the people strewed herbs and flowers before them and sang psalms. I was at the side of the road and saw them go by, though I could not see well, and I followed them not to the palace. They say they are martyrs.

Her voice shook still more at this, and I wondered that she should be so moved for this scourger of bishops and the other two who had done as much if not more.

Dr Bastwick, said she, took out his own scalpel and gave it to the executioner to cut off his ears with, and the blood ran all down his white damask doublet. And then his wife picked up the ears and kissed them and hugged them to her breast.

Well, said I, wishing to console her, they were not my ears.

No, said she, but if they had been, I would have done the same as she did.

Then she told me of the doings in Scotland, how the Archbishop of Canterbury had made a new prayerbook and caused it to be read in St Giles's Church in Edinburgh by the two Scottish archbishops and eight or nine bishops, at which there was a great stirring of the people against all these bishops, and especially by the women, who called them traitors, belly-gods and deceivers, and stood up and threw their wooden stools at them.

If the bishops in Greenwich Palace had heard me, I said, none of this would have happened, but as it is I am justified. Wife, go to Sir Francis Windebank and tell him how my prophecies are coming to pass.

Then she was gone, and the candle with her, and I thought I must have dreamed her. But later she returned with a letter from Sir Francis Windebank, which she read to me, and the message was, *Sir, I have spoken with your excellent wife and received tidings of you. Pray tell me, are there not some that account you to be distempered in mind?*

Wife, said I, what does he mean by this question?

I know not, said she, but you had better answer it.

So I sent back, shortly, to say that there were. And with that, my wife appeared again in the prison, and I could by now see better past or through the candle, so that there was a semblance of a face about her as she read the Secretary's letter: *Sir, God forbid that I should be of their judgment. But howsoever, we will get a certificate from them, for it will be a means to get your liberty, and to secure me.*

We fell to talking of freedom and how we should live when I was released, but my mind returned from time to time to the certificate that Sir Francis had promised for I had no wish to be accounted mad.

But, said she, you will be away from this place and its foul odours, and the danger of disease, and we shall be together again.

Yes, I said, that is true (and marvelled at the thought that I was married, and to this small person with a face wholly bright and a body which was but a gown-shaped shadow). Then we must have the certificate. But, wife, when I am released I must prophesy, even though I am called a madman.

There will be no need, said she, for your prophecies will have come true by then.

At this I marvelled still more, for I suddenly thought that my life as a prophet would be over, and I could be like other men, with a wife, a family and a trade. And my wife leaned over and kissed me, her face round and soft against mine like the surface of a cushion, and was gone once again into the darkness.

The next time she came, she was crying.

Why, wife, what is the matter?

I have the certificate, says she, and you are to be released.

You are sure? said I. When?

At once. Here is a letter from Sir Francis.

Sir,

Allow me to congratulate you upon your release from your unfortunate incarceration. Be assured that it was no will of mine that you should suffer, but all was for the good of the kingdom and the safety of the state, as I then thought, for which error I ask your forgiveness. I rejoice now to say that you offer no threat to that security, or at least none compared with others that you may have heard of, and therefore you may go about your business without further hindrance. Only I desire you, Sir, if indeed you have some credit with the Almighty, as I am persuaded you have, to pray for us, above all for His Majesty the King, and, if you will, for myself, who remain &c.

Sir Francis Windebank.

Thus was my martyrdom brought to a more satisfactory end than Dr Bastwick's. And thus, too was I made free to explore that raw edge Hugh Jones had spoken of, and to finish it as best I could. For what did I know, a married man these three years, of women?

Chapter XXXVIII
A Buttonhole Cut, Barred and Oversewn

A tailor is judged, Hugh Jones used to say, by the exactness of his buttonholes: why, I could tell from any buttonhole in Westchester which was the tailor that worked it, and my own above all, for they are the finest.

A button is a bauble of wood, tin or stuffed cloth for the securing of a garment, and a buttonhole is a slit in the material for holding it; in its natural state it is close and secure, but with a little prompting or forcing with the finger it can be opened to a roundness corresponding to that of the button. You must cut your buttonholes with your smallest and sharpest scissors, but first, Mr Jones used to say to me, we measure, then we mark, and only then do we cut. I outraged him when first I tried to do it because I made my buttonholes parallel to the edge of the garment, whereas the proper way, he said, is always at right angles. If you are making them for the Lord Mayor of Westchester, said he, then you may make them slantwise, but never parallel. A buttonhole, Arise, like any hole, is a hungry thing, and unless you govern it well, it will go on to devour the rest of your cloth. Therefore you must sew over the two ends of it to stop it opening too far, which we call barring it, and next you must sew all round the edge, keeping your stitches small and even.

I had forgot till this moment how Mr Jones explained to me about government of buttonholes, and I blush now that I remember it. For what is an unfinished buttonhole, said he, but a raw edge in miniature? And like the raw edge it is a feminine or womanish thing. Indeed, Arise, we may say that a woman's whib-bob, which I told you of before, is not a simple raw edge, but more precisely a buttonhole, and for these reasons...

Whereupon he fell to speaking of Mrs Windrush, and I stopped my ears as best I could without his seeing, because I always thought of my mother at such times and how she would reproach me if she knew I was studying such mysteries in my unmarried state, but I kept at least half an ear open so I could hear when he returned from Mrs Windrush to the buttonhole and began to instruct me in barring and sewing over it.

And I was glad of this half-ear's worth of instruction when I arrived back with my wife and we set up house together, in a humble room like the one we live in now, for we were, in this business of buttons and buttonholes, still unknown to each other. I had had occasion to see my lady customers take off their outer clothing to be fitted for a gown or a waistcoat, so that the sight of my wife standing before me in her smock was nothing new. I was more moved by her hair, which had been always before imprisoned beneath her kerchief and a cap or hat. Only in the hornbook had I beheld this zealous freedom of hair, there being much more of it than I had expected beneath its linen confinement, and of the blackest and softest in the candlelight. Being in my shirt and drawers myself, I went to her quickly and embraced her, that we might not see each other further. She held me strongly, pressing her head against my jaw as if she wished to burrow into it, and her body, separated from mine only by two thicknesses of clothing, felt, not raw and unfinished, but full and manifold.

She was murmuring, more to herself than to me, and I could not at first make out the words.

Husband, she said, Mr Evans. Arise Evans. Husband.

Then I saw that she was seeking to understand me as I sought to understand her, which I wondered at, but it pleased me. Wife, I said, Mrs Evans. Maud Evans, it is time for us to go to bed, as husbands and wives do. We have been married long enough, and it is cold in this room.

The sheets clung icily at first so that we were frozen together side by side, yet warmth grew swiftly in them and soon we could move again. Now, the candles being out, I grew bolder in reaching out to her, and found first a knee, then an arm, then a shoulder, and somewhere in the distance behind them I heard an anxious laugh. Well, I thought, I can have done nothing wrong yet. Come, wife, I told her, for we are commanded to be fruitful. Will you not obey God's commandment?

There was silence in the darkness for a while, and I became fearful. Then –

Very readily, said she, and it was strange to hear her voice so close to my head. I made to move in its direction then, but hearing her continue to speak resolved to remain still a little longer.

I fear I will not have many children, the voice said. My having abundant hair and small firm breasts is a sign of excessive heat in my person, and therefore I am unlike to conceive as easily as a woman with large breasts and scant hair might do. It is true that I am pale of complexion and so less hot than a ruddy woman, but there can be no doubt that much of my inward moisture has been diverted to the growing of hair instead of to the making of, of that blood with which an unborn child is nourished.

Mrs Evans, said I, where did you learn such things?

Why, said she, all women know them, or I suppose they do. I had them from my mother when I first reached womanhood. But she enjoined upon me never to talk of them with men, unless with my husband.

And what did she tell you more?

Do you not know of these matters yourself? Did your father not...

You forget, wife, my father died when I was not seven years old.

Your stepfather, then. One of your stepfathers, I mean.

My master in Westchester, Hugh Jones, used sometimes to talk of women, or of one woman especially, but I stopped my ears.

She said nothing for some time, and I thought she was ashamed, but when she spoke again it was slowly and carefully as before. Well then, said she, you should know that men are hot and dry and women are cold and moist. And because we are opposites each needs the other to be complete. The seed of procreation is produced by men and women both, only men produce theirs with their outward organs and women with their inward. The seed of the man being so hot and lively, its nature is to create a boy, but when it enters the woman it meets there the female seed, which is cold. If the man's seed is strong enough the woman's is overcome and she conceives a boy, but if the man is weak or old or sick, or the weather is too wet or cold, then the man's seed fails in its task and a girl is conceived. You knew none of this, husband?

None of it, said I, but the hearing it makes me bold. Mrs Evans, your seed shall not triumph. And though you be hotter and dryer than you should be, yet is my own heat and dryness so great that you will dissolve into fertility before it.

So I explored further with my hands and found that zealous hair of hers, and stroked it many times, trying to think which material it most resembled, but I had never had satin in my hands before, which was the most likely comparison. She was not displeased, as I could tell by certain small noises or breathings she made, and by her moving her body closer. Putting an arm across her shoulder I pressed my face down to where I thought her own lay, and my lips wandered over her face until they found hers. I had intended only a little kiss, for there was other business ahead, but she held me to it, her arms being around me once again, and I was breathless until I became used to it. But I recited inwardly the Song of Solomon, Thy lips, O my spouse, drop as the honeycomb: honey and milk are under thy tongue, and so continued a while longer.

When this kiss was concluded, it seemed to me time to speak again, for if it is proper to say grace before eating, how much more so is it to speak God's word at such a time. There being no more appropriate text than this same Song of Solomon, I recited: A garden enclosed is my sister, my spouse; a spring shut up, a fountain sealed. Thy plants are an orchard of pomegranates, with pleasant fruits; camphire with spikenard, spikenard and saffron; calamus and cinnamon, and all trees of frankincense; myrrh and aloes, with all the chief spices. A fountain of gardens, a well of living waters, and streams from Lebanon.

There was much wriggling of both of us all through these words, and by the end of it I lay on her as on a couch, whatever there was of clothing that had been between us being cleared away. Then I made of her a pattern as a master tailor does, but instead of chalk I used my fingers, my face, my knees and every part of me that could feel, until I knew where all of her lay, even to the raw edge or buttonhole as my old profane master would have it. And having absorbed what I might from Mr Jones's sayings, I said to myself, after all, it is simple enough, for it is naught but tupping such as I have seen a ram doing with a ewe. Button and buttonhole, whib-bob and todger-pin.

She cried out as if in pain, which discommoded me somewhat, but I cried out myself soon after, though it was not pain that caused it.

After we had lain in silence for a while, she told me there was a wetness in the bed where she was.

Well, said I, it is the seed of procreation, that you told me of just now, and that we read of in Scripture. And also the blood of virginity.

I shall wash the sheets in the morning, said she.

Chapter XXXIX
An Old Harbinger Set Aflutter

Another thing I should have said to my son while he was here: this Dr Bastwick whom you so revere, what was he but a setter-aside of authority? For they who started by slighting the authority of the bishops, as Bastwick, Prynne, Burton and the others did, continued by slighting that of the King himself, whom God had placed over the bishops and all men. I know not, my son, if you had a hornbook, growing up as you did in this city of rebels at a most rebellious time. If so, it must have been defective, for I am sure it did not show these mighty figures: a Bishop wearing a pointed hat and carrying a shepherd's crook in his hand, or God himself wearing a crown and seated on a throne, for the Puritans like not such images. Even my own hornbook failed to show a King, so I suppose the only image of authority you had was a Father raising his finger in the air. Nevertheless, this image, my son, implies all the others, for a Father is Bishop of his family, a Bishop is Father of the Church, the King is Bishop of the nation and God is King of all. This is authority, and if you slight one part of it you slight the rest. I understand this better than you, for I have met two Kings, and was courteously received by both of them, and felt the radiance of their greatness. These, and not your Puritan doctors, are the men you should do honour to.

His Majesty King Charles Steward the Father, when he entered into the Parliament in January of the year 1642, behaved most becomingly as a guest in that place (even though he was King of it and had a right to be anywhere he pleased in his kingdom), and it is said he addressed the Speaker thus, By your leave, Mr Speaker, I must borrow your chair.

This courtesy he had no need of, for he had at his back some two hundred men armed with swords and pistols, yet he might well feel abashed in the chapel of St Stephen, which, though used now for state business and not for worship, was high and shadowy, illumined by candles and the litter of light from the stained-glass windows. He must have looked small in his borrowed chair, talking in his soft stammer to the bearded men who craned on the benches to hear him, their ruffs and falling bands so well bleached they glowed more than the candles themselves.

I must declare, said he, that no king that ever was in England shall be more careful of your privileges of Parliament, yet you must know that in matters of treason no person has a privilege.

He had come there to seek five members, the most active in demagoguery and shouting against him, Mr Pym, Mr Hampden, Mr Holles, Sir Arthur Haselrig and Mr Strode, but all were forewarned of his arrival and long gone, so he had a wasted journey. Then there was a great outcry from the men in the stalls all round him of Privilege, privilege, and the King, seeing how things stood, not merely in the chapel of St Stephen that day, but in the whole city of London, and in much of the nation beyond it, and fearing, rightly, for his future if he remained any longer in this troublesome capital where a man could not even arrest whom he wished to, left the place.

The birds, said he, have flown.

When it was reported to me that the King had spoke these words, I felt a coldness rush up the length of my back, for I remembered the bird I had helped my mother chase in the hall at home, and I was at once sure that the report was mistaken, and that the words His Majesty had spoken were these:

The bird has flown.

It was the corpse bird he must have seen flapping around the top of the windows. The King's mother, who was Danish, was not like to have brought him up to know of this bird, and thus he must have had only a vague notion of its portentousness. Nevertheless, a bird indoors is acknowledged everywhere to be an ill omen; its flutterings and blunderings against beams and walls, returning again and again to the windows to beat with its wings, feet and beak against what must seem to it a solidification of the air, are the very emblem of desperation. And did any one of those men there, so statesmanlike in their beards and black doublets, offer to stand on a chair and catch it for him, or to chase it hence with swishings of their hats and swords? It was not seemly for the King to do so, having borrowed the Speaker's chair for a quite other purpose. I see his gaze pass from one member to the next, seeking the faces of the five wanted men, then reluctantly leave them to drift upward to the highest panes where the tiny creature was raging in the light, perhaps, of St Stephen's halo. Was it long-bodied for a sparrow? Was it winged at all, or was it a mere stub of bird moving and complaining within an invisible disturbance of the air? And what was its cry? Certainly nothing more than *Whee* or *Wheedle*, as I remember myself from my childhood, for why should it call *Deuwch, deuwch*, to one who understood not the language of the Britons?

It is not for a humble tailor to catechise a King, and, as I have related, the only time I met him I said nothing at all, being content to hand him the letter in which my own warnings were set forth, but when I think of this bird's visitation I wish I had been there to question him, that I might know whether these signs and portents come to all men as death does.

Q. Your Majesty, have you heard the little bell? Have you heard a screech-owl calling outside the window at night as you lay in bed? Have you found any bruises or marks on your body, not caused by any accident you know of? Was there a dog that howled all night in the grounds of Whitehall Palace or of Greenwich Palace, a dog that was not one of your own hunters, nor one of the Queen's pets?

It was early for such warnings, Charles Steward having seven more years to live. But perhaps there is after all no term or date of expiration on them; perhaps they notify us as long beforehand as is fit. And what better time than now, for it was at that very moment of entering Parliament with armed men at his back, for all the world like a King courteously declaring war on his people, that he started the events that led to another January morning outside the Banqueting House at Whitehall. I had given my own warning, as I have related, long since. Nevertheless, my son, I wish I had been there, to explain this bird whose import is so little understood outside our own country. And I cannot help but reproach myself that, as once before, I could not speak the words he most needed at the time he needed them:

Q. Your Majesty, have you thought well on your worldly affairs? Is the settlement of your kingdom in order? Have you remembered all your people, even down to the least of them?

I never saw the King after my visits to Greenwich. But when I think of the calamities that befell him after, it is always this moment I bring to mind: the coloured light of the chapel, the black beards of the indignant members of parliament, the soldiers with their swords and pistols, and the bird flying again and again against St Stephen's haloed head as if it too was trying to stone him to death.

Chapter XL
The Equivalence of Plackets and Gussets Asserted

No man may call himself a tailor who cannot make a placket. I say not a placket is as essential to tailoring as a seam, no, I say not that. And there are garments that may be finely and completely made and yet have no placket in them, that is so. But to be a true tailor a man must understand plackets. Consider this: when a woman pulls on her petticoat, it passes easily over her feet and ankles, which are narrow, then over her shins and knees, which are somewhat narrow, then with more difficulty over her thighs, which are somewhat broad. Now is the aperture of the petticoat arrived at the buttocks and hips of your female customer, which are broad. If you have made this aperture large enough to pass easily over these same buttocks and hips, then it must pass easily in the other direction too, and fall down again. If you have made it not large enough, then she must struggle to enter into it, for it is easier for a camel to pass through the eye of a needle than for a broad woman to enter a narrow petticoat, and but few struggles of this kind are needed before your red flannel begins to lament and stretch its fibres. And this is the use of your placket, which is a slit or opening in the side of the petticoat, underneath the waistband, such that, the band being unfastened, the petticoat falls open and the woman is easily admitted.

Having writ thus of plackets, I remember that my wife in our younger days was wont to complain mightily at the intimacy with the female person that my trade requires. For this, she was hardly to blame; many others unschooled in tailoring would be shocked at the necessary corporeality of my matter, and this writing of buttocks and hips, should it fall into the wrong hands, might prove combustible. As with my disquisitions of the raw edge and the buttonhole, however, my purpose is not only practical, but also moral, being the right government of cutting. For what is more dangerous than a blade, be it shears, scissors, knife, sword or axe? And what catastrophe is more absolute than the severance of one thing from another? As a cut must be governed as to its edge, to prevent bleeding, so must you govern its extent and all its dimensions, measuring and marking first. For if a cut goes too far, you may botch it again but not perfectly. Even I, Hugh Jones would say, cannot mend a cut so that the stitches will not be seen by one who knows where to look for them, therefore, Arise, think not to do what your master cannot, but approach each cut with trepidation, knowing you can never uncut it. A placket, said he further, is that which *place*t, which is as much as to say it pleases. And mark, Arise, from the same Latin root do we obtain the words *placid* and *placable*, which signify varieties of peacefulness. And thus we see how a cut, well-governed, may be a pleasing and peaceable thing.

No man may call himself a tailor who cannot make a gusset. And though a gusset be not as essential to tailoring as a seam, for I say not that, and there may be garments that are finely and completely made and yet have no gussets in them, a man would be no tailor if he made only those garments that have no gussets. Therefore to be a true tailor, a man must understand gussets, as indeed he must understand many things, such as plackets. I find, however, that there are no plackets in the Bible, and no gussets either. How can this be? Are we to suppose there were neither plackets nor gussets in the Holy Land, or is it rather that the prophets and evangelists knew them, but wrote not of them? Whichever of these is true, I am perturbed by it, for if the Israelites wore none, it may be that the purest and best and holiest of garments require neither placket nor gusset, while if they had them but wrote not of them, it may be that the prophets and evangelists deemed that plackets and gussets were not suitable matter for writing of. Nevertheless, I believe gussets and plackets alike are worthy of my pen, for there is moral wisdom to be had from their contemplation. To expound therefore: a placket is, as I have said, an absence of cloth where cloth would otherwise be, while a gusset is a superfluity of cloth, for at the place where you have cut an opening, as a sleeve or the leg of a pair of breeches, there do you sew in a triangular piece of cloth, so that the opening may be enlarged on the entrance therein of the arm or leg, and this superfluity of cloth also reinforces the rest.

And that is why I say the gusset is the reverse of the placket. Therefore it is in the interest of the world's harmony and order that the number of gussets and the number of plackets should be balanced, or else the world's garments must contain either too little cloth or too much.

This notion of balance was of the greatest import to Hugh Jones. All things, my boy, said he, must be in balance, else the universe will not stay in its place. And this means that by however much one thing is too expensive, so must another thing in the world be too cheap, and if one tailor, for instance my son-in-law Eldridge, be poor, so must another, for instance myself, be rich. This is in accordance with the celestial music of the spheres. And if a customer brings too much cloth for a gown, then after cutting and sewing of it, it is fit that the excess cloth be removed to hell in the form of cabbage, else will the customer's excess of cloth overbalance her. For every person, Arise, has either too much or too little of worldly goods. Therefore look you always that you have more than sufficient for your immediate needs, so that some unfortunate man elsewhere be not overbalanced with his own excess.

It was like Mr Jones to take wealth as his example in this matter, but it is not one I have ever given much mind to, in which, no doubt he would have been mightily disappointed. But if the kingdom was out of balance at the time of which I wrote just now, there were worse deficiencies in it than poverty, even though I was greatly impoverished myself. I believe there must have been too many plackets, for the fibre of the nation was sadly rent. But this is no consideration for my readers, now that the balance has been restored. Make your plackets peaceably, and make your gussets, too. Only, if it be in your power, my son, look that you make as many of one as of the other.

Having writ the above, however, I feel a terrible misgiving, for I bethink me suddenly of gores. Is not the gore the true contrary of the placket? As we have seen, the waistband of a woman must be tight around her person, else the petticoat would fall down; but her skirt must move freely, so that she can walk and go about her business, therefore it is necessary to enlarge the skirt, just as we enlarged the hip region underneath the waistband. But if you put a placket in the skirt the effect would be unseemly, for whenever she walked or sat or did anything, then would her stockings be revealed. Therefore you must make a cut and fill it in again with a gore, which is a triangle of material with the narrow end uppermost and the wide end underneath, so that it makes the skirt wider at the bottom than the top. It seems to me now that the gore, at least as much as the gusset, is the contrary of the placket, but I know not where this leaves the harmony and balance of the world, whether the sum total of plackets therein must be equal to the gussets and gores added together, or whether there be another tailorly quantity I have not yet thought of to be stitched into the calculation. It is very vexing. But I say this in any case: no man may call himself a tailor who cannot make a gore.

Chapter XLI
The Great Proved Ungrateful, or A Prophet Slighted

There was a great press of people going into and out of the Parliament, and more walking up and down the hall outside, and I walked with them until I saw a thin pock-marked man stepping out to cross New Palace Yard, in deep converse with two others. I ran to him and seized his cloak, crying, My lord, my lord, at which he wrenched back his head as if to avoid a blow, and the other two put their hands on their swords.

My lord, said I, do you not remember me?

And he said nothing but gave a giggle that was half shudder, and, reaching down, gently detached the hem of his cloak from my grasp.

It is Arise Evans, said I. We spoke nine years since, in the days before your greatness, which I prophesied.

You prophesied...?

I am a tailor, and a prophet. I came to see you at Essex House, and your man Jeffers showed me up. He is less obliging now and affects not to know me and therefore I came to find you here.

I think, said he, I know not...

But my lord, said I, you had many friends to dine with you that day, and a great swan for a centrepiece, and you offered me a gold Jacobus but I would not take it. And then you told me to go to Lord Brooke and showed me part of the way thither, as far as St Clement's Well.

He laughed again in that wincing way he had, and shook his head, not looking at me directly. Leave us a moment, gentlemen, he said to his friends, for I see this fellow means me no harm.

At this the friends took their hands from their sword hilts and walked on, with a glance or two backward. Then the Earl led me over towards the stables where there was a mounting block and sat on it carelessly, his cloak blowing about his knees.

Now said he, what is it you want from me? Money?

My lord, said I, there was a Jacobus you offered me at my earlier visit to you. I refused it then, but I thought to have it now by reason of all I foretold for you and the truth of it. For work is hard to find now the land is at war, and I have small children to support.

A Jacobus! You aim pretty high, fellow. Why should I give you so much? Indeed, why should I give you anything? I (and he shook his head with a smile that was somewhat abashed, despite his high words), I must confess that I do not recollect you at all. Evans, did you say your name was? Welsh, are you?

When the kingdom is shaken, I repeated to him, some will fall, while others will rise. None will rise higher or more swiftly than the Earl of Essex. I have seen you, my lord, riding at the head of a great army. You will be General of all England.

He looked up at me doubtfully from his mounting block, his hands on his knees, as he must often have sat on some convenient block or stump to direct his men in battle.

This was my prophecy to you, I said. That you would be General of All England. It was nine years ago, and you laughed at it then.

General of All England, said he. Yes, I suppose I am. General of All England except the part I am waging war on, anyway. But, my good man, you should tell the Parliament that, for they do not seem to know it. Tell it to my Lord Manchester and Sir William Waller while you are about it. A Jacobus, you say? If you are a liar, you are a very bold one. But what makes you think I should be grateful for your prophecy as you call it?

Indeed, said I, you were grateful at the time for the glory I predicted for you. How is it you do not remember me, my lord? I am a Welshman and a tailor, both which particulars seemed to give you some gratification at the time, though I know not why, and you took me into the banqueting hall to meet your guests, who were taking out the feathers from the swan and strewing them everywhere.

He laughed and shrugged. Glory was it? said he. I know nothing about that. The mercury will tell you that I won a great victory at Newbury Fight. Do you know what a battle is like, Evans?

Mercurius Britannicus, the broadsheet of the Parliament faction.

I have seen them, said I, but only in visions and in dreams.

That is the way I have seen them, said he. Only in visions and dreams, and yet I am, as you say, General of All England. I do not think a battle can be seen any other way. By the time the army comes to fight, it has been marching for days, perhaps with nothing to eat at all, or the stalest and driest of pease bread that any civilian would crack his teeth on, and nothing to drink but foul water, and at night sleeping, if they can, in the mud with no covering but the clothes they have been wearing all day. Do you remember the weather we had early in September, day after day of freezing rain? Being the general, Evans, I had the glory of a flask of wine to take a sip from every now and then, and a tent to sleep in, which, let me tell you, is not as glorious as all that, but I am accustomed to it, and it is better than a ploughed field. And the glorious duty fell to me of riding from one regiment to the next telling them to keep their courage up, whereupon they all waved their hats and shouted, Hey for Robin, which is what they call me. I wonder who told them to do it. Or perhaps they really love me. What do you think, Evans?

I said nothing.

We found some sheep one day. I know not where they came from, but someone must have seen them and decided that an army on the march must forage where it can. As his general I commend him, whoever he was, and he showed fine initiative in commandeering these same sheep and causing them to be driven along in front of the men. You see,

Evans, if you require the sheep to march behind you, they will soon drop off the rear and become first of all stragglers and afterwards lost sheep. Therefore my army was briefly led by sheep, bleating their way forward through the little country lanes, and the men following after them, picking the haws and blackberries off the dripping hedges and singing psalms. And myself thinking with half my mind that someone somewhere must make a command decision about those sheep, whether to milk them or slaughter them for mutton or shear them for their fleeces, for God knew some of my men could have done with new cloaks. And so when I should have been thinking of the whereabouts of Sir Jacob Astley and his foot, behold me, Evans, riding along wondering which if any of my commanders had experience of sheepfarming.

I grew up on a sheep farm, my lord.

Did you indeed? You should have had a Jacobus for your counsel, then, I promise you. As it was, the matter was taken out of my hands, for one morning we awoke to find the sheep had treacherously deserted in the night. And then I thought I really had dreamed them.

He sat a while with his elbows on his knees and his chin resting on his hands, staring past me to the rest of the yard where men were crossing to and from St Stephen's Chapel. It was beginning to rain but he heeded it not.

Where, said he finally, do a man's bowels belong?

I made no answer.

The bowels, he said, belong in the body, do they not? They were never intended by God to be seen. But I have seen them many times, at Newbury and other places. You will be directing your men into battle, which is for the most part a matter of trying to get them all to run in the same direction at the same time, which they seem incapable of doing. Not that I blame them, the field being so muddy and full of smoke, and great barriers everywhere they turn, which are the pikes of the two armies pressing against each other, so that much of the running they do is along the alleys of a sort of labyrinth of wooden poles. And when they can run freely, such things as hedges and ditches keep appearing suddenly in front of them so that they have to stop and double back, and then they forget themselves and begin running somewhere else. The enemy are running also, those of them that are not shooting or on one end or the other of a pike, and they look no different from ourselves. At Newbury I ordered that every man in our army should wear a green bough in his hat, but there were some among the enemy who noted this and put similar boughs in their own hats. You may try to distinguish the battle cries: Religion from our men and Queen Mary from theirs, but with so much crying out going on all around, it is hard to hear who is crying what. Then there is a small flash of lightning and a noise like a low cough sounds through the smoke and rain, which betokens the firing of a drake. Several of the men fall over; they always look as if they are doing it on purpose. And only then do you notice that some of the other men are wearing the bowels of these fallen ones across their faces. They look like pieces of rag, Evans, bloody and befouled pieces of rag.

My lord, said I, hoping to bring him back to the matter, but he heard me not.

The brains also, said he, but they resemble bread to my eyes, white bread, I mean. How does it feel, do you think, to wipe your brow and find sodden white bread there that a moment earlier was another man's fear and rage and hunger and pain and weariness and longing for his wife and children and love of God and hatred of idolatry? For myself I am on horseback, and most of the fighting takes place somewhere else, so that I have to keep riding to keep up with it, but I see it happen to others. Every few moments I see one or two or three discover what it means to be a soldier, which for the most part they knew nothing of before. Shoemakers, perhaps, or blacksmiths, or tailors like yourself. And by the time it finishes, all this piking and shooting and running and falling over, it is night, and I am angry to see how dark it has become, because, do you know, I was becoming accustomed to it? Had we been able to fight a few more hours, I believe I should have had all the infantry running where they should have been running, and deployed my cavalry on the flanks. Then we should have swept through their army and carried off their standards and captured their generals, and the day would have been ours. But it became dark, and no one could see to fight. And so everyone, on both sides, withdraws from the field and goes to sleep, no matter what I or any other of their commanders would have them do. As if it were a day like any other, as if they had spent it making shoes or coats. The only ones who stay on the field are those who cannot leave it, the dead and dying and the ones who groan and snivel all night because they have lost some part of themselves they can ill afford to lose, a leg or an arm and a pint or two of blood. And next day, some officer or other goes round the field counting and afterwards comes to me to say there are so many thousand of their men dead and only so many thousand of ours, and thus we have gained the victory. What is more, the enemy have withdrawn themselves to Reading, leaving to us the fields we so much desired. But I know, I know, mind you, that given another few hours I would have had it all ordered in my mind, and then it would have been a victory indeed. A Jacobus, did you say?

Yes, my lord.

I have not such a thing about my person. I know not why you should think I have. Why that of all things? Merely for being a prophet and having foretold my glory? You may have a shilling if you want it.

My lord, said I (feeling my anger rise, for he had kept me standing in the open all this time and the rain was falling harder now), I prophesied your glory, and I can unprophesy it again, for such is the power God has given me. There are other men in your faction of lesser rank than yourself, but, it may be, of greater parts. Such men can and will supplant you, and the greatness shall be theirs. I see them taking the field instead of you, and the glory falling on others. The victory you long for, my lord, will not be yours.

Hmph, he said, the shilling poised in his hand, half-smiling. Who do you mean, Waller?

I shook my head.

He put the shilling back in his breeches pocket.

It seems I am destined to disappoint you, Evans, and to have my kindness spurned. Good day to you.

I felt the tears starting in my eyes, half from rage and half for the lost shilling, which I was almost ready to ask him for again, but he rose from the mounting block and gestured to his friends, who were watching us from a distance.

We lost at Reading by the way, said he as I turned to go. Only no one remembers that.

Chapter XLII
God's Message, in Two Parts, Explicated in a Domestic Whisper

I awoke to hear a voice speaking in my ear. It was yet dark, and I could see the shape of my wife kneeling on the floor kindling the fire which was starting to throw gores and gussets of light and dark around the walls. My daughters were in bed together on the other side of the room, still asleep. I knew the voice of old, sharp and shrill, but no woman's voice, nor no man's neither, speaking not harshly, but like one who gives a command that must be obeyed at once. And I knew too that this voice, closer to me than either wife or children, could not be heard by them, loud as it was to me:

Thou must maintain a succession of ministry, and the right of infants to baptism.

I shook my head a little, for the voice had sounded so close to my ear that I felt a buzzing there as if some of the words were still in my head. When I was satisfied that it would not speak again, I got out of bed, saying, Wife! Wife!

What is it, husband? said she. The fire is not yet lit. Go back to bed. It is Sunday.

Wife, said I, have you heard of a sort of people called Anabaptists? I must find them this very morning, wherever they are. There is no time to be lost. God is calling me to speak his message again.

Oh, said she.

She said no more than that, but it stopped me in the search for my clean shirt. This Oh is a very zealous word, for it was what my mother used to say all the time: Oh, I know not, Oh, he is tired, Oh, I hope it is a sparrow, *&c &c.* When she uttered it, it was as if she was moving a heap of fleeces in her mind to get at something else she knew was underneath, but coming from my wife it seemed rather a sinking or collapse.

What, wife? What is this Oh? I remember when you thrilled at my prophesying. Nay, you went so far as to abet me in it, saying God's command must be obeyed at all costs. Do you not recall the day we spoke together in Wrexham market, how you urged me to find a way of prophesying without speech and I bought the platter there and then to take to Mr Cradock's sermon?

I was a maid then, said she, and, mark you, I contradict you not, but I am so tired now.

You do not even ask, said I (having found my shirt and being for the moment in the midst of its whiteness, which is not the most dignified posture from which to carry on a dispute), you do not even ask (emerging) what word I am to impart.

Oh, said she again, and poked at the fire, knocking a great ragged piece of coal off the top of a smaller one and causing the most promising concentration of redness to be dispersed in a catastrophe of sparks. Well, said she, regarding the mischief she had wrought with bitter satisfaction, say on, husband, What word is it?

It is in two parts –

Hush, said she. Keep your voice down or you will wake the children. They will sleep another hour or more as it is.

This is too bad –

Hush.

It is in two parts, I whispered sternly. The first part is that I must maintain a succession of ministry.

What sort of thing is that?

Do you not see, wife? I mean (whispering) do you not see? Before the present unlawful rebellion, King Charles Steward was acknowledged by the nation as head of the English Church. Which is to say he was head of God's Church throughout the world, for the Church of England is the only true and rightful Church, instituted of Christ and the Apostles, as I have proved –

I remember, said she. Go on with the rest.

Even the godly, as they call themselves, acknowledged the King and were loyal to him though they very wrongly disputed everything else, such as bishops and the prayerbook and the Queen and the Book of Sports, all of which they explained by the King's being badly advised. But now these same godly have driven the King from his own palace and capital and are waging war against him, so that his rule runs not in half the country. And now they have their way with the Church also, having imprisoned the Archbishop of Canterbury and dispensed with the other bishops, and each of them trusts to his own conscience for the truth instead of to the Church and its appointed leaders. There was a succession of ministry that came down from Christ himself through St Peter and his appointed successors to the English church. Christ laid his hands on the Apostles, the Apostles on other ministers and so on, passing his authority through generations of the Church. But now this Church is broken and scattered. Some are Presbyterians, and some Independents, and every day new sects and schisms arise, each one calling itself the true Church and claiming for itself the right to appoint its own ministers. Thus is the succession of ministry assailed, and myself called to defend it.

You are no minister yourself.

No, said I, but I am God's prophet and he has spoken to me just now, and told me to do it. As he did on former occasions that you know of.

Yes, said she, in much the same way as she had said Oh. She was squatting on the hearth now, her russet petticoat tight over her knees and her arms wrapped around them, a posture more becoming her daughters. Behind her the fire had slumped back into hissing blackness, but I forebore to remind her of her duty. Yes, said she again, what is the second part?

One of the worst of these sects is called Anabaptists. They are called thus because they deny the right of infants to baptism.

I know, said she. My friend Mrs Russell is of their belief. Only she says their right name is not Anabaptists but General Baptists, for they do not forbid baptism. Rather, baptism is of so great dignity that it must only be entered into by grown persons in full understanding of the commitment they make. Our Lord himself, Mrs Russell says, was baptised by John the Baptist when a man grown. And all who join their church must be baptised again, for the baptism they had as an infant counts not for their salvation.

What – ?

Hush.

What, wife? You never told me you were consorting with heretics.

She is not a heretic. She is our neighbour. You have met her.

I do not recall her, and in any case I forbid you to see her more.

You cannot forbid me to see her, my wife said, for I cannot choose whether I see her or not. If she is at the pump when I am fetching the water, I must see her, for I cannot carry water with my eyes closed.

Then I forbid you to speak with her.

My wife pressed her lips together and rolled her eyes upward and to the side, only briefly but I saw it. You asked me, said she, whether I knew anything of them, and this is what I know. Their leader is one Mr Lamb, a soap-boiler of Lincoln.

A soap-boiler!

I have heard men say A tailor! in the same tones, yet people need clothes, and they need soap, too. God may speak to a soap-boiler as to a tailor, may he not?

Saying which, she turned and gave the fire a vicious posthumous poke, causing a small cloud of ash and coal dust to issue into the room.

Chapter XLIII
A Sign Blazing Forth in Spital Yard

This very fortnight in Shoe Lane, a woman gave birth to a child without a head. Can there be any surer sign of schism than this? And yet you continue your arguments, some for mortalism and others for immortalism, and disrupt the sermon with your arguing; some of you are for laying on of hands and go round fondling the heads of any who let you, saying that you are imparting the Holy Ghost and that those you have touched now have the power to preach the Gospel and to lay on hands in their turn, while the rest of you deny it; and while you argue God is making his anger known through signs and portents, and through my mouth, who am his prophet. Did you not hear how after His Majesty's army was defeated at Naseby, a pond in that same county of Leicestershire filled with blood, signifying the bloody destruction that was come upon the land? No, for you closed your ears to it, being too busy arguing amongst yourselves. And so you go about the land arguing and preaching, making converts, and seizing hold of them to dip them in ponds and rivers and tubs of water, maintaining that this, and this only, is the sacrament of baptism. Yea, summer and winter do you dip them, the men in their shirts and drawers, the women in nothing but their smocks, to the great scandal of the country, and many of those you dip are punished by God with colds and distempers of the lungs, and some die of them. And yet you persist in your folly, despite these clear omens from God.

Though I was smaller than any there, there was always a circle round me when I spoke at the Spital, and everyone turned to me and listened. This part of the Artillery Yard had been greatly trampled by Anabaptists till there was almost no grass left in it, and so the circle was of mud. All were thickly clad, the men in doublets and cloaks and the women in heavy gowns. Anabaptism is a very chilly religion, for though they held their services in one of the houses on the edge of the Spital, which they laid open to any who would come there, yet they were happiest standing around in the Yard before and after. Beyond the jostling group was a great expanse of wet grass, which sometimes two or three persons splashed across towards one of the meetings round about. I could see such a group on the far side, a cluster of Independents listening to one of their preachers, who stood under one of the almost leafless trees waving his hands in a godly way. Behind him, beyond the far wall of the Yard, I could see the pointed roof of a building with a cross on the top. The old church and monastery of St Mary Spital had been abandoned hundreds of years since, and now the worship of God had fractured into these knots and clusters.

And women, said I, you persist in allowing them to speak out as men do, as if God, who came into this world in a man's form, would deign to express himself through the weaker vessels. And in this you defy the word of the Apostle who says, Let the woman learn in silence in all subjection, but suffer not a woman to teach, nor to usurp authority over the man.

There was much muttering at this, but none spoke out against it.

All these wrongs, said I, are brought about by schism, which is the splitting away of sects from the Church of England, the one true Church established by God to be ruled by the King and by his bishops. And this is proved by the apparition that was lately seen in Newmarket, of three men struggling in the air, one of them having a drawn sword in his hand, a figuring of the three kingdoms of England, Scotland and Ireland, which shall never have peace until King Charles Steward is restored and stands again at the head of his Church. And all you sectaries, yes, I call you sectaries for that is what you are, all you sectaries will be destroyed in time unless you return to that Church, as God has revealed to me.

Why should you be more confident than any of us? a man's voice said from the back. You bring Scripture for what you say, and so do we.

I have the same spirit to declare the Scripture as did pen it.

If it be so, then you are a prophet. How shall we know this? Give us a sign here, and we will believe.

Yea, they all said, a sign, a sign! All of them shouting at once, and at the same time talking and jostling and explaining among themselves.

I am the Way, the Truth and the Life, said I. No man comes to the Father except through me.

Then some among them cried Blasphemy, these are the words of Jesus Christ, he is not Christ *&c.*

As I tried to shout over them, the ring of mud around me wavered, lost its shape and finally disappeared altogether with their jostling, and I was pressed against the gowns and jerkins. Then a woman pushed through the others, shouting, This is he that speaks against Mr Lamb. Away with him! Why do you listen to him?

She beat at me with her fists and clutched at my face and hair, and the others shrank away from us. She was tall and broadshouldered, though hampered by that shyness women show in fighting, as if wondering whether any would mock her for hitting me the wrong way. I fended her off and covered my face against her until she grew so shy she could hit me no longer, for the whole Yard was watching now; the group at the far side having dispersed, and some of the remnants and other passers-by having joined us. I especially noticed a tall thin young man in a black cloak I had seen often of late, who always seemed to make his way to the front when I was speaking, and never talked to the people around him. Breathing heavily, I put down my hands and felt my face for scratches and bruises. Satisfied that I was not badly hurt, I tried to look her in the eye, but she would not look back. The Anabaptists and Independents now moved off a little and a few of them laughed or started to sing psalms under their breath, but I knew they were watching to see what I would do. I searched my mind for the right passage of Scripture but I was still shaken and the thoughts would not come, though I chided myself for my weakness. I felt for a moment, not as if I were about to fall, but as if I had already fallen. Then with a warm rush inside my being I recognized that God had taken me into his own hand and that whatever came from my mouth now would be his words, not mine.

> Woman, thou shalt not be here this day seven night at this time to rail against me for declaring the truth.

One of the Anabaptists said, That shall be the sign. If she comes here this day seven night, then you are a false prophet, but if she come not at that time then you are a true prophet.

The woman smiled narrowly and made a little curtsy: I will be sure to be here to prove him a false prophet.

I waited for God to speak for me, but the warmth had gone and I was empty and somewhat weary. I will refer it to God, I told her. Let it be so, now that you have taken it for a sign to prove me.

The next Sunday we met there again, and discoursed as before, but said nothing of the sign.

The second Sunday we met as before. There was a peace upon me that day. Though it was as cold as ever, I felt no physical discomfort, nor did God move me to stand in my circle and declaim, but I stood with the others discoursing quietly of Scripture, and none sought to dispute with me. Then there was a stirring at the back and the same rush inside me, and I knew that God had returned with more work for me to do. This time I did not feel as if I had fallen down: if it made sense I would say I had fallen up. All the same, I reached out my hands to the people that stood around me, thinking to hold myself in place by taking a grip on their arms or shoulders, but they moved back, and I saw the woman approaching from the other side of the Yard, people standing aside for her as for me. She moved quickly, yet took longer to reach me than seemed natural, and she looked also smaller than she was formerly, but held herself as erect. When at last she stood before me, she hesitated as if trying to decide whether to hit me again or to address me, and then did neither, but turned to the others beside me and spoke to them instead.

Ah, said she, this villain has slain my child.

They all looked at each other. After a while, the man in the black cloak stepped forward. What mean you? said he.

At the same hour this man said I should not be here, my child departed, so that I could not be here for all the world.

I saw now that her eyes and face were red, and not just from the cold, for there were the marks of tears on her cheeks. Then God spoke through me again.

Woman, the Lord knoweth that I knew not whence thou art, or whether thou hadst children or not. Now the Lord hath met with thee, why dost thou go on railing still? I am persuaded thy child is happy, for he was ordained to glorify God. Take heed and leave off this way, lest a worse thing happen unto thee.

At this, the woman reeled back, and one or two of those around us caught her arms to steady her. She pulled her right arm free of them and rubbed at her face with her hand, then looked at me again, blinking, and made to speak, but, finding she still could not meet my eye, she looked at the hardened mud beneath her feet, and muttered something I could not hear. She shook her head and pulled her other arm free from those who still held it, wiped both hands on her apron, and turned and hurried back the way she had come.

Once again, I felt the emptiness of God leaving me, and a sadness that I now knew had been locked in my mind for a long time, but I could not tell what it was for. There was a cold wind blowing even in this walled Yard and just then the sun went behind a cloud. I perceived then I was no longer alone in the midst of the throng: the man in the black cloak stood beside me, handsome and long-faced.

You are Mr Evans? he asked.

That is my name.

Yes, said he quietly. I thought so.

Chapter XLIV
There Goes Christ!

He spied on us for the Presbyterians! said they. This is the Welshman who speaks for the King and against true religion! This is he that said he was Christ!

What am I supposed to have said?

When I raised my hands for silence they batted them down and tried to seize me, and I could see both men and women nudging and looking sidelong at each other, nerving themselves to do some violence. Being unbalanced, I staggered backwards a few paces, slipping on the frozen mud, and found there were others standing behind me, some of whom caught me, but hesitantly and seeming as if they were more concerned to prevent my falling than to apprehend me, and one man bent down, picked up my hat, and handed it back. When I tried to thank him he shrank away and hid behind a couple of others.

You, friend, said I, you that brought me my hat. You seem a decent fellow for a sectary. I have disputed with all of you many times, I do not deny it, but you always suffered me to come among you. What have I done now, that you all cry out against me and will not suffer me to speak?

It is Mr Edwards, said he, from behind the bodies of his fellows.

And who, said I, is this Mr Edwards, and what has he said against me?

He is a Presbyterian minister, and writes that you have maintained yourself to be Christ. And thus he finds excuse to condemn all of us, Anabaptists and Independents, for he says we are all as wicked as you are, for consorting with you. For these Presbyterians have the church to themselves now, and would condemn all that are not of their opinion.

What? said I. Where are you? Come out from there and explain yourself.

Yes, said he (emerging, or it may be that the people around him stood off from him so that he must needs be exposed). It was in a book called *Gangraena*, which attacks all of us, Mr Lamb included. But yourself most of all, for he cannot accuse us of blasphemy.

Never have I said I was Christ.

You did so, said he. I have read of it in Mr Edwards's book.

I am his prophet, and the prophet of God and of King Charles Steward. God has been pleased to speak through me at times, and most often in the words of Scripture, and then I know not what I utter, for it is God who speaks and not myself.

The woman whose child had died was standing beside the man, though I had noticed her not before.

You said it, said she. Many times, and we all heard you.

All of them grunted and said yea to this, their breath steaming.

I tried to speak again, but they shouted me down, and their steam rose up against me. Then one or two came forward and made to seize me, but I pulled myself free and began to move away. After I had gone a few steps, however, they began to follow me, moving no faster than I did, so that I seemed to be pulling them on a string. I looked away from them and quickened my pace, passing unhindered from the Artillery Yard into another field, so that I could now see the gate that led to Bishopsgate Street. I fixed my eyes on it and said to myself that once I had reached it all should be well.

It was the middle of the afternoon, but the roofs were still white with frost. A freezing mist mingled with the smoke in the air and as I turned into Bishopsgate Street I could feel the people still coming after me, and hear them too, stamping their feet against the cold. They called out to me to stop and face them, and so far from giving up now we had left the Spital they shouted out to the people who lived round about, There goes Christ! Stop him! Stop him!

A door opened on the other side of the street, and a man's voice called out, What is it? A thief?

No, it is Christ!

What?

There goes Christ! Stop him!

Doors and windows opened the length of the street: What did he say? There goes Christ! Christ is come! Men, women and children came out of their houses on both sides, most without hats or cloaks or any clothing suitable for the weather; one was smoking a pipe, a few had mugs of ale in their hands, and one man carried a shoe that he had been interrupted in the middle of mending. I thought they would apprehend me but they stood back and let me pass, then fell in behind, still shouting to the others.

There goes who? Christ! It is Christ at last! There were some among the Anabaptists and Independents who understood the mistake they had caused with their jeering, and I heard them arguing and trying to explain, but the others were more numerous. The mob pressed after me, some still trying to seize me in anger, others crouching and reaching out for me, seeking to touch the hem of my garment. I could see the steeple of Bishopsgate Church ahead of me. The door was open and as I approached more closely I saw a churchwarden look out, then turn back as if to say something to another. By the time I reached the door I could see that the church was full, it being Sunday. The churchwarden came out and his fellow after him and they pulled the door to behind them.

What is it, goodman? The service is started.

I must enter the church.

Who are these folk with you?

They have followed me. From the Spital.

From the Spital? the first warden said. The mob had stopped a little way off and was watching quietly for the present. These, the first warden continued, gesturing at them with his head, these are Independents?

Independents and Anabaptists.

You have enraged them against us, the second man said. He was taller and younger than the other, but seemed more afraid, perhaps understanding that in any fighting he would be obliged to do most of it, for his friend was fat.

We are good Presbyterians here, the first one said. Take your Independent mob and go back to the Spital.

They are no mob of mine, and it is myself they are enraged against.

I heard them calling on Christ, the younger warden said. Independent blasphemers!

They believe the Day of Judgment is come, said I, or some of them do.

Blasphemers! the young one said. They will tear us to pieces.

You come not into this church, any of you, the first man said. He had a sweetened voice like one striving to confer a blessing, but he stared fiercely at each of the foremost members of the mob in turn.

They will tear me to pieces, said I, unless you let me in.

The two men looked at each other. Come with me, said the first one, and we will go in by a back door. His friend turned pale and flattened himself still more against the door he was guarding. The warden took me into the churchyard, shutting the gate behind him, and we picked our way between tombstones to the side of the church.

I took my seat in an empty pew in the north aisle.

The minister stopped for a moment upon seeing me come in, and looked vexed, but it was hard to be sure in the dimness. He was beardless and his voice had not the ring and roll of Mr Cradock or Dr Gouge. So we see, brethren, said he, resuming at last, that Our Lord has given his word, which he never breaks, for which of us, on earth, would keep his own word, or, um, any word that he gave to another, if he knew that keeping of promises was, um, a thing of no importance to God? He has given his word, I say, that he will, infallibly...

I leaned against the back of the pew and waited for my heartbeat to cease its throbbing against the inside of my ears. The sermon would not last more than an hour, then there would be a psalm and concluding prayers, and all the worshippers would make their way out of the West Door, which I had first tried to go in by. I would go out among them, hoping to hide myself among their number. Doubtless the mob would have dispersed by then, or at any rate it might be less numerous and I could make my way home unhindered. But if instead it had gathered strength, perhaps the fears of the churchwardens would be justified. The mob would set upon the congregation, demanding my person, and there would be a riot.

The door opened with a muffled scraping, and I saw the tall churchwarden standing in it. The people from outside began to file past him, some of them taking empty places in the pews while others stood at the back. The worshippers turned their heads and muttered, and the minister lost the thread of his sermon again. So, thought I, they have bribed the churchwarden, or threatened him so that he could keep them out no longer. Well, they cannot harm me in a church.

And so, the minister continued, so he promised that he would return among us, and we, all of us, await this, um, this second coming, as we call it, of our Lord, when he shall come, so the Apostles tell us, as a, a thief in the night, which is to say we shall not, those of us who are unwary, know that he is there at all. And indeed he may be among us at this very moment –

There was a rush of fidgeting and murmuring at the back of the church.

Yes, said he, you do well, you do well to look about you, for Christ may be, um, he may be sitting next to you, or in the next pew, even as I preach these words. For think on it, brethren, the days are short, they must be short until Judgement. Never has there been so much upheaval and, um, evil, in the land. Those of us who are godly, who follow in the Lord's way, have cried out with, um, a loud voice, we have set our hands to the plough, we have unfurled our banners and we have marched forth and fought the

Lord's battle. Yea, and we triumphed, or it seemed so, but when we returned we found that strange heresies had sprung up like poisonous weeds in our own gardens, and thus we find in our midst, where we least looked to see them, men who call themselves Quakers, and Independents, and Ranters, and, um, Familists, and Adamites, and Anabaptists. Yes, you may well murmur, for while the godly have never been so strong or their victories so glorious as they are today, yet our enemies, too, are stronger and more insidious than ever before. And therefore it is now, more than at any other time, that we should be looking to see Christ in our midst. He may, as I said, be here at this very – what?

The people at the back were now murmuring no longer, but crying out, Christ! He is here! Heresy! *&c &c*, and the minister put his hand to his brow, smiling timidly as one unsure whether to be pleased or afraid of the sensation he had created. He tried to continue his sermon, but the noise in the church was so great that I heard none of it, nor the psalm or the prayers which followed. It seemed to me that some of those at the back had commenced to fight each other, but I dared not turn around to see, nor move at all until the congregation was dismissed. By this time there was shouting and striving all round the church, and I heard people call out Where is Christ? Christ is come! Find him! *&c*, and other voices rebuking them as blasphemers. When I looked up from my prayer I found the fat churchwarden beside me.

Come, friend, said he. We will go to the vestry.

He pushed through the crowd, who seemed not to recognize me in the dimness, and indeed some of them, I supposed, had never seen me at all. So we reached the vestry and the warden shut the door.

The minister was sitting on a bench, his head in his hands. Was I too strong, Robert? he said. This has never happened before.

This is the man, Robert said. He said he was Christ, which enraged them.

Who are you?

He is some Independent, Robert said, but his blasphemies are too much even for them, and I was obliged to bring him into the church to prolong his life.

I am no Independent, said I. The one true Church is the Church of England, and –

The minister scrubbed at the roots of his hair with his fingers. Which church do you go to, fellow?

I am a communicant with Dr Gouge's people in Blackfriars.

Ah, said the minister. I have heard Dr Gouge preach, a most saintly man. But why did you say you were Christ?

I have said nothing. The people are mad.

Why did you let them in, Robert? They are Independents, all of them. I see it now. I thought it was my sermon that maddened them, but they were maddened before.

It was Edward let them in.

Where is Edward? Go and get him, Robert. No, do not leave me alone with this man, go to the door and see if you can see him. Call to him. I want him to take a message for me.

Chapter XLV
A Prodigal Received with Soup and Reproaches

When I returned from my walk to Paul's Yard this afternoon, I found my son seated before the fire and his mother ministering to him with soup. This, says she, ignoring my entrance, will restore you, Owen.

What, Owen, say I, does the cold still afflict you?

No, father, says he, probing the soup with his spoon and peering into its depths as one who fears what he may find there. The Lord has withdrawn his phlegm from my sinful passages and I rejoice once again in his pure air, undeserving as I am. But there are other afflictions than those of the body, and I fear the sins that have brought them upon me are worse than those former ones.

His voice dies away at the end of his speech, and he lowers his head like one respectably dejected, but his cheeks are aglow with firelight and the warmth of the soup, and I never saw a youth look so comfortable as he crouches over the bowl.

Owen, says my wife, has come to stay with us.

How? He cannot stay here. What of my book? And what of Mr Greenhaugh and your apprenticeship, Owen?

He looks up from the bowl as if about to speak, but only hesitates a few moments and then drops his gaze again.

Will you, says my wife, take some soup, husband?

Why, whatever should I want with soup? I do not recall that I ever committed such sins as Owen speaks of, that would merit a punishment from God that can only be assuaged with soup, say I, noticing now that the steam from the pot hanging over the fire has filled the room with the warm savour of roots and onions, and that I am hungry and cold from my walk.

Well, father, there is the matter of your nose, Owen says, looking quickly at his mother and then at me. You never to my knowledge asked what God meant by afflicting you with that. Is it better, by the way?

My nose, my nose –

Now, Owen, says my wife, you must not reproach your father with his afflictions, though I fear it will never be as it was formerly. (She is looking at me too, now.) I think it is almost healed, however.

It was healed long since, by His –

Owen laughs in that whispery way he has, as if he must give vent to his mirth, but does not trust his voice with it. It is a family resemblance, says he, that God chooses our noses to punish us with.

It seems to me, says my wife, that you talk a little too much of God, Owen. That was partly the reason Mr Greenhaugh cast you out, for there are some who cannot abide such talk, especially in this new age. After all, how do you know what God wills and what is a mere accident or natural occurrence? I have gone among our neighbours these many years, and have seen all sorts of people cruelly struck down, with agues and dropsies, with toothache and spitting of blood, and even with plague, and I never saw that –

Mr Greenhaugh cast him out?

I never saw that any of them deserved their suffering more than their friends and kin who were well.

That is because you do not know God's will, mother.

And if they recovered, says she, if I was able to cure them, as I was with some, was it not because God gave virtues to these creations of his, to adder's tongue and sowthistle and sea coleworts, which I, through talking to the wisest among my acquaintance and studying in Mrs Lowndes's bookshop and trying out their benefits for myself, have grown to understand? For I have observed, Owen, that where a remedy succeeds with one patient it succeeds most often with another, not always but enough to make me think that the virtue lies in the medicine more than in the patient. And if there are virtues in nature, may there not be vices also, which we call sicknesses? It seems to me, and I only speak now as a – I know not how to describe myself – as a sort of domestic woman physician, that the illness is a part of the world, as the remedy is, and therefore we ought to look to the world to understand them both. It could be that if we knew the virtues of every herb in the world, we would cure all sicknesses forever. Have your finished your soup? she concludes, though, standing as she is behind his left shoulder, she can see as well as I that his bowl is still half full.

Owen raised both hands to cover his ears during this speech, but, finding that he had his spoon in one of them, he was obliged to lower it, so that he covered only the left ear. Now, somewhat abashed, he lowers this one also, and glares at her. You are a woman, says he finally, and it is not for a woman to speak on these matters.

And you, say I, (glad to have an opportunity to speak), are a son, and it is not for a son to rebuke his mother, however perplexing her utterances may appear. Besides, Owen, it is not my nose or your cold we have to speak of but how you come to be here at all. Is it true that Mr Greenhaugh has cast you out?

Mr Greenhaugh is not a fit master for one such as I, he mutters. And if it comes to that, tailoring is not a fit profession.

Indeed it is. It is vindicated in Holy Writ, and, and, answers to a general need, and, as for Mr Greenhaugh, he is one of the best of his kind. The apprentice does not choose the master, and the son does not choose his own profession, or the world would be turned upside-down.

You thought as I do when you were my age, says he. I have heard you say you should never have been a tailor, and yet you chose this trade for me, which you were no more suited to than I am. And you hated your first master, too, and he cast you out, as mine has.

He went broke and I had to leave him. But my second master I loved, and he taught me that tailoring is a worthy profession, for it is the joining of one thing to another thing, than which there can be no greater or more necessary accomplishment (wondering, as I say it, whether this is true and indeed what precisely I mean by it), as you would know if you had read my *Book of the Needle*, which I trust you will when it is finished, as I hope – Why, what is this?

The pages of my latest chapter are scattered across the desk where I left them, but there is another on top of them, inscribed in a strange hand.

It is a letter, my wife says, from Mr Greenhaugh to yourself, to explain why he has cast out Owen from his shop. I have not read it, she adds, seeing as it was addressed to you, and as it was more proper for me to busy myself about my son, in making him welcome and consoling him in his distress with the making of this same soup. Will you take some? she concludes, smiling vaguely.

Wife, there are more important things afoot than soup, but I will take some presently. First, I must read Mr Greenhaugh's letter.

> *To Mr Evans in Long Alley. Sir, I send you this by the hand of your son, trusting you are in good health. I have, Sir, been very patient with him, and have done my best to instruct him in all he will need to know as a tailor, not only the forward stitch and the back stitch, the overhanding and the oversewing, the seams and the hems, but even to the rudiments of cutting, such as he needs not to know till he is a master, which is no more likely than to be King of Spain. Well, I shall not go further into these matters, knowing you to have been at some time in the past a species of tailor yourself, but suffice to say that I never met with a worse apprentice in all those skills, and for most of his work I have had to finish it myself or get a journeyman to do it for him. Now, Sir, all this were bad enough and plentiful reason for*

casting him out, but what makes it worse, and has left me, Sir, at the end of my endurance, is these sermons of his. I will not abide being called a sinner by my own prentice, and I care not if he call himself one, too. America is welcome to him, for he will not even stand my justified correction, but when I beat him he says he is a martyr. He thinks he is above tailoring, which no man in his station of life may say, for it is a worthy trade for anyone, and far too good for himself. Besides which, he is not a fit person to be in the same house as certain females, even if they be only servant-girls. Therefore, Sir, with regret, I must ask you to take back your son, and to seek a new master for him. His indenture with myself is at an end and I purpose to keep the sum of money you gave me, as payment for the labour I have put into this unworthy cause. I remain, Sir. &c.

Owen, say I, what does he mean about females?

It is a lie, says he. I would never have carried the letter to you if I had known he was going to calumniate me in it. I am a bad tailor, I confess it, and I have had my quarrels with this man, who would not countenance my trying to counsel him, when all my purpose was the easement of his soul.

If I thought, Owen, that you were guilty of any uncleanness –

Come, husband, says my wife. You know Owen abominates uncleanness as his parents do, more perhaps, godly as he is. Here, you may have your soup now. Mr Greenhaugh was angry and knew not what he was writing. I dare say, there being girls in the house, Owen was apt to joke with them as young men will, and Mr Greenhaugh took it amiss, especially from one who displeased him with his work. And it is the work which should concern us most, all of us. For how is he to live without it?

And how can we live with Owen, say I, who have not enough to live on ourselves? Hssp – !

This last is the noise I make taking a spoonful of soup and scalding my tongue on it. I catch Owen's eye at the same time, and, seeing him about to pronounce a judgement on my just punishment by God, I rejoice that I am still able after all this time to silence him with a look. His days of moralizing on his elders are at an end.

Chapter XLVI
Love's Treachery Revealed

In the Keeper's Lodge a great fire was burning. Accustomed now to the darkness of the prison I could see little else but the flames, yet I made out dimly that there were two chairs in front of the hearth, and a dark figure in one of them who rose to greet me.

Shw mae, ffrind.

Pwy ydych chi?

Ffrind ydw i, a Chymro.

I knew not where I was, hearing the language of my childhood spoken, but the man led me to the other chair, and I sat in it, and my gaze was drawn straightway into the heart of the burning, and I thought, as I used to as a child, that with a little courage it would be possible to live in those glowing and hissing caverns between the logs. The Keeper was still there behind us, and the stranger spoke to him.

Friend, pray bring us some beer.

This was a wonder, for he returned directly with the two mugs, the Keeper of Newgate waiting on the lowliest of his prisoners, and I looked hard at the man on the other side of the fire to see who had this power, but, being still dazzled, I saw only that he was ruddy-faced, smiling and either clad in black or it was the firelight made him appear so.

Drink, said he, and laughed, and though I could not see what was comical about my situation, I laughed along with him, and drank as he instructed me.

Q. What is your name?

A. Arise the son of Evan the son of Arise the son of Owen the son of Arise the son of Evan the son of David the son of Arise the son of Griffith the son of the Red Lion the son of the Ren.

Q. You are from Merionethshire, I believe?
A. I was born in the parish of Llangluin, a few miles off from Cader Idris, which is the highest hill in the world. My father was a sheepfarmer, and I should have been one myself but he died and I was left disinherited, that was his darling while he lived.
Q. A fine county I have heard. I am myself from a town in Wales called Cardiff. But tell me, how do you come to be in prison?

I turned to him then and tried once more to make out his features. I could see now that he had no beard, but only a thin, dark moustache which hung down almost to his pointed chin. His face was round but somewhat bony at the same time, and his hair under the cap was bushy and long. He smiled as if greatly delighted with what I told him.

A. I know not, for I have done nothing wrong. I was called by God to speak his word, and so I held forth at the Spital to all who would hear me, and God brought about a miracle to prove me right.
Q. What miracle was this?
A. A woman's son was stricken when she disputed with me.
Q. Stricken?
A. God suffered him to die so that my prophecy might be fulfilled, but the child is happy now in heaven.
Q. Good, that is very good.

He laughed again – indeed, it seemed as if he was always laughing, as much when he was speaking as when he was not, as a man breathes at all times – and called for more beer. I would have refused, for I was weak from my confinement, and I thought the unhealthy airs of the dungeon had made me ill. I was dizzy and the fire was hot on my cheeks and forehead.

Q. But I have heard that some persons of discerning judgement believe that you are more than merely God's messenger or prophet. There are those who believe you to be the Messiah himself, are there not, friend? I have heard it said that Arise Evans is none other than Jesus Christ, returned to live among us. How I would rejoice if that were so! And it may be so in truth, I cannot deny it. Is it so? Drink your beer.

A. I never said I was Christ. But if the voice of Christ speaks through me, then that voice may say it is Christ and speak truth. That I know nothing of, for it is not myself who speaks. And there were those at the Spital who were so amazed at the power that is in me that they followed me all the way to Bishopsgate Church, crying, There goes Christ!

Q. But you have the power to work miracles?

A. It is true, I have seen visions since I was a child. I have flown over the mountains, and watched the sun on Whitsunday morning dance and turn about like a wheel. An angel came to me at the shopboard and stood over me with a fiery sword. I was fed by God in a cloud hued like the rainbow, and many times he has spoken to me in my ear, closer than you are to me now, to give me my instructions. But the power is God's, not my own.

Q. There can be no doubt of it, any of it. More beer!

He rose then and stalked about in front of the fire, a short, broadshouldered man with calves that seemed too thin for his bulk. He seemed lost in thought for a while, but seeing me watching him, he turned and smiled again.

Q. How right you are to mistrust the Presbyterians! For I never heard any good of them, did you?

A. It is not only the Presbyterians I mistrust, friend, but all religions except the Church of England, for that is the only true Church. I have most of all a horror of the Anabaptists.

Q. Indeed? I had heard you were an Anabaptist yourself. Or else some kind of Independent. But perhaps I was wrongly informed. If you are Jesus Christ, you need not belong to any church, for it is the church that belongs to you.

A. I never said I was Christ.

Q. Forgive me, it is our friend the Keeper's excellent beer muddling my thoughts. You are not Christ but you are a believer in the Church of England. What, you hold with bishops?

A. With bishops, friend, and the prayerbook, and bowing the knee at the altar, and music in church and infant baptism. But it is God who holds with these things, and I must hold with them if I hold to God. This is his Church and he has set King Charles Steward to be at its head.

Q. Ah, the poor King! But I wonder that you are not better disposed to the Presbyterians, for I have heard they have hopes that the King will come to their beliefs in time, now he is defeated in battle. And these Presbyterians have taken the Church of England unto themselves, as they did the Scottish Church, so it would seem to me – but forgive my confusion – that you, as a member of the Church of England and a lover of His Majesty, should be a Presbyterian yourself now.

A. No, for I hate the Presbyterians as much as the rest. Or rather, as a good Christian I should say that I hate their errors.

Q. You interest me much, friend. What errors are these? But have another mug of beer first.

A. Why, they have put the government of the Church in the hands of some people they call Elders, who are so arrogant that they catechise everyone who would come to the Lord's Table to take communion, and those that cannot answer their senseless questions they turn away, contrary to the word of God. And if anyone should ask Dr Gouge at Blackfriars any question of doctrine, he asks them first, Have you seen the Elders? Thus we see that even a minister famed for his saintliness is in awe of these tyrannical persons, who are not even ordained, much less called by God.

A. You are right, friend, no one can deny it. And it is for speaking these truths no doubt, and not for blasphemy, that you have been confined in this dark and unsanitary place.

He was seated by now and waved his beermug slowly round to indicate that it was not the Keeper's Lodge he meant but the whole of Newgate. His face, for the first time this evening, was grave rather than smiling, and I liked him better for it, for it showed that he approved my arguments and understood my suffering.

But tell me, said he at last, are there not some who consider you distempered in mind?

I was asked that once before, said I, and my answer is the same, that there are many who think it. But I do not heed them, for I am the sanest man of all.

I think so too, said he. *Hwyl fawr, ffrind.*

When he had gone, I found the Keeper at my elbow, and said to him, This is an honest man. If all men were of his mind I should soon get off.

The Keeper laughed. You are mightily deceived in this man, for if he had his will you should not long be alive. He and the rest of his fellow ministers say that you ought to be put to death for what you have said and done.

He is a minister? said I. What is his name?

His name is Love.

I looked at the Keeper to see if he was jesting.

Yes, said he, Christopher Love, a Presbyterian and a famous enemy of the Independents and all who depart from what he calls orthodoxy. And his errand was to trap you if he could.

Chapter XLVII
A Voice Crying Among the Mighty

Cromwell was a stocky, ruddy-faced fellow, sitting at his supper table with his legs stretched out in front of him, his longish hair tangled and a couple of buttons on his doublet undone, and answered my questions crisply, like a man of business reminding me how much they cost. Two others sat at his table that evening, a boy of prentice age with a face like Cromwell's but smoother and handsomer, and a man in his thirties, who seemed tall even though seated, and was dark-complexioned with bushy black hair and an expression like one worrying a piece of meat from between his teeth with his tongue, which he may indeed have been doing, only I thought the expression was habitual and the irritation in his mind rather than his mouth. Both these younger ones looked up at me as I stood before the table, willing me to be gone, and then glanced at Cromwell to see whether he had marked their impatience.

And what of my son Henry? said he, indicating the boy with his thumb. What do you prophesy for him? What of my son-in-law Ireton? Both of them, I warrant, have brighter futures than myself. Prophesy for them, Mr Evans.

I know nothing of them, my lord.

I am no lord, said he. I am a farmer and a soldier, but if God has a message for me I will hear it. I will say one thing for you anyway – you know your Bible better than any man I ever met, which makes me the more inclined to listen to you.

I have heard, said I, that you are not proud, but that you receive instruction many times from mean men, and therefore I could not rest until I came to you.

Instruction? said he. I receive many petitions, if that's what you mean. People seem to think I can do things for them. Are you one of them, Mr Evans? Is there aught I can do for you, eh?

God knows I have been treated unjustly, I said, but I came not to ask reparation for myself.

You have enemies, though? Cromwell said, with a little snort.

Yes, my lord, many, and the chiefest among them are the Presbyterians.

See, he said, looking at Ireton, I told you he would be worth our time. He can quote the Bible and he hates the Presbyterians. Say on, Mr Evans. What have the Presbyterians done that aggrieves you so mightily?

Then I told him how Mr Edwards had put me in his *Gangraena*, falsely maintaining I had claimed to be Christ and stirring up the populace against me, and how Mr Love had visited me in prison, deceiving me into thinking him a friend, to amass evidence against me.

And I was sent, said I, guarded by a company of marshall's men, to Bridewell. And when the Presbyterians saw that no one came from the Spital to witness anything against me at Sessions, they saw now that now they could not get my life. So they got some of their agents to draw a petition to the Bench, giving out that I was distempered in mind, and got many hands to sign it. They sought to persuade my wife to appeal to the Bench to send me to Bedlam by telling her that there I would have good warm meat every meal and good usage. Their plot failed and when the Sessions came, I got out of prison. But these Presbyterians, though they call themselves Christians, will not forgive me for defeating them. They still seek my life.

They seek our lives also, said he, for we are all Independents here. We have done the service of the kingdom, and now we are looked upon as enemies, and instead of rewarding us they are ready to take away our lives. What shall we do?

Sir, I said, the King's Majesty is at Holdenby House, a prisoner in great distress under Colonel Graves. You have men enough under your command.

Get the King unto you and treat him well. For the King is in the hearts of the people, and so you will draw all the kingdom to side with you, and have your enemies under your feet.

Enough, Ireton said. Sir, we have heard you patiently, but you must not think to advise us on matters of state. Be assured, we have all such concerns in hand and in due time –

A king, said Cromwell, poking at a mutton bone on his plate as if to see whether it would stir of itself when sufficiently provoked, and what is a king after all?

A king, said I, is the father of the nation, appointed by God to lead us, and more especially when the nation is England, which is the greatest of all those on earth, and which he chose especially for his Church. It is for this reason His Majesty is named Charles Steward, for he is Steward of the Church. I have met this King, my lord, and I tell you I never met a man more endued with power, though it was not outward show but a gentle shining forth of glory from his person.

You met him, eh? Did he speak to you?

He said thank you, my lord, when I handed him some writings, and I observed that His Majesty had a slight halting of the tongue, which I thought was a sign of God's special attention towards him. For just as the angel touched Jacob on the leg, and the sinew shrank at his touch, so this infirmity of speech seemed as if his tongue had been touched by God. Though now I think on it, there was a shrinking in the King's leg, too, for he walked with a limp, so it must be that God has touched him twice.

I have not met His Majesty, said Cromwell, which is a strange thing to think on, seeing that I have spent so many years striving against his armies. I met his father, though, King James, when I was but a young man in the Fen country. Have you visited the Fens, Mr Evans? They are a flat and marshy region, most unlike Wales, for you and I come from opposite extremes, both geographically and politically and in every other way, save that we believe in the same

God. You from the western hills, me from the eastern marshes, eh? But they are a very poor people for the most part, for they can no more grow wheat in that swampy earth than I dare say your people can in the rocks and brambles.

My father was a sheep farmer, my lord, and owned sufficient land for his purposes.

Well, they are poor, he continued, his eyes never leaving the bone, which had a protuberance on it like the blade of a mattock. I made it my business to speak out for them, and, hearing that he was about the selling of the Fens to some Dutchmen, I went to see him, and had at my back a number of countrymen on stilts, which they use for getting about in the watery land. He was not a small man as I have heard his son is, and seemed bigger than he was, for he was muffled in thick robes, which he wore always to prevent assassination so that the knife should not penetrate them. And I know not whether God had touched his tongue but he spoke very outlandishly, being a Scot, so that I found it hard to understand him. Still, I dare say he was thanking me as his son thanked you, and he took the petition, but here is a strange thing, Mr Evans. The moment he took it, his nose fell a-bleeding.

Henry laughed. You never told me this before, father, said he.

As I say, he was of a somewhat ruddy complexion, as I am myself, and his nose bled very profusely, which discommoded him a great deal, running on to his robes, and for a little while none of his courtiers knew where to look, until one of them came forward with a handkerchief, for if he had one himself I doubt he knew where to find it in all that padding. And there was the King muffling his nose in fine linen and still speaking as best he could, but no one could understand him in that condition, whether they understood him before or not. Well, thought I, you may protect your body from outer strokes, but none may stay the Lord's blow, for he strikes from within. Mark you, Mr Evans, I was no rebel, but only a petitioner like yourself, and I know not why the Lord wished to strike him, or what sins he had committed, but a king may sin the same as anyone else.

He picked up the bone then, between his thumb and index finger. It was clean and white, every scrap of meat having been sucked from it, and he looked at it as if it bemused him, then put it down again. Ireton was staring fixedly at the opposite wall, and Henry's lips were pressed together, like one who must not permit himself to laugh.

So I went away with my stilted men, he continued, and afterwards I heard that His Majesty thought it a very ill omen, and had said he wished he could hang the fellow that gave him that paper. Perhaps he should have done, for it would have saved his family some trouble in later years. I had no thought of politics then, or soldiering. I must have been a little older than Henry here, perhaps twenty-four, for I think it was the year 1623, yes, it must have been.

And what season was this, my lord?

He looked at Ireton as if expecting some help there, then smiled. Summer, he said, about midsummer. Why do you ask? Did you prophesy that?

No, my lord, for God had not yet called me to be a prophet at that time. I was then but a prentice, living in Westchester. But a wise man of my acquaintance told me that, the golden number being nine, the moon having changed on Low Sunday Eve, there was a prophesy of Taliesin that announced a woe in Britain in the year 1623. Tell me, my lord, was this the second Thursday after Midsummer Day?

Cromwell shrugged, still smiling. You are a curious man, Mr Evans.

For if it were, I said, then this must have been the fire upon the land that the prophet warned of, a metaphorical fire and not a real one. Mr Jones thought it might be the Day of Judgment itself that was foretold, but I see now that it was a different judgement on the King and the nation. For all such prophesies must come true, only it requires much shrewdness to interpret them.

He nodded slowly, pursing his lips, and I thought he had apprehended my counsel and was ready now to add it to his calculations. Ireton pushed his plate into the middle of the table, as one preparing to rise after a meal, and Cromwell looked at him and marked the gesture.

Well, Mr Evans, said he, which I took to be a dismissal. But before I could take my leave, a new thought seemed to occur to him. The Scots, he said.

Yes, my lord?

You say I should get the King to me and so I shall have the love of the people. But what will the Scots say to that? For you know, Mr Evans, it was to the Scots that he first surrendered, and they still hope to make him a Presbyterian like themselves. Their army lies at Newcastle and if I provoke them by seizing His Majesty, there is nothing to stop them marching on London. I doubt the New Model Army would care for another war so soon after the last one. What shall I do about the Scots? Do your prophecies say aught of that?

The Scots, said I, have not been paid for the fighting they did in your cause, and that makes them rebellious. Give the Scots their money, and they will depart the kingdom.

Ah yes, he said, money. I did not think of that.

Chapter XLVIII
A Botch Hardly Begun

I think to write today of botching, which is oftentimes the greater part of tailoring, and yet I have hardly mentioned it so far. But I cannot write of it unless I do it, and I cannot do it unless I have cabbage, which, as I have writ elsewhere, is a thing all tailors have in plenty. For one of the skills in botching is to have a perfect memory of every scrap of this same cabbage (which, as I told you, is a collocation of rags and not a vegetable): of its size and shape and fabric and colour and degree of wear, so that when his customer hands over the garment and shows him the part that wants mending, he knows at once that he has the very piece to botch it with, and may even be able to say to a fair degree of nicety how deep it is in hell (or his chest of snippets). Hugh Jones said that he knew every piece of cabbage that ever came into his shop, for all the cloth that was brought there had passed under his hand. I remember, said he, the customer that brought it and the garment he asked for and the price I charged him, and how much of his cloth I got away with at the end, and so must you, my boy, when you are a master like me.

But a journeyman cannot do it so well, for he goes from master to master, and so never gets a full knowledge of the scraps that are to be found in any one workshop. Many is the afternoon I have wasted up to my elbows in hell, looking for a piece of blue broadcloth so long and so wide, and with a small diagonal tear in one corner, only to remember that I saw it two years ago in some shop the other side of London. But however that may be, I had the chest of cloth to fumble in, and I have nothing of that sort here. If I had but Owen's piece of rag, I could stitch it to my doublet above the place where I took a snip to try out my scissors in my chapter of appurtenances, but he is gone out and no doubt taken the rag with him.

In any case, it is so cold in this room I can hardly write, for my wife says that we must save the coal to have a good fire at Christmas. What, say I, you mean to mark Christmas with lighting of a fire? And what does our young Puritan say to that?

We need not tell him it is for Christmas, says she.

She is on her knees rooting in her chest of remedies, not in search of any particular decoction, but because, says she, it is long since I was at the bottom of it, and I wish to put all in order. It is for Owen's sake, as much as my own. He says he can never be a tailor, and though I told him to read your book, he says there is nothing in it he can make head or tail of –

You sent him to my book? That must be why it is become so scattered of late. You did very wrong, wife. It is not finished yet.

You are writing for prentices, are you not? says she, muttering under her breath, Duckmeat, archangels, pellitory of the wall, and ranging the jars and bottles on the floor according to no logic that I can see. Owen is a prentice, and if he cannot understand it you are failing in your task. Worse than that, he says it is full of heresy, and he fears it will harm his soul. You know, husband, his soul was always a thing he was most careful of. Look, a jar of bluebottles. I did not know I still had them. I wonder if they are much corrupted.

Heresy –

I should take all these jars down to the pump and wash them, for some of them have become sticky on the outside, and I should not wish Owen to touch them in that condition. Well, you know, husband, I like Owen's beliefs no more than you do, but you should not write so much of God in a book of tailoring. However that may be, he says he learned little of the craft from Mr Greenhaugh, and nothing at all from your book, and now he thinks to become an apothecary, like myself.

Like – ?

Of course, says she, I told him you would not countenance it, and I told him also that we have paid Mr Greenhaugh for him to be made a tailor and so he must go there and plead with him to have his old position back, but it would be foolish, would it not, to neglect to plan for every eventuality? For if Mr Greenhaugh will not have him and Owen will not seek elsewhere, and indeed we have no money for another prenticeship, then he may as well help me at my work, and be, so to speak, my own prentice.

Your prentice? How may a woman have a prentice? It is ridiculous.

No more ridiculous than a boy of Owen's age moping around the house praying and reading the Bible because he has no position. Have you seen my conserve of bugloss, husband? I am sure it was here a year or two since.

Just then the door opens and Owen comes in. Seeing us both looking at him, he shrugs and makes a great show of rubbing at his arms and shivering. It is like to snow, I doubt, says he. I never was so cold in my life. What, is the fire not lit?

We cannot afford a fire in the daytime, Owen, I tell him sternly, or at least, not until – What of Mr Greenhaugh? Did you ask him to give you back your prenticeship?

He was out, Owen says. I waited for him an hour, and talked to Susan, and so departed.

How out? say I. Why was he not in his workshop, a master tailor like him? Or if he was not, there must have been some journeyman there you could have spoken to about it.

What Susan? says my wife.

He had some business with the Guild, so Susan told me, But I made her promise to be sure and let him know that I had called and that I repented of whatever it was he thought me to be guilty of, and humbly besought my old position back, if it did not too much inconvenience him and he had not given the work to someone less Godfearing than myself. You have taken all your physic out of the chest, mother. Is someone distempered?

Well, Owen, you always said you liked to hear of my potions and cures, so I thought... But what of this Susan? Is she one of those females Mr Greenhaugh wrote of in his letter, that you were making yourself so troublesome to?

Oh, females, says he, getting down on his knees beside his mother, Susan is no female, and besides there were no others, but only her. You know what Mr Greenhaugh is like. Show me the potions, mother. What is in this one? It looks like a heap of dead flies.

But I meant to write of botching.

Chapter XLIX
The Author Senselessly Distracted by Bluebottles

My son Owen being in the room as I write (for he is there most of the day at present) I thought to ask him for the cloth my wife very wrongly gave him to blow his nose in, meaning to practise the botching I started writing of in my previous chapter. For, said I, this is a skill every tailor must learn, and it may be that Mr Greenhaugh's dismissing you was partly on account of your deficiencies in such skills.

Owen is sitting on the floor among my wife's jars, vials and boxes, which she has not put back in the chest since last she took them out, nor removed to the pump for washing, but has charged Owen with the inventorizing of them as the first task of what she is pleased to call his apprenticeship. This task goes forward very slowly, for many of the receptacles bear no inscription, or the inscription is illegible, or else she has told him she does not believe it, and so Owen must open each one and inform himself of the contents. The opening is sometimes troublesome, especially when the bottles are old and grimy; then he wrenches and strains at the stopper, or beats it against the wall, uttering between gritted teeth his Puritanical imprecations: O Lord I thank thee for this test of my industriousness, and O Lord I rejoice in my struggle, and Give me strength, O God, to do thy work. (At the beginning, he presented one to me to test whether age and wisdom might prevail where youth and vigour were thwarted, but I told him to leave me be, for I had writing to do and was no apothecary, neither master nor prentice.) After opening them, he must ascertain the contents, which my wife tells him must be first by sight, then by smell, then by touch, and finally by taste, and has made him remember a catechism of qualities thus:

Q. What is its colour?
Q. Is it liquid or solid?
Q. If liquid, is it viscous or flowing?
Q. If solid, is it dry or moist, soft or granular?
Q. Is its smell fruity or flowery, acrid or fœtid?
Q. Is it warm or cool to the touch?
Q. Is its taste sour, salty, sweet, bitter or burning?
&c.

Each of these qualities he must record with pen and paper, and he has taken some of my ink in a dish for the purpose (for I would not have him returning to my desk to dip his pen with each new bottle he opened), and he is to present her at the end of the day with their descriptions that she may identify them and thus know the extent of her store. But often when I look up I see him sitting crosslegged with the bottle on his lap (proving that he has acquired one tailorly habit at least) and staring at the dents he has made in the plaster of the wall by striking of bottles, his lips moving like one in prayer. At other times, he paces about the room or comes and looks over my shoulder as I write, which discommodes me mightily. Then he returns to his labour, which he cannot do silently, but mutters his catechism as he works: What is its colour? Green, no, blueish with somewhat of green in it. Viscous, warm. Flowery, or more like leaves than flowers. Sour and burning both, *&c.*

He looks up when I address him, the bottle in one hand and his pen in the other. What cloth? says he.

It was a cloth of mine I used for practising stitches, and which you took for your affliction of the nose.

I know not, says he. What shall I write of the bluebottles? They are not so blue as they were in life, but more nearly black. And I would call them dry and granular, but there is a little fluid with them also, which (sniffing) I take to be some spirits or strong waters they were formerly suspended in that is now mostly dried out. Shall I call them moist? Father?

But seeing me regard him reprovingly, he drops his pretence of busyness.

Affliction of the nose? says he, shaking himself a little like one roused from abstraction. Surely that was yourself, father? I had naught but a little stuffing cold, which the Lord took from me in good time. And I do not recall any cloth.

This is too bad, Owen. The cloth was only lent you, and I need it now for my book. Is it not on your person?

He looks at himself, raising his arms as if to examine underneath them, then makes a great show of patting his clothing. I have it not, says he at last. Indeed, now I think of it, I believe it went in Mr Greenhaugh's chest, for the botching. But I meant, father, to speak to you about this book of yours.

This is impossible, say I. I cannot write if my own family, who should be a support to me in my labours, my own family, my wife and child, do everything in their power to hinder me. And it was my wife, mark you, my wife, who –

Owen takes the jar of bluebottles from his lap with thumb and forefinger and places it carefully on the floor beside him. This book of yours, he says again, which my mother would have me read. I have tried to obey her as a dutiful son must, for we read in Scripture –

I know what we read in Scripture, Owen.

To say truth, he says, seeing the last few chapters lying readiest to hand, I started with those, and I must say, father, I was greatly disturbed by them. I say not they are blasphemous, but, but... (He reaches again for the jar of bluebottles, then seems to notice what he is doing and puts it back on the floor.) There are passages in them that seem to me to be departures from your tailoring matter, and, besides that – I mean no disrespect, father – I was not altogether sure they were, well, true.

You doubt me, Owen? My word, my written word, the word of your father? First you read the book when you have no business to do it – yes, I know (seeing him about to speak, and raising my hand to stop him), your mother told you to, but it was against my will, who am your father as I said before. Then you start at the wrong place, and lament that you cannot understand it (raising my hand again). Then you call me, the father who begot you, a liar. And to cap it all you have taken my cloth and given it to Mr Greenhaugh, without which I can write no more and may as well go and be a tailor myself, for someone must keep us from starving.

He has the cap off the bluebottles again and is stirring them with his finger. Seeing that he means not to speak further unless he has to, I continue.

Well, Owen, I have reproved you as you deserve. But what, for the sake of argument, did you mean by that remark, impertinent as it was? The remark, that is, about the book's being untrue.

You said you spoke with the Lord Protector, says he.

What of it? The Lord Protector – though he was not Protector at the time I first spoke with him – the Lord General was not a man to bar his doors, but would dispense his small beer and bread-and-butter to any that wished to advise him. I met him often after that, and he was always glad to listen to me. Besides, I have spoken with many others in my life, as I told you, with kings even.

But you said Ireton was there, and Cromwell's son Henry, that was governor in Ireland after.

Where else should they be but at his table, being his son-in-law and his son?

But, said he, you are only my father. I mean... In any case, if you truly met with the Protector, you should have reproved him for the wicked man he was. For did he not kill the King?

Now this is very confusing, Owen. It is not long since that you were lamenting the passing of that Commonwealth of yours, and now you reproach the leader of it, and for killing of a King that your own faction overthrew. Besides, it was not the Lord General who killed the King, but others of his party. Cromwell was a worthy man for one of his persuasion, for he always listened to me with respect, and I believe he would have saved His Majesty if he could.

The minister says that the King would have realized his errors and come to the true church in time, and should never have been beheaded. We Presbyterians were no disloyal subjects, only we could not abide bishops. But this Cromwell you write of so fawningly was a tyrant and a great enemy to the Presbyterians, though he did good service to the cause in winning many battles against the armies of idolatry. And another thing, father, in the earlier chapter you wrote (only I read it after) you said that you spoke with Mr Love, that he visited you in the prison when you were confined there.

That is so.

And this was Mr Christopher Love, the great martyr for truth and freedom? It must have been he, for you said he spoke Welsh (only I could not understand those parts), and Mr Love was indeed a Welshman. It was bad enough that you wrote unkindly of Dr Bastwick, who lost his ears, but Mr Love lost his very head in the cause of godliness because he resisted the tyrant Cromwell, and you show him laughing and drinking beer and trying to deceive you. Mr Love was the purest and holiest man of our time, and died on the scaffold after making a noble sermon, which I have read, for the minister lent it to me. Besides which, I have read his sermon on hell, which is very bracing and terrible, and no man could have spoke it who told lies while drinking beer by the fireside. And Susan says that besides all this, Mr Love was a prophet and foresaw many things that have come to pass and are still to come.

A prophet!

Well, he mutters, I am not sure I believe that part, though it is Susan who says it.

He is abashed now at having spoken so much and so thoughtlessly, and so says nothing for a while, but looks about him at the wilderness of bottles, many of them still unstoppered and giving forth a great disharmony of odours, fruity, flowery, acrid and fœtid.

How shall I describe the bluebottles? he asks finally.

What is this? Why should they need any description? Your mother knows they are bluebottles. It is only the things she has forgotten about that need be described. I swear, Owen, you are as ignorant of writing as you are of everything else.

Chapter L
Remember

My son, I was at Tower Hill on that hazy August day, among a crowd of people who were loosening their collars and unfastening their buttons as if oppressed by something they scarcely knew was there, for the sun was more felt than seen. I stood for hours watching the stage where all would take place, believing that it would happen every moment and that it would not happen at all, that its happening was a sort of dream that all of us were dreaming at the same time, and that if any one of us woke and cried out in protest there would be no dream and no death. I was not one of the foremost, but I saw well everything that passed, for the scaffold was not built at the highest part but on the flatter ground a little below it, and I was at the same height as the platform, which was thickly scattered with straw like the floor of a stable. I watched that emptiness while men and women talked all round me, merriment and fear contesting in their voices. The scaffold was bright even at those times when it was dull everywhere else: though it was naught but straw and wood and air, it seemed full of some holy meaning, and my mind worried at it as a man worries at a passage in Scripture he understands not. Every now and then there were movements among the crowd, as if the execution party had arrived; there would be a gasp as the rumour spread, and a laugh when it was seen to be false. Then we would go back to loosening of collars and not believing in any of it.

I was not among the crowd on that bitter January day two years before, waiting for the King to appear through the window of the Banqueting House and step on to the black-draped scaffold erected in front of it. I had seen it many times in my visions, and had no wish to see it more.

My son, I did not notice at first when they finally arrived. If there was a commotion among the crowd or a recurrence of the general sighing, I missed it, for my thoughts had turned inward and no doubt I was more than half-asleep where I stood. When I came to myself, half the party were already on the scaffold, and the others were climbing the steps to join them somewhat haphazardly; indeed, as I watched, I saw one go back down again and speak to another at the foot, as if he had forgot something that must be done on the ground. Nor could I tell easily which of the persons was which. I had thought the prisoners would be shackled and the executioner wearing a mask, but apart from the soldiers with their halberds and helmets, I saw only a group of men, wearing hats and cloaks despite the heat, moving confusedly and talking among themselves. One or two more went down the steps and stayed there at the bottom. Then I began to distinguish one from another; a burly fellow with a great bushy moustache whom I had mistaken for a soldier was carrying, not a halberd, but a long axe with a great blade, much bigger than any I had seen used on the farm for chopping wood. He looked about him for somewhere to put it, since it was evident he had work to do before using it. Finally he leaned it head-down against one of the posts at the side of the scaffold, but it fell, which he did not regard, but went to help a couple of others with a large square burden that I understood was the block. This they hauled to one end of the scaffold and adjusted it several times, for it seemed to be never quite positioned as

The King's hair long and soft, his nose straight and delicate, the eyes brown as a sparrow's, no other part of his person visible. The crowd steaming, stamping their feet. The head hesitating, seeming to turn back, as if speaking perhaps to someone in the room behind, as who should say, is this the place, is now the hour? Not through fear but knowing that on this of all days proper ceremony must be observed, for any clumsiness or slip will be remembered for ever.

they wanted it. Then the executioner went over to another man who stood there and took from him a bucket. There was sawdust in it, as I could tell by his scattering a few handfuls in the general vicinity of the block, which fell like a mist in the hazy air.

I recognized Mr Love by his stocky figure and by the important way he had of standing with his thin legs apart. So I had seen him in the Keeper's Lodge at Newgate Prison, and as soon as I knew him, I made out the face I remembered, ruddy cheeked and bright-eyed as if still flushed with firelight and beer. He wore the black cloak of a minister, and there were three others with him wearing the same, whom I asked my neighbours about; they told me these were not to be beheaded but were fellow ministers the condemned man had brought with him to comfort him. And that man who hangs back, said they, is Mr Gibbons, another conspirator, and he is to be done away with after. This Gibbons stood at the top of the steps, not as one afraid but as too modest to put himself forward when his fellow was at the heart of things, for Mr Love now stood in the centre of the scaffold and all others had shrunk away to the sides, save that a man approached him now and spoke seriously with him for a while, and then they shook hands, and the man stepped back again. This, I learned, was the Sheriff, Mr Titchburn, and I saw him bend his head and speak to the men beside him as if he had business that must be attended to presently.

When the Sheriff retreated, Mr Love straightened his shoulders and doffed his hat sweepingly. Beloved Christians, said he, I am this day made a spectacle unto God, angels and men, and among men I am made a grief to the godly, a laughing-stock to the wicked and a gazing-stock to all, yet, blessed be God, not a terror to myself. Although there be but little between me and death, yet this bears up my heart, that there is little between me and heaven.

Angels, thought I, why does he speak of angels? It was I who told him at Newgate of my meeting with an angel.

Isaac said of himself that he was old and yet he knew not the day of his death, but I cannot say thus. I am young, and yet I know the day of my death, and I know the kind of my death also, and the place of my death also. It is such a kind of death as two famous preachers of the Gospel were put to before me, John the Baptist and Paul the Apostle. They were both beheaded: ye have mention of the one in Scripture story and of the other in evangelical history... Beloved, I am this day to make a double exchange: I am changing a pulpit for a scaffold and a scaffold for a throne; and I might add a third: I am changing this numerous multitude on Tower Hill for the innumerable company of angels in the holy hill of Zion, and I am changing a guard of soldiers for a guard of angels. This scaffold is the best pulpit I ever preached in, for in the church pulpit, God through his grace made me an instrument to bring others to heaven, but in this pulpit he will bring me to heaven. These are the last words that I shall speak in this world, and it may be this last speech upon a scaffold may bring God more glory than many sermons in a pulpit. Before I lay down my neck upon the block, I shall lay open my case unto the people that hear me this day, and in doing so I shall avoid all rancour, all bitterness of spirit, animosity and revenge.

So, my son, did Mr Love speak: angels, again, always angels. All the time of his sermon, while he was vindicating himself of the charges against him, I observed that the sun did not shine. The day was growing cooler. I saw the people beside me look around uneasily as if they felt it, too. Only Mr Love seemed unaware of it, waving his hat to illustrate his points, firstly, secondly, thirdly, fourthly, fifthly. His voice was as firm as ever, his face ruddier still.

Such a one as I, born in an obscure country in Wales, of obscure parents, that God should look upon me and single me out from among all my kindred, single me out to be an object of his everlasting love; when for the first fourteen years of my life I never heard a sermon, and yet in the fifteenth year of my life, God through his grace did

As for the people, says His Majesty, truly, I desire their liberty and freedom as much as anybody whomsoever; but I must tell you that their liberty and freedom consist in having of government those laws by which their life and their goods may be most their own. It is not for having share in government, sirs; that is nothing pertaining to them; a subject and a sovereign are clear different things. And therefore until they do that, I mean that you do put the people in that liberty, as I say, certainly they will never enjoy themselves. Sirs, it was for this that now I am come here. If I would have given way to an arbitrary way, for to have all laws changed according to the power of the sword, I needed not to have come here; and therefore I tell you (and I pray God it be not laid to your charge) that I am the martyr of the people.

The King has suffered all his life from an impediment that caused him to speak haltingly, but here on the scaffold his voice is firm and unhesitating.

convert me, and I here speak it without vanity (what should a dying man be proud of?), for these twenty years, though I am accused of many scandalous evils, I speak it to the praise and glory of my God, for these twenty years God hath kept me, I have not fallen into a scandalous sin; I have laboured to keep a good conscience from my youth up. I magnify his grace, that he hath not only made me a Christian but made me a minister, judged me faithful and put me into the ministry, and though the office be trodden upon and disgraced, yet it is my glory that I die a despised minister. I had rather be a preacher in a pulpit than a prince upon a throne. I had rather be an instrument to bring souls to heaven than to have all the nations to bring in tribute to me. I am not only a minister and a preacher but a martyr too, I speak it without vanity.

The day was no longer hazy, but shadowy. I knew it was noon when Mr Love began to speak, but no one can listen to a sermon long without losing his place in time. There was a disturbance of the people at one point, for something he said, and they had to be calmed, and twice he was interrupted by the Sheriff: there was another man to execute after, and the business must be finished by six o'clock. I knew not how late it was when he turned to the Sheriff and said, May I pray?

Yes, but consider the time.

Mr Love knelt down on the straw and bowed his head. He was silent a long time, so that I thought his prayer would be an inward one, but then he began to speak and his voice was as loud as before.

Lord Jesus, receive my spirit, and Lord Jesus stand by thy dying servant, who hath endeavoured in his lifetime to stand for thee. Lord, hear, pardon all his infirmities, wipe away his iniquities by the blood of Christ, wipe off reproaches from his name, wipe off guilt from his person and receive him pure and spotless and blameless before thee in love. And all this we beg for the sake of Jesus Christ. *Amen.*

He rose to his feet. One of the ministers who was there on the scaffold with him stepped forward, and they clasped hands.

You make a Christian end, I hope, said the other, his voice raised so that all might hear.

Aye, I bless God. Then Love turned to the Sheriff. I thank you for this kindness, said he. Where is the executioner?

When the whiskered man came forward, Love said, Art thou the officer?

Yes.

Then, one by one he took leave of all those who were on the scaffold with him. I thought he would shake Sheriff Titchburn's hand, but he kissed it. Turning himself about to the executioner, he said, Friend, are all things in readiness?

Yes, sir, replied the executioner.

He took off his cloak and hat, unbraced his doublet and gave it to a friend, and then pulled out a red scarf from his pocket and gave it to the executioner, saying,

The executioner is terrible in his black mask, like a headless man himself. Seeing him trying the edge of the axe, the King says, Hurt not the axe that will hurt me. He turns to the Bishop and asks for his white satin nightcap. I go says he, from a corruptible to an incorruptible crown, where no disturbances can be; no disturbances in the world. He asks the executioner, Is my hair well? He takes off his cloak and hands his pendant of St George to the Bishop, then taking off his doublet, he puts on his cloak again, and looking upon the block, says to the executioner, You must set it fast.

It is fast, sir.

It might have been a little Higher.

It can be no higher, sir.

When I put out my hands this way, then -

Then having said a few words to himself, as he stands, with hands and eyes lifted up, he stoops down and lays his neck upon the block; and the executioner, seeing the hair coming out from under his cap, tucks it back in again, whereupon the King, thinking he is going to strike, bids him, Stay for the sign.

Yes, I will, says he, an it please Your Majesty.

Remember, says the King.

My son, how can I remember what I never witnessed?

I was not there to see the axe fall and his blood spurt out, which I assure you it did, a veritable fountain, his heart having so much vigour. You are a tailor as I am; our cutting is done on the shopboard and not the scaffold, and the instruments of it are shears and scissor, whose blades are so puny that each needs another up against it to sever the fibres effectually, and this is the only raw edge we see in our days' labour, the threads and thrums of cloth raggedly

Dispose of this upon the block as thou think it convenient. Which, accordingly, he did, spreading it upon the sawdust and laying it upon the block. Then Mr Love put his hand in his pocket and took out some object wrapped in white paper, and gave it to the executioner, saying, Friend, here is three pieces for thee. Do thy office and I beseech God to forgive thee as I freely do. Then Mr Love kneeled down and laid his neck upon the block, and sitting up again, said, Friend, upon my next lying down, when I lift up my left hand do thy office.

When the man raised the axe above his head, I found I was shivering. It was cold for August, and a great cloud had been rising up from the west all the time of Mr Love's sermon. At the moment the axe fell this cloud covered the sky directly above us, so that it became dark for a little time.

protruding when we have cut it. And after such cutting, my son, the raw edges must be finished by sewing them over again, and thus it is also with a severed head, for when the body is taken away, the head must be sewn back on before it may be buried, and yet as Hugh Jones said, once any material has been cut, no tailor, however skilful, can truly make it good again. He said also that every word has another beneath it, and would no doubt have insisted that re-membering is the replacement or readhesion of a member, but I cannot think this is what His Majesty meant by the word, a sewing on again of what has been severed, for it is too mean a business for such a mighty spirit. My son, when your grandfather died, the word in his mouth was stranger still, being *Woolach.* It may be that the dying have their own language that we are not yet ready to understand, so that this *Remember* of His Majesty's may have some different meaning altogether from what it signifies in the mouths of the living. But no doubt he did indeed mean me to recall his death as I do that of my father when there was no longer air enough in the world to sustain him; this is no easy matter for a prophet, for whom time is not as it is for other men. I saw this death before it happened as clearly as I see it afterwards, so that I cannot tell now whether I behold it in a forward or a back stitch of my memory. Nevertheless, it is not for me to dispute the King's command, but I must try to obey it, and so must you, my son.

Remember, says the King.

He stretches forth his hands -

Chapter LI
The Lesser and Greater Botching Distinguished

I now perceive a deficiency in my chapter of botching, for I wrote only of cabbage and sewing on of patches, my reasoning being that it is better to start any explanation of complicated matters with their simplest aspects (only I did not even finish my treatment of those). Thus I have given the impression that botching is naught but a mending of tears and a filling up of holes, a making good, that is, of things that are old and worn and damaged by the accidents of existence. This is to take a garment that has become less itself over the years, and restore it to its former nature, and it is trivial work, such as any housewife might do. If a tailor also performs this lesser botching at times, the work that is more proper to his station is what I shall call the greater botching, which is the taking of something and making it into something else. Even my son Owen, that least tailorly of tailors, showed an understanding of this greater botching a while back when he said to me that every man was making his cloak into a coat, though what he really meant was that they were paying Mr Greenhaugh to do it for them. For it is one of God's mercies to the craft that nothing we do is ever final, and thus a cloak may become a coat or a coat a cloak, a gown may become a petticoat, a petticoat a shirt, a shirt may become lining, and lining may end as cabbage for the patching of cloaks, coats, gowns, petticoats, shirts or linings as the case may be. The same piece of cloth may change garments half a dozen times, and change sex into the bargain. But if the lesser botching requires a perfect memory for the size and shapes of odd bits of cloth, the greater demands more formidable mental powers, for in every garment that passes before you, you must see all the others, both those it has been and those it may be in the future. Thus, instead of remembering, the skill of the greater botcher is both in dismembering and in re-membering what he has previously dismembered. Sleeves and legs come and go, hems are taken in and let out again, seams are unpicked and resewn, gussets are stitched into plackets, waists narrowed and widened, inches cut out and added on. Truly we may say of tailoring as the Scripture says of the making of books that it hath no end, save at the Day of Judgement when all things must be concluded.

I rose this morning much heartened by my reflections on the greater botching and ready to begin a more particular exposition of it, only to find Owen at the desk before me with a page of my writing in one hand and my small scissors in the other.

How now, Owen, say I, you are up betimes. You never wont to rise this early when you lived here formerly, or not without a deal of shaking. But I am glad to see you showing such application. Are you studying my chapter of plackets and gussets, and trying out the instructions for yourself? You will do better with a real piece of cloth than an imaginary one.

What say you, father? says he, holding the paper before his eyes and frowning at it.

An imaginary piece of cloth, for I see you are cutting at the empty air –

He begins cutting at the paper, and has taken three good snips before I understand what he is about and rush to take it from him. Owen, what are you doing? My book! It is paper, not cloth.

Leave me be, father, you will tear it.

And indeed it has begun to tear at the end of the long jagged cut he was making. But I have it in my own hand now, holding it on the other side of my body so that he cannot get at it, which seems, now I think of it, to be at odds with my paternal dignity.

Why, this is not even a chapter of cutting, or one of my more tailorly chapters at all! It is the chapter I wrote lately of Mr Love's execution. What were you doing with it, Owen? Are you mad? Or did it offend you in some way that I wrote of the death of such a man, whom you very wrongly regard as a godly martyr? The chapter was in some measure intended for you, as a means, a means of informing you, of explaining to you what –

My mother, says he putting down the scissors, is dissatisfied with my work as an apothecary. She says my listing of qualities is amiss, that I call a thing sour when it is bitter and salty when it is burning. She says further that I have spilled too many drops of her medicines on the floor, wasting their precious substance and polluting the matting. I told her I cannot be content with such labour, for I am a man of the spirit and this is worldly business. We quarrelled over it yesterday when you were out for your walk.

She said naught of it to me.

No doubt she is ashamed that she tried to force me into so unbecoming a vocation. I can never be happy with dabbling among pickled insects and the juices of weeds, and trying by such means to thwart God's will. You heard what she said, that diseases were of the world and therefore the cures for them should be of the world also. It would be a sin in me to live by such a doctrine, even if the work gave me pleasure, which it does not. I can still taste some of those tinctures now. Sour or bitter or burning, I know not which, but they are noxious on the tongue.

This is nothing to the purpose, Owen. I am fully in accord that you are not suited to be an apothecary. All the more reason why you should return to Mr Greenhaugh and take up tailoring again. But why do you cut my chapter? This is madness.

He gathers himself together like one who knows he must make a complicated disquisition.

When I resolved to give up apothecarying, I took up your book again with the intention of obeying my mother and learning what I could of tailoring from it. But it is hard to find the tailoring matter among all the other things. Not that I reprove you for it – no (seeing me about to speak), far from it, father, for the other matter is in some ways more... interesting than the mere writing of needles and stitches. But, the truth is, the more I read, the more I felt a want of order in the words. There is a chapter here and a chapter there as the fancy takes you –

Owen, the writer finds the order in his words afterwards. The first writing is, as it were, the weaving of the cloth, and later there is cutting and stitching to be done. In any case, when I have finished the book I shall take it to Mr Lowndes at the White Lion, and he will have suggestions of his own about which chapters should be left in and which cut out. For him, Owen, a book is what it can never be to one such as myself, a commodity, and he knows what will sell and what will not.

As I say this, I think of Mr Lowndes sitting sadly among his piles of unsold and unsellable books, *An Anti-Brekekekex-Coax-Coax, An Account of the Last Hours of the Late Renowned Oliver, Lord Protector &c, &c,* and lamenting the hard times in the book trade.

Mr Lowndes, say I, will cut and stitch my words, and at the end of it there will be a true book, with covers and title page and fine black type, a handsome book that the public cannot help but covet. For Mr Lowndes is a master of his trade as Mr Greenhaugh is of his.

I was reading your book, says he, and thinking that this and that might be better ordered. And when I came to your chapter of Mr Love's death, it was as if I heard God speaking to me, or as if an angel appeared at my side.

Now, Owen –

No, father, let me speak, I pray you. I heard the words in my head: YOU ARE AN AUTHOR. For, do you not see, I have been trying to make myself into a tailor to please you, knowing the substance of a tailor was not in me? It was like trying to make a coat when you have not enough cloth for it. And then I tried to make myself into an apothecary to please my mother, knowing that for me it would always seem more proper work for women and those of weak faith. I followed you in this, and my mother in that, because it is proper for a son to follow after his parents, but after all, father, you are an author as much as a tailor.

Well, I will not deny that what you say is more lucid than most of your utterances, and more pleasing, too. It is true that I am an author of a sort, having writ books and published them. But, Owen, that was because God required me to do it. I must be an author because I was a prophet, and in these times the best way to prophesy to the nation is by writing of books (thinking, as I speak, of Mr Lowndes: *The public will not read as they did formerly*).

But God has instructed me to write also. And because my writing must be for the glory of God, I shall write an account of my own life from infancy on, telling of my sufferings at the hands of my fellows and my family, pardon me, of the trials of a godly youth growing up among heath–, among those who have not received the blessing of God's light. It is true that little has happened to me outwardly yet, save sitting on a shopboard and being beaten by Mr Greenhaugh, but the best writing, it seems to me, is of inward things. The journey of a soul, father, or the struggles of a soul against temptation and the devil, or the growth of a soul from pettiness and worldly concerns to its full flowering into the sunshine of faith and fulfilment. A tailor only keeps his customers warm and covers their nakedness, soberly or immodestly according to his inclination, but a true Christian author may act as a beacon to them in their wanderings through the darkness. It is as good as being a minister, no, better, for it reaches more of one's fellow men, and touches them more deeply, and in the quiet and loneliness of their own chambers where no sermon can be heard. What a privilege that my words and my sufferings can go out and find them there. Father, I could hardly sleep last night for thinking of it, and as soon as it grew light –

You rose, say I, and began to cut up my book.

He stretches his hand out and begins to gather up the papers, then looks through them with a puzzled expression, as if searching for the one he cut, which I still have in my hand. He reads a few lines of the topmost page, then puts them all down again.

Oh, says he. Well, father, I thought to learn what I could of authorship before I began my own writings, for truly it is a special grace that the Lord has provided me, in my own house, a species of author from whom to learn some of the skills of my profession. Therefore I resolved to continue reading your book, and I began this morning with your chapter of Mr Love, whom I greatly honour both for his life and the noble manner of his death. Most of it I knew before, having read his final sermon as I told you, but nevertheless I was moved to read it again, and it seemed to me now, with my new eyes of an author, that Mr Love might have been talking of myself, how he was born in an obscure country –

You were born in London.

I am Welsh, anyway, or of Welsh blood, which makes me somewhat obscure. And how God converted him in his fifteenth year and singled him out from his fellows, because it was in my fifteenth year that I was converted and I am sixteen now, though I tried to lead a godly life before that, yet I had not the certainty of my salvation until I was fourteen, all which you shall read in my book. And how he had rather be a minister in a pulpit than a prince upon a throne, only for myself I had rather be an author. The tears came into my eyes as I was reading it. But it was vexing at the same time, for, even though I knew the story I could hardly make out what was in it. It was all jumbled up with some other matter, of the late King, and *his* execution. Look.

He looks at the topmost page again and is about to hand it to me when he remembers the page I am holding and gestures towards it.

You see, father, where I was cutting. I was trying to cut the narrative of the King away from that of Mr Love, and keep them separate.

Why, Owen, they are intertwined.

He frowns at the page in front of him, and his fingers move as if he were still wielding the scissors.

They are intertwined, Owen, because the one story makes me think of the other, for thoughts do not pass through the mind singly, but grow round each other like ivy round the trunk of an oak, and thus I wrote it as I thought it, interconnectedly. When Mr Lowndes receives the manuscript he will know what to do. Have you never looked at a printed book? The body of the text appears in large type running down the inside of the page, but there are margins, too, which the author uses for scriptural references, translations of foreign words, notes on this matter or that, and any of those intertwining thoughts of his that will not fit into the body of the chapter. Mr Lowndes will take my narrative of the King's death and put it into the margin wherever he can find room for it, using a smaller type so that the reader is not excessively distracted, for this is a part of his trade.

When I am an author, Owen says, looking with longing at the scissors lying on the desk next to his hand, I shall write only one thing at a time.

Chapter LII
A Basket of Summer Fruit

You were a boy then, Owen, screaming and quarrelling with your sister Megan, that is your sister Willis now, and your mother trying to quieten you, for, she said, your father must have silence to write. I wrote every day, my book growing shapelessly, an armhole, a skirt, a gusset, not knowing what kind of garment it would be when it was finished. To say truth, I do not think your squalling and lamentations much disturbed me, for I had grown used to them over the years, and besides I knew not what I wrote. I was not even sure that writing was what I was doing, or that it was myself doing it. I listened to God's word and transcribed it while you and she fought, or while the two of you played at jackstones and cherry pit, for you were not then too godly to play, nor too manly to play with a maid when there were none of your fellows to play with. I was fevered with writing, yet at rest in it; I was in my screaming room in Blackfriars but I dwelt at the same time in the silence of my words. What was it to me, then, when the sounds of the room became different, when there was a disturbance in the vicinity of the door and the children's voices were put to flight by deeper, more measured ones? But there, when I made to dip my pen, was my wife putting forward her hand as if to stop me, and when I looked up, her face had the frozen expression of one who would utter a warning, but may not.

Husband, here are some gentlemen to speak with you.

They looked too tall for the room, though I suppose only the younger one was above ordinary height. Still, it was strange to see two men standing there, both plainly but not cheaply attired in broad-brimmed black hats and good frieze cloaks. The tall man took off his hat, looked about him for a moment, then began turning it round and round in his hands.

He was about five-and-thirty, with a broad, small-featured face on the verge of losing what handsomeness it had had, and stood like one used to vigorous action though he was a little heavy. His friend was older, with bandy legs, which I noticed when he lifted his feet to avoid treading on you, Owen. His nose was crooked, too, and his eyes had a squint, so that he looked like a man who had been put together badly.

I am William Satterthwaite, said the first man in a milder voice than I expected, and this gentleman is Mr Samuel Starling. We have come, Mr Evans, because we have heard you may be able to enlighten us about – he leaned a little closer and nodded encouragingly, as if he expected me to understand what he was saying before he had even spoken it – about a basket of summer fruit.

What is this? said I. Who are you? (feeling foolish as soon as I said it, because he had just told me who they were).

We are friends.

He said it as though *friends* had a special meaning to him. It was Mr Starling who nodded this time, in token that the meaning was familiar to him also. Both of them then looked hard at my wife, but she did not see them, for she was shepherding her children away from their feet towards the far corner of the room.

This, I said, is my wife (feeling more foolish still for saying it, but they were staring as if they had never seen a wife before, so that I thought she needed explaining). But tell me, gentlemen, how do you know about this basket of fruit? Did Mr Peters tell you of it, or Mr Lilly?

Hugh Peters was chaplain to the Lord General Cromwell, and William Lilly called himself a prophet, and I had shown my book to them both.

Mr Peters, said Mr Satterthwaite, is no friend of ours, nor Mr Lilly neither. Bur we have read your book nevertheless, for it has travelled further than you think. Mr Starling?

Mr Satterthwaite laughed,

and Mr Starling gave a smile that showed his upper teeth only and yet made him look unexpectedly boyish, and reached inside his cloak.

Here you are, Mr Evans, said he, looking at my wife again (who still had her back to him).

I took the papers and read the title page: A VOICE FROM HEAVEN TO THE COMMONWEALTH OF ENGLAND writ out in my own hand as fair as I had been able to, with a fine flourish on the capital Ns especially. For, Owen, a book need not go to the White Lion or to any other house in Paul's Yard to be distributed among the people. It wants only patience and a good supply of pens, ink and paper to copy it out as many times you have friends to read it.

Many of us, said Mr Satterthwaite, have read this book, and marvelled much at what we learned from it. It has been flying about, you might say (he smiled again) in our circles, and let me tell you it has caused a great stir there.

You have not the final book, gentlemen, said I and leafed through it, mortified to see how much that I now thought essential to my matter was not there, as if someone had torn those pages out.

Nevertheless, Mr Satterthwaite said, it made us very joyful to read it.

Very joyful, Mr Starling said.

And what are you writing now? Mr Satterthwaite continued, gesturing at my desk where the pen lay across a half-written sheet and had marked it with a small oblique dask of ink. – Is it another book, of the same kind as the first?

It is the same book, sir, for it is not finished yet. Thank you, gentlemen, for bringing my pages back. It will save me much labour, for when I have made the changes and additions, I shall have another complete copy to give out. (Saying which I cast my eyes down upon the desk, by which I hoped they would understand that I wished to return to my work.)

Well, said Mr Satterthwaite, and nodded again. It has been an honour, sir, to meet the author of these words. And Mrs Evans, he said, bowing to my wife, for she had left the children now, sensing a departure. A basket of summer fruit, he added, chuckling and shaking his head, as if admiring the words for an ingenious jest.

He walked past Mr Starling to the door, and my wife hastened after to open it for him. I thought Mr Starling would follow, but he looked at me with his head on one side and showed his upper teeth again. Come and take a glass of wine with us, said he. It will do you good, for you are very sad.

It is true, Owen, I had been sad a long time, but I hardly knew it myself. I must write whether sad or not, and I pushed the sadness away with scratching and dipping of my pen and muttering of words under my breath and searching the perfect copy of the Scriptures I kept in my mind for the right verse for my purposes, but as soon as I left off these tasks for a moment I felt the sadness again, a numb feeling in my forehead and cheekbones and a heaviness in the eyes where I would not allow any tears to form.

Which was in the Mitre in the Strand the day I was arrested.

Now, seated in a private room in the tavern, I raised the glass of sack to my nose and thought, as I had done the last time I tasted a fine old wine, that it had the smell of books.

What ails you, Mr Evans? said Mr Satterthwaite.

Why, said I, I cannot get my manuscript printed.

Then I told them how I had been walking from Whitehall to Charing Cross one day last July, meditating upon the eighth and ninth chapters of the Book of Amos, when I looked up and realized that I was passing the very spot where they had built the scaffold two and a half years earlier: where His Majesty had stood before the people and found his tongue loosened, so that he could speak clearly and boldly of the difference between a subject and a sovereign, and between a corruptible and incorruptible crown, where he had taken off his cloak and doublet, knelt down, tucked his hair into his nightcap, and stretched forth his hands. Now it was sunny, not freezing, and there was no scaffold in front of the Banqueting House, nor did I know which of the many windows he had stepped out of. But as I stood and watched, I heard a voice coming from the place:

Be stirring in what thou art about.

God was speaking to me again as he had spoken to his prophet Amos, asking, *What seest thou? And Amos replied, A basket of summer fruit.*

I saw the berries piled up in the basket, bruised by their own weight and leaking red juice, for the fruits of summer are cherries, strawberries, raspberries, blackcurrants, redcurrants, all of which are soft and bleed readily. The blood of the King was as nothing to this bleeding of fruit, yet it was a pleasing harvest, very delicious to him who tasted it. The generation of the world was ripe in sin, ready to be cut down. And God said further to Amos, *The end is come upon my people, I will not pass by them any more.*

I hurried home, took pen and ink and began to write of the eighth and ninth chapters of Amos, for I realized now that every word in them pertained to England, the Parliament and the King, and only I could explain them. *I saw the LORD standing upon the altar: and he said, Smite the lintel of the door, that the posts may shake: and cut them in the head, all of them; and I will slay the last of them with the sword: he that fleeth of them shall not flee away, and he that escapeth of them shall not be delivered.* This Lord, I saw, was the second King Charles, now rising up after his father was slain to take vengeance upon his murderers. He stands upon the altar, that is, the scaffold, and commands us to smite the lintel, that is, the Speaker of the House, and to slay the Members of Parliament. All these visions were recorded in Scripture: they had happened in another country thousands of years ago, but they were happening still in our times, and to us.

I will not deny, Mr Satterthwaite said, sighing, that there were those among us who were downcast after His Majesty's recent defeat at Worcester. We had thought we should have a new King again very shortly, and now behold him fleeing for his life and the land once again in the hands of his enemies. So you see, Mr Evans, when your book began to be circulated among us, we were much heartened at your prophecies, for you told us all was not lost and the King would indeed return to our shores. If your prophecies could only be circulated throughout the land, then His Majesty's supporters everywhere would feel that same courage you have made us feel.

How may that be? said I, feeling the warmth of the wine rise up inside me.

Mr Starling? Here, said he taking the bag from his friend and putting it on the table in front of me, is forty shillings from His Majesty's Exchequer. Meet me tomorrow in Paul's Yard and we will go and find a publisher.

I raised my glass to them, but said nothing for I was thanking God in my heart, for his providence that had brought it about.

Tell me, said Mr Starling, will your book, when you finish it, name a date for His Majesty's restoration?

I had not thought – I began, and saw a look of disappointment pass across both their faces. Then I remembered the Book of Daniel, *until a time and times and the dividing of time*, and the Book of Revelation, *a time, and times, and half a time*. Why had God put those words in my mind now, and what did they mean? St John also says in Revelation: *The holy city shall they tread under foot forty and two months*. The prophets spoke in mysterious language yet there was always a plain meaning behind or beneath their words for one who had been granted the wisdom to interpret them. *A time* meant one year; *times* meant two years; *the dividing of time*, or *half a time* meant a half-year, which is six months. A time, and times, and half a time was three and a half years or forty-two months from the day the first King Charles lost his head on the scaffold, which was 30th January, 1649.

The date you look for, said I, is later this very year. After the end of July, 1652, look for mishaps to the State's affairs.

Chapter LIII
King Charles His Star

You have seen the moon shining in the daytime. There it is with the clouds flitting round it just as if this were its natural abode, a moon such as you are used to seeing in the night sky, waxing, waning or full as it may be, and yet it has something of the blue of daylight about it and something of the wispiness of clouds, as if it were a moon the sky had made for itself out of its own ethereal substance. I have never seen this without thinking for a moment that it was a blur on my eyes that might be cleared by rubbing at them with the sleeve of my doublet or that it was one of my own daydreams that had slipped outside my mind and floated into the heavens. This is common, but a star in the daylight sky is far stranger. For we are used to beholding stars in multitudes, or if there is only one it hangs low in the evening sky soon to be joined by all its fellows, or in the morning sky soon to be extinguished by the brightness of the sun. But suppose it midday, and a single star directly overhead, not wispy like the moon, but sharp and golden, a pin passing through the centre of the heavens, transfixing all who behold it.

A daylight moon portends common events, but this was the first daylight star in the history of the world, saving only the one which led the wise men to Bethlehem and hung there over the stable both day and night. That star announced a nativity, and so did this, for the year was 1630, the day May 29th, which was the day the Queen gave birth to a son, named Charles after his father. To my great sorrow I was within doors stitching in my master's workshop when this star shone forth and so I never saw it; but there were many in London that day who did, and a poem was writ of it, and presented to the King when he came to Paul's Cross to give thanks for the safe delivery:

When to Paul's Cross the grateful King drew near
A flowing star did in the heavens appear.
Thou that consults with divine mysteries,
Tell me what this bright comet signifies?
Now is there born a valiant Prince i' th' West
That shall eclipse the kingdoms of the East.

We see by this that poets are not to be relied on, for it was a star and not a comet, nor was it flowing but standing still, and in any case it appeared at the Prince's birth and not when the King came to Paul's Cross afterwards (otherwise how could the poet have writ it out fair in time to present it to him on that occasion?); nevertheless, the gist of it is true, and it may be more accurate in the original, which was in Latin, for translations are still less to be relied on than poets. I wish, sir, I had brought this original text with me, for your master would have been able to read it, though I cannot.

The interpreter turned and translated all this for the smiling man who had nodded all the way through my explanation, not so much like one who understood as like one who hears a tune and though he restrains his body from dancing to it yet his head dances a little despite him: I caught a couple of words that I remembered from the poem I had copied down when I wrote my book about this same star: *stella, lucide, princeps*. Yes, thought I, for all I can tell he is rendering my speech faithfully. But how curious it is that some of these words have gone from Latin to English and are now returned to Latin again.

Menasseh Ben Israel more resembled a merchant than what I had supposed a Rabbi to be. He was a man of middling height, solid though not corpulent, well dressed in a black doublet and falling bands. Beneath the large skull-cap his face was somewhat plump in the cheeks, as if he had always eaten well, but his eyes were heavy-lidded as if he stayed up reading late into the night. He had sidelocks and his beard and moustache hung down longer than an Englishman's would, but it was not the great mane I had pictured on a fellow-countryman of Moses and

Abraham. I had thought, too, that the place where I called upon him would be hung with Hebrew scrolls and adorned with candlesticks, that there might be a smell of incense or of bitter herbs in the air, but it was only a plain panelled room with chairs and a desk, equally fitting to a scholar or a man of business.

The interpreter's speech was a long one, which Ben Israel interrupted frequently with questions. Both talked rapidly and excitedly, with many gestures, smiling and frowning by turns. Ben Israel's reply was long also, and he looked hard at me all the time, seeming by his expression to be willing me into understanding him. When he had finished, he turned and looked questioningly at the interpreter, a man younger than himself and thin with a long white bony face.

The Rabbi is most contented with your utterance. He has heard you are a great philosopher, as your words confirm. And also that you are an honoured friend of the Lord Protector, whom he esteems highly.

I waited for him to say more but he only turned and looked at his master again, who nodded, smiling.

When I said nothing, the interpreter addressed me again, in a more modest voice which made me think he was speaking for himself now.

The Rabbi is also a philosopher. He was the teacher of Spinoza, whose fame may have reached these shores.

Ben Israel sighed and pursed his lips on hearing the name.

No, said I, I have never heard of this Spinoza, but I have read your master's book, *The Hope of Israel*, which I had from Hugh Peters, the Lord Protector's chaplain. I found it in Mr Peters's house while I was waiting there to see him, and so began reading it and when he came in I found I could not leave off reading, though he was very anxious to have me out on account of some other business he had that day. I told him I could not go hence till I had read more, and he said, Take the book with you, which I accordingly did, and was very glad of it for it made me understand the Jews and what they long for.

The interpreter repeated all this, and I heard: *Hugo Peters, librum* and *Hebraei.* The Rabbi bowed.

There is no true Christian but must acknowledge your nation of old to be the people chosen of God. It was the Jews that made the Tabernacle and the ephod, and Solomon was a Jew, who asked for wisdom in a high place and God granted it to him, and Jacob, who struggled with an angel at the ford Jabbok and vanquished it, and all the great prophets we read of in Scripture, as Amos and Daniel and Isaiah. The Jews should be honoured by us Christians; I never saw a Jew in person before this day but I have spent my life in reading of your people. When I heard that you were come to England to speak with the Protector, I could not rest, but must come here at once and speak with you. And look, here is a book which I have writ out fair in answer to your own, and had it translated into Latin.

He raised his arms on being proffered the book, the palms out, in a sort of dumbshow of joy, then took it and began to leaf through it, frowning now, more deeply as he turned the pages.

I have called it *Light for the Jews*, which light is the one gift your people, for all your wisdom, still lack. You refused the Light of Jesus Christ, who was the Messiah you looked for: you would not acknowledge it, and continue to wait for a Messiah to come in our times. You believe that the Last Days are at hand, and in this you are justified, but when the Messiah comes it will be his second coming, and not his first. This is the light you lack, which I offer you in this, my book.

He smiled and shrugged, holding the book now closed in his hand.

This, sir, is why I told you about the daylight star which appeared when the present King was born. That King is Charles II, who is now in exile, but will return again to rule over us. For we read in the prophecies of my own people, the Britons, who are specially favoured by God like your own, that a

Dreadful Dead Man shall come to the throne. King Charles is a dead man, who was made dreadful by the striking off of his head; King Charles shall rise again. Then shall all nations live in peace, for this Charles is the Messiah whom you seek. You seem doubtful, sir. But you may know King Charles is the Messiah by his description in Holy Writ, for we read in the Book of Esdras that he is taller than those about him, and such a man is our present King who is as much taller than others as his father was shorter. And you may know him also by his name, which is Charles Steward, which signifies he is the steward appointed by God to rule over yourselves and us.

I who tell you this have been a prophet these four and twenty years. I foretold the late troubles when the people rose against their King and slew him, and was imprisoned for it three years, which also I foresaw. And all this you may read of in my books *A Voice from Heaven* and *An Echo to the Book Called A Voice From Heaven*, which, by the grace of God, have gone out among the people and made me famous. (Or rather, you, sir, may read them and translate for your master.) In those books also I foretold that Charles Steward would be restored to the throne. It is true that I said, as you may have heard from others, that he would be restored in the year 1652, and in my next book that the restoration would be in 1653. I was in possession of the true date, but could not reveal it for fear his enemies should be enabled thereby to prevent it. But the day shall not be long now. Charles shall be your King as well as ours, the Messiah you are seeking, and shall rule over the whole world for a thousand years, before the Last Judgement shall come. That was the meaning of this star that was seen over London that day. You are a Wise Man, and you have followed that star, though you know it not, for England is the Holy Land now, and London is both its Bethlehem and its Jerusalem.

Menasseh Ben Israel had put the book on his desk, no doubt intending to read it later. He sat with his hands folded across his stomach, nodding still, though smiling no longer, while the interpreter spoke: *Carolus, rex, stella.*

Dies quando venerit Messias adest, the Rabbi said. The day when the Messiah shall appear is at hand, but I cannot believe that King Charles Steward is he. It may be indeed that the Messiah shall be a gentile and from this part of the world, for (he reached out his hand to tap my book as if to make his peace with it) I put much credence in an ancient French author who wrote as much. But it seems to me more likely to be Oliver the Protector, or else the King of Sweden, for this Charles you favour is much eclipsed. And the King of France is likelier than any. Honoured philosopher, I have been much enlightened by our colloquy, and if you have the ear of the Protector I beg that you will speak to him on behalf of our people, for whom, I am persuaded, you feel a respect which does you great honour. It is nearly four hundred years now since the Jews were wrongfully banished from England. Go to your mighty friend and beg him that we be permitted once more to live in this land and go about our business here.

He nodded again, so deeply that it was the whole upper part of his body that moved back and forth, and not merely the head.

Yes, said he, if you truly wish my opinion, I would have to say the King of France. But we shall see very soon.

Chapter LIV
A River Running Both Ways

Some time ago, my lord, while I was lying in bed thinking on the struggles between Lord Lambert and the Parliament, I heard a loud voice like a mob shouting outside my house, *The King is come with an army up towards Windsor, but no war intended.* So I went out and found myself beside the Thames, ready to take a boat to go and see the King, as once I took a boat to Greenwich Palace to see his father. But when I looked at the water, there was something strange about it, for the current on the far side towards Southwark was running in the wrong direction, upstream, while the current this side ran its usual course. The watermen and bystanders wondered at it, saying, *We have seen two tides in one day, but such a thing was never seen before, the water running both ways at once.* They began getting into boats, intending to sail up the river to see the King. There were some men there that I knew from Blackfriars Church, and from my days waiting about Parliament with the other petitioners to tell some of our great men about my visions, and they put their fingers to their lips and held up their hands in warning that I should not tell of their going, for they seemed to be in great fear. Then I was alone, walking along the road towards my home with a drawn knife, long and bright, in my hand, and a grim woman in dark clothing came towards me furiously, but seeing my knife she turned and fled. I was on horseback now, in the countryside south of London, riding towards it, and there in a little village I met my wife, and we made our way to the river to get a boat home, but when we got there we found the water was almost dried up, so that we could have walked across it without it going over our shoes. Nearest the banks it flowed through long grass, so that it looked more like a flooded meadow, and even in the deepest parts of the central channel it was not more than a quarter of a yard deep. I could not see how a boat could take us anywhere, and as I was discussing it with one of the watermen, I awoke.

Lord Lenthall had his hand over his brow, and his eyes were closed. There had been a great gathering at his chambers that evening, and I wondered if he had drunk too much wine or tired himself out with talking. I began to feel awkward sitting there, and was about to rise and steal out of the room, when he opened his eyes.

I am glad, said he, that these visions of God continue with you as they did formerly, but I confess this one baffles me. What does it mean?

Well, my lord, the river that runs both ways signifies the nation contending against itself.

Yes, he said, yes, I see that. But yourself with a drawn knife, and the grim woman, and the Thames overgrown with grass... It is an uneasy dream and I like it not. I cannot think it portends any good for the nation.

He shook himself and straightened his clothing. I had not seen him so at ease before, for there was always a guarded look about him and he held back in any conversation, waiting to hear what others would say first. I was once brought before a Secretary who had no pen, and here was the Speaker of Parliament who preferred not to speak. But he was familiar with me by now, and would talk when we were alone.

Your nose looks painful, Mr Evans.

It is a trial to me, my lord. My wife says that it is fungous but I believe it must be the King's Evil, and can never be cured until His Majesty comes in. I am sorry to disgrace your chambers with my unsightliness, and worse, for the smell of it is very polluting.

I assure you, I can hardly smell it from here.

You must think, my lord, what it is like be as close to it as I am, for my nose is the organ most sensitive to its own corruption: it both gives off the foulness and receives it. But I was ever an outcast, and the nose is but a bodily sign of that condition.

Lenthall smiled. I should hardly describe you as an outcast, Mr Evans. There are times when I think you know more of the great men of the land than I do. As I recall, you were hardly ever out of the late Lord Protector's company, who was a man most of us lived in fear of, yet he listened to you. But I am afraid, now I think on it, that I have, after all, some bad news for you. I have spoken to my friends in the Customs, and they tell me there is no position for you there after all. I am sorry.

He drew out a handkerchief from somewhere inside his black velvet doublet, and I thought he was going to hold it before his nose, but he merely wiped his eyes with it, shook it a little, stared at it sadly and put it back. His face must have looked weaselly when he was younger, but now his beard was white and the brown cheeks crisscrossed with lines.

I never expected it, my lord. To say truth, it was only my excuse for first coming to visit you, for I had more important things to discuss, and knew that you would never admit me if I told you my real reasons. And, with respect, sir, you are wrong to say that I may make free with all our great men. For I went to Lord Fleetwood and Lord Lambert, and both of them turned me away, and only yourself consented to see me, who had more reason to reject me than any after the prophecy I made of you.

Yes, I heard about that, said he. You wrote that the Lord would smite the lintel of the house, or rather that was in the Book of Amos, I think it was, and you maintained that it signified the Speaker. And then that fellow flung a stone in my face as I was going into the House.

I am glad it hurt you not.

Thank you, Mr Evans. As mishaps go, it was not as great as some. Who would have thought I should still be here, after all that has happened? I was Speaker on the day it all started, when His Majesty entered the Parliament to summon the five members.

I have seen it, said I, many times. There was a bird fluttering about the windows.

Was there? I do not recall it. But I was there when Colonel Pride came with his soldiers to purge the House of those who would not support the Independents, and I did nothing. And again five years later when Cromwell told us we were no Parliament and dissolved us. He called my mace a bauble and had his men carry it away. They pulled me out of my chair you know. His Majesty had been more courteous, for he asked my leave to borrow it. Did you prophesy all that? No? Well, I daresay you had other things to concern you.

I was much concerned with the Jews then, said I. And I can only prophesy as God instructs me.

Well, said he, now we have the Rump Parliament back again for the time being, and perhaps we shall have another Protector after. What do your prophecies say of Lord Lambert? Is he stronger than Parliament? He is stronger than I am, anyway.

General Monk is stronger still, for his army is better fed and better paid than Lambert's.

You think so? But why should he leave Scotland? He has no wish to govern, has he?

He will come, said I, if Parliament is threatened. And when he comes, you must persuade him to bring in the King, otherwise it will always be the same: one will be getting up and others will be pulling him down, and confusion and destruction will follow.

It is true, said he and sat up straighter in his chair, his hands to his temples. Now if we try to bring in the King, can you show me any assurance from God that it will come to pass?

Yes, said I. I have had many visions to that effect.

Pray tell me one, said he.

I was talking and laughing with a group of friends, and going a little way off from them intending to come back presently I heard a pleasant sound of music in the dead of night, and I thought it was the City Waits playing to the Lord Mayor, as it seemed to me they did every night. I went to a window with my candle and saw them all in a low chamber, playing on their viols and sackbuts and recorders as they lay in bed together. When I left them and went seeking my friends it was daylight and I came to a place where a company of bricklayers, labourers and such men were building a high brick tower and making fine walks, and as I turned about and looked at the tower again, the builders were all gone. Then I asked a man that was alone there, trimming a green bank belonging to a great old house, why they had left work. *Because it is Saturday noon*, said he, and he went on trimming the bank till it looked like a strange creature lying on its back. Then he took it in his arms and raised it on end and I saw that it had a face like a real woman, and I praised the workman, saying, *Never did any limner the like*. But as I looked, the bank became a real woman indeed, speaking and walking about her business, with her maid to attend her. At this, I was amazed and said, *Surely this is God's work*. And then, meeting my friends again, and telling them with much joy what I had seen, I awoke.

Yes, said he, I like that one. But what does it mean?

Chapter LV
The Burning of the Rump

The sky was red. I had to press against the wall as far from the middle of the street as possible, because of the heat of the bonfires, so many that there was no longer any darkness between them. St Margaret's was ringing, and St Martin-in-the Fields and St Clement Danes, St Dunstan's, St Andrew's, St Bride's, the Temple, Blackfriars, Bow Bells, the great bells of St Paul's, all ringing together and out of step, like a battle fought by angels. In King Street, they were marching up and down holding long poles like pikes in the air; a few drops of something splashed into my face as I passed. I tasted what I thought was rain, and understood suddenly that it was blood. I was seized by the fear that the things on the end of the poles might be human heads. They were hunched and reddish, and seemed to be gripping the poles by their own will, like squirrels. Then I recognized them – the men were parading pieces of meat, the biggest steaks I had ever seen.

At the place in the Strand still called the Maypole, though the Maypole itself was torn down by order of the Parliament some fifteen years previously, I met with a troop of aproned butchers all holding a great knife in each hand, and clashing them together to make a peal to rival that of the bells. Having finished their ceremony, they turned to a red and white carcass they had dragged with them on a hurdle, and one carved off its haunches very lovingly while the others held it, slipping the meat from the bone. A boy seized one, tied it to a long pole and hung it over the flames while the men shouted at him over the din, Don't you burn it, Nathan. Some of us are hungry.

No, said another, let the bastard burn. We can eat any day.

The boy must have been a year or two younger than Owen. Feeling me push past him, he seemed to take offence, and pointed to his backside. Kiss my Parliament, said he.

I staggered on, my face stinging, and above all my diseased nose, which always pained me most when it came close to any fire. The air was savoury with the smell of roasting beef and mutton, which reminded me that I too was hungry. At Temple Bar, they were executing a piece of meat over a bonfire, hanging it from a small gibbet they had built for the purpose.

Further along Fleet Street, they had just finished roasting, and a woman came up to me with a platter full of hot beef. I ate two slices with my fingers, and took a cup of ale with it.

It is the Rump, said she.

You mean the Parliament? It is overthrown?

We will not have any of them any more, said she. Not Speaker Lenthall, nor Lord Lambert, nor any more Cromwells. We have had this one and that, one after another, and they were all the same.

Then the King must come in.

We don't hold with the King neither. But they are all the same. We shall rule ourselves now.

Where did you come by all the meat? asked I.

We won't need...

What say you? I cannot hear.

Will not need food any more. Parliament...

She was carried away by the press of people. I had eaten and drunk too quickly, and felt the unchewed meat lurking in my gullet, waiting its time to return.

At Ludgate Hill I rested by another bonfire where a man was turning a spit and another was basting it viciously with some liquid that angered the flames and made them strike out at him. Both men were too close to the fire but perhaps they could not be burnt now any more than they would need food tomorrow.

From this eminence, I could see a dozen more splashes of fire reflected in the Thames, and others beyond in Southwark and Lambeth. The shape of the city could be seen in the sky, darkness at the horizon where the surrounding fields were, and a circle of glow within, a glory. They do not know yet that the King is coming in, thought I. They are happy without even knowing the reason of it, thinking it is enough to burn the Parliament. But he is coming, and sooner than they think. There is his crown.

Chapter LVI
A Devil Cast Out

It was not raining now, but it had rained as I was making my way here, and would do so again later this morning, for rain was where we had lived these past two months. I looked up at the sky out of habit, and so did the people around me, but there was nothing there, not even a mass of clouds, only the same vague greyness we saw all around us. Yet all were dressed for a Sunday or a holiday, gowns and cloaks in red, green and sky colour, though darkened somewhat by moisture, and the dye running in some of them. The children had brought their toys with them and ran about the park with balls and windmills. I heard a woman behind me asking, Will His Majesty come soon? and thinking it was myself she addressed, I turned to reply.

I have been attending to that question these eleven years, goodwife.

She made an effort to smile but I had seen her flinch when she saw my face, though she was plain herself and had a great wart on her right cheek. I have heard, said she, that he walked in the Park last Saturday.

I believe he will come today, said I, for I know something of these matters. And when he does, I shall solicit his healing touch for this nose of mine.

The man she had first spoken to nodded to me. It is not the King's Evil, said he. I have seen the King's Evil, and it is different.

I raised my hand to my nose, as I did sometimes when I was reminded that this fiery orb at the centre of my being had also an outward form perceived by others. When I touched it very gently there was no increase in pain, only the familiar sensation of finger on skin which for an instant crowded the other feeling out of my mind and made me think that this swelling of my face was, after all, mostly nose, and that, though it was larger, less shapely and warmer to the touch than my nose had formerly been, these qualities were rather a curiosity to be explored than a source of agony. Then I would let my finger wander over it, hoping to prolong this experience, but the slightest excess of pressure would cause a flash of pain, and in any case the inward tolling began again almost at once, as if the nose were a white-hot horseshoe that a blacksmith was hammering from the inside.

If it were only my toe, or the little finger of my left hand, some part of me that I could cut off in my mind from the rest of my body. But the nose, being in the middle of the face, was impossible to escape. It was an organ I had not thought of much before, save when I had had a cold, but I now understood that everything a man feels is felt, to a great measure, though his nose, and everything he does is done, to some degree, with the nose. For the nose breathes, and breathing continues for so long as we are alive; so that we say something is as natural as breathing, meaning that we do it without thinking about it. But when the nose is diseased, breath becomes pain, and pain gives rise to thought, which, when it concerns what we were never intended to think about, is as painful as pain itself. I had felt something like it at the death of my father, when, despite my mother's cry of Give him air, it was myself who had to breathe all of it, until the breathing became a great burden to me; but even that had been an abstract ordeal rather than an endless succession of burning pangs. When I remembered, I would breathe through my mouth instead, but this was a decision that had to be renewed at each breath, for the body does not willingly do it, and this deciding over and over again left no room in my mind for anything else, for as soon as I let my thoughts wander the anguish was renewed. Nevertheless, I had succeeded enough to cause some distress in my mouth and throat also, which were so worn out by unwonted use that their tender skin had been rasped sore, so that it hurt me to eat or speak.

Notwithstanding all this pain and thinking and thinking about pain, there were times, not when I forgot it all, but when my mind seemed to have grown enough to contain other matters as well. For instance I had spoken to this woman in my normal voice, in spite of sore tongue and lips and agonized nose. My words had been a sort of pleasantry, and I had even, I believe, smiled back when she tried to smile at me. I was a little indignant with the man who cast doubt on my ailment being the King's Evil, and had to check an urge to speak sharply to him, saying, Do you not know that all evils belong to the King, who has the power to cure anything so long as God wills it? For he is anointed of the Lord, and it is written of such that they shall cast out devils and drive away serpents, and that they shall lay their hands upon the sick and heal them. At the same time I was looking at the sky and considering the prospect of rain, which would make it necessary to come back to the Park tomorrow in the hope that His Majesty would take his walk then, and looking around me at all these people in their finery and wondering what they had come to petition about, and whether all of them would be admitted to the royal presence before me. With another part of my mind, I observed these two kinds of thinking, one that was all suffering and the other concerned with the business of the day and marvelled that I could think both ways at once. But as soon as I did so, I was back to pure pain again.

Besides, said the man, His Majesty does not touch for the Evil in St James's Park. If he comes here, it will only be to take the air and display himself to the people.

I would not argue with him, knowing that was what he hoped for. Besides, I had had my argument with Mr Knight, the King's chirurgeon, a few days earlier, when I had joined the mob at the door of the Rose Tavern and almost been crushed in the press for tickets. When I was finally admitted, Mr Knight told me that my inflamed nose was not the King's Evil, and indeed it was very different from the great bluish-purple swellings I had seen among the crowd outside the door, that looked as if a rat had burrowed under the skin of the neck. It was got in the King's service, said I, so it is His Majesty's Evil, and only he can heal it. But Mr Knight would not be persuaded.

In any case, I did not want to stand in the Banqueting House among all those rat-necked others, and file up to the stage to be touched when my turn came, in the smell of incense and mumbling of priests, and to be given a gold Angel to hang around my neck. That was for common sufferers, and there would be no time then to say who I was and what I had done for him, before I was ushered away so that the King could touch the next.

I left the man and the woman and found a tree to lean against. It was wetter here than elsewhere, for the leaves dripped on me and I had to stand on mud rather than grass, but the crowd was accordingly thinner and, being at a slight elevation, I had a good view to the east towards Whitehall Palace where His Majesty would be coming from. There were people passing along the path from that direction now, in clothes that caught what brightness there was in the daylight and gave it back in colours so garish that they must be of satin, but I knew it was not the Royal party yet. I had seen a King and knew what to look for. So many times I had stood before the great and been moved to speak to them. What would I say this time? Before I had always had prophesies to give, but, the future having already happened, I had nothing to tell him of now but the past.

Your Majesty, my name is Arise Evans. I am a man of humble origin, you would say, yet not so humble, for my father was a considerable man of the parish. But he left me disinherited that was his darling before, and so I became a tailor. Nevertheless, Your Majesty, I have moved among the great, for I met your sainted father and told him of the calamity that was to befall the land. The Lord has spoken to me and shown me visions. I have flown above mountains and watched the sun turn about like a wheel, and been fed in a rainbow cloud, and driven off a witch with a pin. I have been imprisoned twice for your sake, nay, thrice if you include my incarceration for three days in my mother's house in Wrexham. I have writ some fourteen or fifteen books telling of your restoration, when the Dreadful Dead Man should rise and the Chicken of the Eagle take wing. The very rocks and mountains where I grew up told me of this miracle, for they were called BELIEVE, ASCEND THE GAP, and THEY WILL GIVE LIGHT and ARISE THE HOUSE OF CHARLES. Your Majesty, I have been sustained in my labours these last years by your servants Mr Satterthwaite and Mr Starling, but I am a poor man, and sick, as you see. I ask only–

It was the King. The party had almost reached my position before I understood what was happening, for he was among those lords and ladies in satin after all, only I had not perceived it. I had been unwittingly picturing his father who was a small man and very well favoured, and gave off a sense of compressed power, but here, in the midst of the throng of petitioners who came and went with every pace he took along the path, was a man a head taller than anyone there. His Majesty had a long, dark face, with a long nose and heavy eyes, a face that reminded me of a horse. He was older than I had imagined – indeed he had the kind of features and complexion that must never have seemed young. He walked a little ahead of the rest of his party (though there were soldiers before and behind), with long, slow steps, looking from side to side at the crowd, stopping often to speak to some of them, at which time his companions would draw abreast of him and turn towards the people he was talking to, as if to mark everything the King said. For all his gloomy features he spoke lightly and laughed often.

I ran from my tree, slipping on the mud, until I reached the body of people lining the path, where I began to push at gowns and doublets, clawing and elbowing my way through and calling out my name in hopes that the King should hear it and know who I was. Several people cried out and cursed me, but, being of small size, I was generally beneath the level of their gaze and so escaped their grasp. I was crying out myself with the pain of it, for in all the jostling I could not escape some blows to the nose, and the sound I made must have put some of them in fear.

They began to shrink away from me instead of resisting, and I went forward faster, fell almost, until I reached the edge and found myself alone there, the advance guard to the left of me, the King and his friends yet a half dozen yards away. His Majesty was bending over to speak to a woman in the crowd. When he stood up he saw me before him, straightening my doublet and breeches, and his horse eyes held a puzzled expression, like one trying to remember something. Arise Evans, I tried to say again, but I knew not what sound came out.

Nevertheless, he must have heard me and understood, for he did not resume his progress, but slowly raised his great hand in its lace cuff, and beckoned me to him.

I fell to my knees at his feet, and began, Your Majesty, my name is Arise Evans, but being still out of breath and in pain I could hardly speak. He reached down his hand and I was about to press it to my lips, but my mouth was burning and I knew not if I could bear the pain. I grasped the hand and bowed over it. There was a fine ruby ring on the first finger and a gold signet ring on the second, the royal arms which I had seen so often in Blackfriars Church. The fingers were long, the knuckles bristling with coarse black hair, the nails thick and somewhat ridged but clean and well-trimmed. This was the hand of King Charles the Son, and of King Charles the Father, the hand of the Lord God, who rules all, saves all, heals all. Your Majesty, I began again, but was seized at that moment by an anguish so terrible I felt I could not endure it but must die in that very place. The hand was dry and warm; it lay in my own perfectly at ease for the King had made no effort to remove it, though my hands were clenched tightly round it now with all the strength of my suffering. I will kiss it, thought I. It is what I have come for (though I could no longer remember if that was true) and then I will be free to die. And I raised the hand to my face.

Clutched it rather, for I knew not what I was doing, and it seemed to me that I had in any case no lips or mouth or nose any more, but only a furnace where my face should have been, and I pulled the hand violently to that furnace and, to speak honestly, struck myself with it. The moment that sacred skin crushed my nose there was an agony a thousand times worse than I had experienced before; yet it burst at once into cool sweetness. I pressed the hand into the place where my nose had been and wiped it again and again round my face, weeping and saying, Thank God, Thank God.

When I came to myself again I was still kneeling on the path, the King's hand in mine, which I dropped forthwith and looked up at him. The back of his hand was covered with greenish-yellow slime streaked with blood, and he held it before his eyes, moving it a little from side to side and flexing the fingers as if to see if it was still the one he had had formerly, with all its old skills and properties. Then he looked down at me, shaking his head slightly, not angry or revolted but still more puzzled than before.

Your sainted father, said I. King Charles the Father, King Charles the Son. My name is Arise son of Evan–

I will remember you, said he.

Chapter LVII
A Bowl of Plum Pottage

The house is cheerless this Christmas Eve, with no fire and nothing to eat. Finding I could keep warm no other way, I have taken to my bed, leaving the desk and writing appurtenances to Owen, to his great joy. He has lit a tallow candle at a neighbour's fire, and writes by its little light. He now professes to thrive in the cold, for, he has decided, God made the winter to chastise our bodies and enliven our spirits, and we do very wrong to dispel it with fires. I observe, however, that he is wearing all his clothing, even unto the hat, as well as my cloak, and every now and then he leaves his work and paces up and down the room, clapping himself about the shoulders. I observe also that his fever of writing has waned somewhat in the course of the evening; at first he spoke with relish of the journey of his soul and his struggles against temptation, telling me of his writing as he was doing it, but now his pen moves slower, and when he speaks there is a testiness in his voice.

How do you remember things, father?

Why, Owen, what mean you? Remembering comes naturally to the mind. It needs no instruction.

So I should think, and my mind is full of pious thoughts and vivid illustrations of them, but in the interval between dipping the pen and putting it to the paper they flee away. And if by chance I cling on to one and try to write it down, my words seem feeble to me. It is as if I have never lived, father, since I can find nothing to say about my life.

Well, Owen, what have you done in your life, besides, as you say yourself, sitting on a shopboard and sewing?

It may not seem much to the outward eye, says he, but sewing, being a private, intricate kind of labour, allows the mind to be very active. You know this yourself, for I believe you mentioned something of it in those writings of yours, *The Book of the Needle*. (Which book he has gathered together and stowed inside the desk at my own insistence, that my pages may not become confused with his.) And if a thing is worth thinking it ought to be worth writing down. Not only that, but when I sit and sew I am oftentimes praying without words, so that my thoughts are a sort of – I think dialogue was the word you used – only in my case the dialogue is with God rather than with some imaginary master like this Hugh Jones you wrote of.

Hugh Jones, say I, was not imaginary. He was my dear master, who –

Well, says he, I did not fully understand that part, for sometimes you called him Hugh Jones and sometimes *Dominus*, but it matters not. It is still better to have a dialogue with God than with an earthly master, for when God makes his reply there will be a part of my book that is of divine origin and so cannot be criticized by any. Only when I come to write it, I cannot remember any of the things God said to me.

Perhaps, Owen, it was not God speaking to you at all but your own thoughts and dreams.

Blasphemy! says he, and puts his hands over his ears, but seeing I do not heed the gesture, he takes them away again and affects to dip his pen in a carefree way. Thank you, father, says he, for your words fill me with rage, and rage is a great spur to writing. I make no doubt but that my autobiography shall go on apace now. And I shall put you in it.

Nevertheless, he does not lift the pen from the ink bottle but sits, resting his chin on his left hand and regarding the other hand, still holding the pen, with a sort of meditative admiration.

And my mother, too, says he after a while, and my sister Megan, that is Willis now. And Mr Greenhaugh, who shall be a sort of evil principle. And Susan. Father (his outrage now seems much abated), father, is not this the best part of writing, before you have writ any of it? Because then it may still be perfect, whereas no sooner do I put pen to paper than the distractions and temptations of the world rush in and mar everything. Being an author is a noble profession (he draws the pen from the bottle and watches as a drip forms and falls within), and I am only sorry that Susan cannot see me at it. But if it were possible, I would be the sort of author that does not write anything.

Your character is consistent, say I, for I understand you were also the sort of tailor that did not sew anything, and the sort of prentice that did not learn anything.

He nods, pursing his lips. You cannot provoke me any further, says he, for your provocation is the very matter of my book. Look, I shall write your words before I forget them. What did you say again?

In any case, say I, who is this Susan you speak of so often? You always say her name as though I should know it.

Oh, Susan, says he. She is no one much. But it may be that not having Susan to talk to is what is hindering my writing, for if you were she you would be telling me what I could accomplish and not what I cannot.

Hearing a scrabbling at the door, we both look at it, and I believe for a moment both of us think it must be Susan without, as if the mention of her name has summoned her presence. But it is my wife, who enters shortly after, clutching a huge bowl. Will neither of you help me? she asks, but straightway puts the bowl on the floor beside the fire before we have a chance to stir.

Why, wife, what is this?

A bowl of plum pottage Megan kindly gave me for our supper when I told her we had nothing in the house. But it has been somewhat chilled in the journey, so we shall need a good fire to heat it up again.

Hearing this, I get out of bed, abashed to be there at this hour, and fully clothed withal. I remove my nightcap in any case, and go to inspect the pottage. It has a murky look, with prunes and scraps of meat protruding from the yellow layer of congealed fat on top, but I can smell cinnamon and honey, though the aroma seems closed in because of its unheated condition. Owen fingers out one of the prunes and puts it in his mouth. I trust, says he when he can speak again, that this is not an idolatrous pottage. For I have fasted long enough, and I must eat if I am to have the strength to write. But if I thought this pottage had been brewed to celebrate a superstitious festival, I would be unable to partake of it.

Why, Owen, what else – ?

Light the fire, Owen, says my wife. It is already made up against tomorrow morning and it should light easily enough with your candle if you are careful. Indeed, I think we may have another candle this one evening, for I should like to see what I am eating, and whether Megan can make a plum pottage as well as I can.

I cannot remember when you last made one, say I. But if we light the fire now, what shall we do tomorrow? You said we had no more fuel.

We have no more of anything, says she, but we need not worry about cost for this season. My daughter has invited us all for Christmas.

Owen sits up sharply from his crouching position at the hearth. He has just this moment kindled a screwed-up piece of his own autobiography that he had spoiled from too much crossing out, and the flame flies up beside him almost as if it were an utterance of his own.

Christmas! says he. I did not think it of my sister, or of you either, mother, though there is nothing that would surprise me coming from my father.

It is not your father's fault. It is the King himself has made Christmas lawful again, so there can be no wrong in accepting.

I wish I were in America, Owen says. They will have no Christmas there, I'll be bound. Mother, I care not whether it is lawful, Christmas is a wicked and superstitious festivity, as can be seen by the word Mass in its name.

It has the word Christ in its name, too, say I, unwilling to be bested by my son at this matter of the words that lie beneath or behind other words.

Then it is taken in vain, said he. For this Christmas is nothing but a decking of churches in rosemary and ivy, and a singing of carols, and an acting of plays, and a playing of games and an asking in of neighbours for intemperate eating and drinking. If it were a true holy season, it would be marked by fasting and not by feasting. You understand that I can eat no pottage now I know its significance?

Nevertheless, Owen, say I, look to your fire. For your mother has commanded you to do it, and you must honour your father and mother.

He is the more willing to obey this instruction because it enables him to turn his back on us both and occupy himself in building little tenements of sticks and prodding the fire into them, a pastime that has delighted him since childhood. And I know not how it is, but he says no more against the pottage after that, but sits down with us very willingly at table. For a long time we eat and say nothing, and I am stirring the remnants in the bottom of my bowl and considering another helping when my wife speaks.

There are too many raisins of the sun.

That cannot be, say I.

Well, she can afford them, being married to Mr Willis. And I do not deny that she makes a good pottage, though it lacks the subtlety of my own. Owen, will you not come with us to stay with your sister?

No, mother.

He speaks quietly and without rancour now and holds out his bowl shamefacedly for more, which she serves.

Well, says she, this was foreseen. There is nothing for it, then, but for you to go back to Mr Greenhaugh and ask him to take you in again, for you will not be able to live here. I know not whether he keeps Christmas in his household, but I suppose he will not turn you away at this season, and if you insist on working instead of feasting he will be all the gladder. Or you could spend the time in a closet praying, as your father used to.

He will never take me in, Owen says.

In that case, you will have to come to your sister's after all. Which is it to be? What does Susan say of the matter?

Who, I ask again, is this Susan everyone keeps speaking of?

Susan says it is true he has not taken on another prentice yet.

Husband, will you take a little more? Owen, some ale? It is common enough for a man to dismiss a servant in a fit of rage and regret it afterwards. And I dare say much of the trouble was that he took offence at this dalliance of yours with Susan and did not understand its nature.

What dalliance? say I.

Dalliance? It is no dalliance, says he.

He does not understand that your intentions, though they must be remote at your age, are honourable ones in respect of her.

I have no intentions, says he hotly. Susan is my friend, but as to marriage I have no thought of the future.

And yet, say I, thought of the future is what you must have, Owen, especially as you have nothing at all at present save a stomach full of ale and plum pottage. I say not, as Hugh Jones once said to me, that you may be anywhere, but you must be somewhere come tomorrow, and it would be wise to establish once and for all what your wishes are.

Well, says he, I think I could be an author, but there is no money in it. I could write anyway, if I had some employment to keep me, always provided I had strength at the end of the day to work on my book. And if I had, what shall I call it, room in my mind? For a writer must be able to sit and think.

An apothecary has no time for sitting and thinking, my wife says. For when you are not with your bottles you are with your patients, and they, being people, take up all the space you have in your mind.

It is true, says he. I would have as little to do with people as I can. Except Susan, perhaps, and not always her. For people are a great distraction, I find, when I wish to be with my thoughts. I am like my father in that.

And he has done well enough as a tailor and author, has he not? Until today, but now he is old, so his present poverty is not to be wondered at. It seems to me it is settled. You must go back to Mr Greenhaugh. Will Susan plead for you? Does he listen to her?

Everyone listens to Susan, says he, whether they want to or not.

Very well. It is worth trying, and if you fail you must come to us at your sister Willis's, and sulk there as much as you like, and then look for a new prenticeship in the New Year. After all, your father failed in his first position but thrived in his second.

I did not fail. My master went broke.

It is settled, says Owen raising his cup, a half smile on his face (being the kind he most prefers). Only I wish I knew the future.

You already know a great deal of it, says my wife. You will not be an apothecary. You will probably be a tailor. You will marry Susan, or if not I suppose some other woman, for it is clear you have the inclination. You will perhaps be an author, for it may be that such things run in the blood, as certain diseases do. And before next year is out, God willing, you will be an uncle and your father will be a grandfather, for so my daughter Willis told me this evening. That is as much as most people can hope to know about the future, for I never had much belief in this business of prophecy.

Wife, say I, this surprises me much. I had not thought, when I was Owen's age, to have children at all, and now I am to be a father of generations. But what mean you when you say you have no belief in prophecy? That is as good as to contradict me, for the whole business of my life has been to prophesy.

Husband, says she smiling, you know well that I would never contradict you.

Chapter LVIII
The Book of the Needle Concluded

Waking from my first sleep, I found myself thinking of all the words that were spoke this evening and looking for deeper meanings in them. I cannot tell why it took me so long to perceive that my wife's saying she would never contradict me was itself a contradiction. Because she smiled as she said it and I was warm with ale and plum pottage and with Owen's acquiescence in our plans for him, and with my wife's news of a grandchild to come shortly, I let the contradiction pass under my nose without even scenting it. Now, having realized, I thought of shaking her to reproach her with it, but she was sleeping so soundly beside me, her nightcap a-tremble with her snores, that I decided to wait for a better time, especially as any disturbance would also wake Owen, who sleeps in a truckle bed in the corner of the room, and perhaps cause a renewal of our arguments with him. Nevertheless the thought is disconcerting enough to forbid further sleep for a little while, for if a contradiction has escaped my notice here, how many more have passed by me over the years? Consider, firstly, that women by their nature are cunning. The word she used herself was *subtlety*; it is true she was referring to her cookery, but the Bible describes the serpent as subtle, who is the enemy of man; woman, from her communing with this serpent in the Garden of Eden, has received much of his subtlety, and thus become something of an enemy in her turn, as was shown in her disguising a contradiction with a smile. Consider, secondly, that a man being so accustomed to find opposition when he ventures abroad, he is the less inclined to expect it within doors. Thirdly, an author is always much preoccupied with his own thoughts, so that when anyone speaks to him his reply is often a grunt, he having heard so little of it that he dare not venture a reply. These three considerations having been gone over several times in my mind, I conclude that she may well have contradicted me often without my being aware of it. Therefore I think to review the total number of my conversations with my wife over the twenty-six years of our marriage and look in them for other contradictions, but I find it hard to remember the words with enough certainty.

While I am thus preoccupied, a man goes past the end of the alley ringing a handbell and calling out the hour, and I doubt not he is crying Peace on Earth and Good Will to Men also, but he being in Fleet Street and myself in Long Alley I cannot hear it well, not even the hour he is calling. I know only that it is Christmas morning and there are a few hours of winter darkness left before we must rise, my wife and I to go to my daughter Willis's house, and Owen to go to Mr Greenhaugh's. Therefore I have resolved to leave this fruitless pursuit of contradictions, and to light a candle at the embers of the fire and work quietly at my desk, till dawn if need be. For I have *The Book of the Needle* still to finish.

Now, however, seated at my desk in the inward light of the candle, as if the mind itself were casting its glow on the page, I find myself not so much writing as toying with words. And the end of all my toying is this: I have writ a title page for my book, which was a thing it needed, and inserted it before my first chapter. I have given the date as 1661, having regard to the planned festivities at my daughter's, which will allow me no time to take the book to Mr Lowndes before the New Year. Besides, I doubt not but I will think of some small botchings and finishings to be made before then. As to the rest of the title, it is a good long one, and, in keeping with the peaceful principles of this new age, not too argumentative. Sewing, cutting, fitting, pressing and botching: did I include full instructions for all of them? I know not, but if I have left anything out I can soon amend it. And the mentioning in my title of confusion, rebellion and the Commonwealth of England is a most happy stroke, for if Mr Lowndes is right and my wife wrong, if, that is, there be some among the public who will not buy a book on tailoring as finding the matter tedious and mechanical, these same people may find more fire, as Mr Lowndes would have it, in my other theme: the history of our present age. My son Owen was thus very wrong, as he is about most matters, when he said that an author should write about one thing at a time; this is enough for those who expect to have only one reader, but for myself I expect many.

It occurs to me, however, that I may cause some confusion in these readers of mine by my way of addressing them, for I began by writing to the parents of my imaginary prentice, then continued to the prentice himself, and at times I wrote directly to Owen, who is after all, such a prentice as I have in mind for the book, though he has disappointed me much in his understanding of it. I regret it if the goodman and goodwife I addressed at the beginning have been feeling ignored or forgotten in these latter pages, for it is no very comfortable thing to be forgotten, as I have found in my own life. Sir and mistress, do not despair over your son. My book will teach him all he needs to know of the appurtenances and the varieties of cloth, of threading the needle and the forward and back stitches, of seams and plackets and gussets and gores, of buttonholes and of botching. For the rest of the craft, he will have plenty of time to learn it, for our present King, anointed of God, will reign for a thousand years, and he having the miraculous power to drive out disease, which I am myself a witness to, this generation of man will be the longest lived and most prosperous of any that has yet been known. There, I have made my last prophecy. No, I have changed my mind, and I now make one more. I shall never write another book, for the future has already happened, and I find that my mind works better on the forward than the back stitch; I am not specially gifted at remembering, or re-membering, the past.

There was a weather-prophet once who used to walk down one side of the street, and tell all the people he met there that it would rain tomorrow.

Then he would walk down the other side and tell all he met that it would be fine, and in that way he retained his credit with half of the people at a time. Now there is a tempting career for a young man to contemplate! If I had been content with weather-prophecy of that sort, I doubt not I should have been listened to more than I have, and have been rewarded more than I have been for speaking God's true and fiery words. My life would have been a more peaceful, even a happier one, but I would not then, the son of a Welsh sheep-farmer, have spoken with the great and seen the world turned upside-down; I would not have helped to bring the nation to a joyous resolution, or writ what I suppose is now some sixteen or seventeen books; and I would not, with as clear a conscience as I now do, be able to sign myself,

Arise Evans, Tailor and Prophet.

FINIS

Matthew Francis's previous Cinnamon publication, the collection of short stories *Singing a Man to Death*, was shortlisted for the Wales Book of the Year Award. He is the author of four Faber poetry collections, of which the latest is *Muscovy*, published in 2013. His poetry has twice been shortlisted for the Forward Prize, and in 2004 he was chosen as one of the Next Generation poets. He is also the editor of W.S. Graham's *New Collected Poems*, and author of a critical study of Graham, *Where the People Are*. *The Book of the Needle* is his second novel – the first, *WHOM*, was published by Bloomsbury in 1989. He lives in Wales with his wife, Creina, and lectures in creative writing at Aberystwyth University.